FOREVER MAGIC

The Thorne Witches Book 7

T.M. CROMER

BOOKS BY T.M. CROMER

Books in The Thorne Witches Series:

SUMMER MAGIC

AUTUMN MAGIC

WINTER MAGIC

SPRING MAGIC

REKINDLED MAGIC

LONG LOST MAGIC

FOREVER MAGIC

ESSENTIAL MAGIC

MOONLIT MAGIC

Books in The Stonebrooke Series:

BURNING RESOLUTION

THE TROUBLE WITH LUST

A LOVE TO CALL MINE

THE BAKERY

EASTER DELIGHTS

HOLIDAY HEART

Books in The Fiore Vineyard Series:

PICTURE THIS

RETURN HOME

ONE WISH

To Monica B.
Thank you for putting up with me and all my quirks. Your patience and understanding defies belief. I need to find a way to channel your Zen.

*S*omeone was in the house.

In an economy of movement, GiGi Thorne-Gillespie stood, dressed in a stunning black catsuit, and conjured a weapon, all with a simple wave of her fingers. With a few whispered words from old Granny Thorne's spell book, she'd effectively cloaked herself and any sound she was likely to make. She didn't bother to be quiet —there was no need now that any noise would be deadened—and headed for her husband's unused study.

Husband? *Ex*-husband was closer to the truth. The divorce would be final within the next thirty days. A divorce that *she* had requested. For a moment, she wished things could have gone differently. Wished she and Ryker might have continued on as they had begun— deliriously happy.

She shoved aside her melancholy and focused on the problem at hand—*the intruder in her house.* Light shone through the crack in the doorway. GiGi placed an eye to the opening and peered through. Whoever was in there had moved outside the scope of her vision, which meant she would need to enter.

Easing the door open infinitesimally, she held her breath then waited. When the sounds of movement continued uninterrupted, she inched the door wider. Once again, the intruder moved out of her sightline. She swore quietly and pushed the door wider still.

Without warning, a hand came from nowhere and pinned her to the wall. Acting on instinct, she lifted her arms, pulled the air from the room, and blasted her assailant. He grunted but held fast.

"One would think a Thorne would be more powerful than that little gust of wind," the man said lazily. "You can drop the cloak, sweetheart. I know it's you."

GiGi muttered the words to reveal herself and glared at her soon-to-be-ex husband's ruggedly handsome, smirking face. "I could've thrown you into next week if I wanted. What are you doing here, Ryker?"

His eyes dropped to the hand now lightly caressing her throat. Then he ran his hot gaze down her body at a snail's pace. Those dark, bedroom eyes missed nothing. "Nice," he murmured. With a regretful sigh, he dragged his attention from her body and focused on her face. "What would you say if I told you I've retired? That I'm here to humbly ask you to reconsider the divorce."

The deep, sensual quality of his voice combined with his words sent her heart into overdrive. Because her rapid pulse would be a dead giveaway of her feelings, she shoved his hand away and rushed to put distance between them.

"I'd say you're out of your mind." With her back to him, she closed her eyes and willed her nerves to settle. "First, you'd be bored within a week without your precious spy games. Secondly—"

His arm wrapped around her waist, effectively stopping the rant she was warming to. With his large hand splayed across the flat of her abdomen, she found it nearly impossible to think straight.

"I'd never be bored as long as I'm with you."

She bent one of his fingers backwards and smiled at his hiss of pain. "Secondly, I don't want you," she lied. "Pretenders don't interest me."

"I've never lied to you."

"Right," she snorted. "Show yourself out. I'm heading back to bed. I need my beauty sleep. Wouldn't want to subject my next lover to bags and sags."

"You're toying with fire, GiGi."

Yes, she knew she was. Perhaps the reason might be because she hated the cool indifference he portrayed most days. She paused in her grand exit and faced him.

"We'll be divorced in less than thirty days. If you think I'm not going to enjoy the remainder of my life, you're cracked in the head."

Ryker's face turned hard in his anger. The sight made her heart thud faster. Once, she'd have smiled an invitation and cajoled him from his pique with a wicked promise to rock his world, but those days were long gone. Fifteen years gone. But oh, those first years, when love was new and exciting! Then it all went wrong. She was left jaded and bitter with no faith in the man standing before her.

Suddenly emotional for all they'd thrown away, she sighed and turned away. "Stay or go, it's your home until the end of the month."

She'd almost made good her escape when he called her name. Pausing with her hand on the door, she didn't bother to look over her shoulder.

"I never cheated on you."

Facing him, she said, "Didn't you, though? If not the *entire* physical act, then enough of it." When he would have defended himself, she held up a hand. "Yes, you've told me multiple times. 'It was a simple kiss.' 'It was all for the Witches' Council.' You were 'on a mission.' Blah, blah, blah." Opening the door even wider, she said. "I didn't care what your excuses were then, and I certainly don't care what they are now. You destroyed our marriage with your stupid job. *You* did. Let that sink in, Ryker."

She registered his disappointment and shrugged. "I hope it keeps you warm at night."

"According to you, I have enough women for that."

A sharp pang struck her heart. Even now, the idea of him with another cut her like a machete through butter. Wordlessly, she fled back to her bedroom. She shut the door behind her, trying desperately to catch her breath against the threatening sobs. She had sworn to herself the last time she'd cried for him was the absolute *last time*. Giving in to tears now was pointless.

"I'm sorry." His regret-filled voice sounded muffled from the other side of the solid wood panel. "I didn't come here to revive our old fight, sweetheart. I…oh, blast it. I feel like an absolute idiot trying to talk through the door. Open up, GiGi. Let me in."

"Go away, Ryker," she ordered harshly.

The doorknob beside her turned a half inch then stopped. She stared at the metal handle and waited for his next move. She heard the click and saw the knob settle back in its original position.

"Sleep well," he murmured.

Closing her eyes against the sting, she nodded her head as if he could see. A single tear rolled down her cheek, and she swiped at it. Furious with how quickly she succumbed to her wrecked emotions, she went straight to her closet and pulled out her leopard-print suitcase.

RYKER FLOPPED BACK INTO HIS OFFICE CHAIR AND SCRUBBED HIS face with his hands. Goddess, he was tired of fighting with his wife. All he wanted was to live out his days in relative peace with GiGi. Relative, because there were times when he loved to see her fired up. Petty squabbles led to wonderful make-up sex, or at least they had. Once, when they were young and crazy for each other.

He glanced around his personal space. The room she had so lovingly conjured for him from a mental image they'd created together. The executive desk was made of a distressed maple hardwood and stained a deep honey. It had bold, antique metal accents from an old seafarer's trunk. Matching shelves lined the far wall and contained classic volumes from the Gillespie family library. They had belonged to his sister, Trina, but he'd inherited them after she was murdered.

Ryker grimaced. He'd lost so much—his parents, Trina, GiGi— and for what? For an organization that would have continued to func-

4

tion with or without him. For one that was practically irrelevant at this point in time.

His attention was caught by his cigar humidor. Instinctively, he reached for his father's old lighter in his left pocket.

Ryker found himself smiling.

GiGi detested his smoking habit. She made him promise to quit on the day they'd married. Until their vows were exchanged, he could smoke one every fifteen minutes should he care to, but once they tied the knot, that was it.

No matter how many miles separated them, he had honored that promise. Just as he'd honored his promise to be faithful, regardless of how many lonely nights he spent. Yes, GiGi had shown up at an inopportune time during his mission. Yes, she'd found him kissing Marguerite Champeau, but he hadn't really had a choice. If he hadn't shown that cold-blooded succubus attention at that point during his stay at the Champeau mansion, it would have been suspicious. Had his wife shown up even ten minutes later, everything could have been avoided. Marguerite would have been unconscious from the drug he'd slipped into her drink, he'd have raided the safe, and he'd have been back in his guest room, dreaming of making love to his wife.

GiGi's interference had cost them both everything that was important. Topping the list was their relationship. Now, he had less than thirty days to rectify the situation and make his wife fall in love with him again, and he had no earthly idea how to do it.

"Ryker?"

His head whipped up, and his eyes drank in her lovely form like a man dying of thirst. The black spandex catsuit she'd been wearing when he arrived was gone. Currently, she sported a lavender sweater set that brought out the deep amethyst of her eyes, along with a pair of flowing black slacks. He wanted nothing more than to rip those articles of clothing off her body and keep her naked in bed for the next month until she changed her mind about the dissolution of their marriage.

"I've decided to stay at Thorne Manor until the divorce is final."

Her words were a bucket of frigid water on the small flame of hope he'd had that she might've returned to talk things out. "That should give you time to remove whatever it is you want from the house."

He opened his mouth, but no words would come. As he searched for the perfect prose, the one thing that might alter the path of their relationship, his gaze fell to the leopard-print suitcase in the hall.

"For effect?" he asked as he nodded to the case. "It isn't like you couldn't conjure your outfits."

Her expression turned haughty. "You're always looking for some underhanded act on everyone else's part. I wonder, Ryker, is it because you're so deceptive yourself?"

He swung his legs from atop the desk and slammed the soles of his shoes on the floor. In one smooth motion, he was on his feet and charging in her direction. She didn't have the sense the Goddess gave a mule, because she continued to stand her ground as he rapidly approached.

"You are determined to push my buttons, aren't you, sweetheart?" He shook his head and locked gazes with her. "This couldn't wait until the morning? You just *had* to come down and tell me you were leaving? Why? So I can feel more guilt? You're a damned piece of work."

They stared at one another. Neither blinking. Neither moving, except for their harsh breathing. Neither willing to give an inch.

"Let me help you with your bag, dear," he sneered. He snapped to teleport the suitcase to the porch of Thorne Manor. Only, the case didn't go anywhere. He frowned and tried again. *What the hell?* Unsure what had happened to his magic, he tried a third time.

Nothing.

"Um, sweetheart..." He said the words softly so as not to freak her out. "...I don't want to worry you, but I want you to try to send your bag on ahead to the Manor."

She frowned and looked down at her luggage. With a careless wave of her hand, she attempted to transport it to her family's estate. The hard plastic suitcase slammed into the wall and went no farther. She tried again and again with the same results.

Wide-eyed, she faced Ryker. "What the hell?" she whispered in dawning horror. It didn't take a genius to figure out that their teleporting abilities had been neutralized.

"I'm not sure. Could be Blockers."

He shot a pulse of energy toward the light switch, thrusting them into darkness. He reached for her hand and ran with her toward a safe room he'd installed when they first created their home. If Blockers were on the premises, then their magic would be ineffective for most things. Either way, he had to get her to safety ASAP. In their panic room, Ryker had stored a good amount of weapons and a food supply to last them for a few days.

"How did they find us? The wards were strengthened by my brother just this morning."

He stopped short. "Alastair? Alastair was here?"

"Yes. He said you sent him to reinforce the wards because you may have collected another enemy."

He didn't answer. Instead, he continued toward the safety of the panic room as he pulled his cellphone from his pocket. He hit the speed dial for Alastair. The call went to voicemail. "If you did what I think you did, you better call me back, you sonofabitch!" he said in a low, savage tone. He disconnected and shoved the phone into his pants pocket. "That manipulative bastard!"

"Are you sure this is his doing?" She cast a nervous glance toward the floor-to-ceiling windows as they hurried through the hallway. "Is it possible someone means to harm us?"

The tremor in her voice tempered his anger. "It's doubtful, sweetheart. The odds are more likely that if true Blockers were present, the enemy would have been through our front door by now." The metal door shut and the lock engaged. Ryker gently drew her close to him, closing his eyes at the contact. "Also, the coincidence is too great that your meddlesome older brother visited our house today."

GiGi drew back slightly and shot a look toward the wall of monitors.

Ryker put a light pressure on her jaw to turn her head. "GiGi, look at me." Her concerned violet-blue eyes searched his face. With an attempt at cool confidence, he smiled. "I won't let anyone hurt you. Ever."

He watched the screens that showed the area surrounding the house. When no detectable movement could be seen, he nodded. Yeah, he was almost positive this was a prank on Alastair's part. The motivation behind the act was anyone's guess.

"Try your magic again. See if you can send the case."

She focused on the screen that displayed the foyer and lifted her hand. The bag rose off the floor a few feet.

"If there were Blockers surrounding us, it's doubtful you'd be able to use your magic. I'm going to teleport to the main hall. Stay here, no matter what."

He turned up the volume of the security system. No sound drifted to his ears. "Stay here," he ordered again when she refused to answer. He left her to test the front door and got a shock that knocked him on his ass.

"Ryker!" she screamed as she appeared next to him to check him for injury.

Nothing was hurt but his damned pride.

"Yeah, not Blockers or we wouldn't have been able to teleport from room to room. Looks like Alastair's locked us in for some stupid-ass reason," he told her grimly. "I'm going to pulverize your brother."

Wisely, she remained silent.

2

*G*iGi suspected she knew good and well why her brother had locked them in their house together. This was in retaliation for GiGi and the rest of the family locking Alastair in with Aurora a few weeks back. Apparently, her brother felt it would be a brilliant way to reunite GiGi with Ryker. "You'll only pulverize him if I don't beat you to it," she muttered. "Can you stand?"

"Of course I can stand," he snapped. "What the f—"

Surprised into silence, she could only stare as his shoes vanished. They both gaped at his sock-clad feet in wonder.

"What the hell happened to your shoes?" she wondered aloud.

"If I knew that, I…" He growled as his socks went by way of his shoes. Barefoot and livid, he clamped his jaw shut.

She was positive he intended to make a cutting remark. It seemed the disappearance of his footwear and socks was an additional joke her brother had thought up to amuse himself.

Glancing around, she tried to detect the faint tell-tale trace of another witch. Alastair's emotions put off a light pulse of magic, and if a seasoned witch knew what to look for, they could usually detect his presence.

Nothing.

He wasn't in their house. Either he'd utilized a scrying technique, or he'd found a way to tap into their home security system.

"You're unusually silent," Ryker said, careful to keep his voice neutral.

She took exception to the term "unusually," as if she rarely kept quiet at all. "What the hell is that supposed to—oh!" Her footwear vanished.

Ryker shook his head and grinned. "That wily bastard."

"I'm not sure I completely understand what's going on."

Barefoot, they both padded to his study. After guiding GiGi to a leather club chair, Ryker poured them both a stiff drink. With a critical eye, she noted his tumbler was a little fuller than hers. More and more, when she saw him of late, he was drinking heavily. It pained her to see it—his hurt at her decision—but she was unable or unwilling to ease his plight. She had to keep reminding herself the deterioration of their relationship had been his fault.

She accepted the glass he offered and took a small sip. Unlike Ryker and Alastair, she didn't care for the brandy unless it was in tea. Yet times like these, when it appeared her brother was attempting to teach them some type of lesson only he had a clue about, harder alcohol was necessary.

"Your brother is forcing us to settle our issues," Ryker finally told her. "If I had to guess, I'd say the old buzzard is trying to play matchmaker—*again*."

GiGi wanted to swear a blue streak. "Why can't he leave well enough alone?"

"Tell me how you really feel, sweetheart," Ryker said dryly.

She snorted a laugh and almost choked on her second sip. Ryker had always had the ability to tickle her funny bone with his witty comments. Shoving aside her desire to joke with him, she carefully set down her tumbler.

"I don't suppose he is going to risk a tongue lashing, so he won't answer his phone." She focused on the purple polish on her toes. How was she ever going to get out of this situation? Spending any amount of time with Ryker was likely to weaken her resolve. Her overbearing, deceitful brother suspected as much, or he wouldn't have locked them in together.

Finally, she met Ryker's thoughtful, dark gaze. "What do we do?"

The mischievous twinkle brightening his eyes told her exactly what he'd like to do. Yes, she recognized that expression easily enough.

"Other than *that*," she added.

"When did you forget how to have fun?"

Her anger was like a punch to the diaphragm—swift and painful, sucking the air from her lungs. "Oh, I don't know. Let me think. Perhaps when you—*dammit!*" Her sweater went by way of her shoes.

Would Alastair's stupid-ass spell leave them naked and exposed if they continued to fight? GiGi jumped to her feet and ran for the stairs. Ryker was hot on her heels.

"What's going on?"

She didn't answer him. Instead, she whipped open her closet doors. Sure enough, all her clothing was missing. Closing her eyes, she lifted her arms and visualized a stunning white ballgown. Nothing. The realization she would be nude if she continued to fight with her husband clicked into place. How could Alastair do this to her? Knowing how much she needed to be free of this toxic relationship, how hurt she was over Ryker always putting her last, how—oh, what did it matter now?

"It looks like the clothes we are wearing are what we are stuck with," she said. "I'm curious as to how long Alastair intends to play this infantile game."

"Is it so bad being locked in with me, GiGi?"

She wanted to scream "yes," but doing so would cost her another article of clothing, and she didn't relish running around without pants or a top.

"I'm going to sleep now, Ryker. Could you please shut the door on your way out?"

He moved closer. Close enough for her to feel his powerful energy at her back, but not close enough to touch her.

"Please understand, I had nothing to do with this, sweetheart. I wouldn't force my attentions on you. I get that you wish to be free of me."

She gave a short nod, not bothering to face him or open her eyes. "Good night, Ryker."

As he strode toward the door, she asked, "If you had to guess, how long do you suppose he intends to lock us in for?"

"I couldn't begin to speculate. The only person who may have even a slight inclination of the way your brother thinks would be you. While I'm never surprised by what he comes up with, I am always impressed."

Finally, she faced him. It was a struggle to keep the irritation from her voice, but she managed it. "What about this impresses you? This is manipulation and torture. Simple cruelty, really."

Disappointment flashed in his eyes, and sadness took up residence on his features. "Yes, you would see it that way, wouldn't you?"

The resignation in his voice tugged at her heart. GiGi forced that defective organ to shut down all sentiment and lifted her chin to glare. No clothing was lost to her pique. *Thank the Goddess.*

"Sleep well. Tomorrow, I'll try to figure out a solution to break your brother's spell."

RYKER LEFT THE ROOM, FEET LEADEN AND HEART HEAVIER STILL. As he closed the door to the master suite, he wanted to sit on the hallway floor and bawl like a thwarted toddler. Alastair had meant well, but he'd never change GiGi's mind. The woman was as stubborn as a century was long.

With a shake of his head, he turned the knob of the guest room across the hall. The door wouldn't budge. Again, he tried. Again, the door remained closed. Ryker had a sick feeling he knew where this was going. If he didn't sleep in his wife's bed, he wasn't getting any sleep. The damned sofa in the parlor was a cream-colored, nine-teenth-century, fancy French piece with no real back or sides to speak of. It creaked every time he sat down and wasn't meant to be comfortable, much less provide support for a good night's rest. It also wasn't long enough for his brawny, six-feet-two frame.

"Alastair, you can be a true bastard some days," he muttered.

The bedroom door swung open.

"Who are you talking to?" GiGi demanded.

"I'm cursing your asshole brother to Hades."

Ryker's pale blue, button-down shirt went by way of his socks and shoes, leaving him bare-chested and fuming.

"Oh!" she gasped.

A quick glance at his wife's face showed her eyes had widened and zeroed in on his muscled pecs. Okay, so maybe Alastair *did* know what he was doing.

Inhaling deeply as if to sigh, Ryker noted the look of hungry desire flare to life on GiGi's face. As quickly as she could, she banked her emotions and cleared her throat. He struggled to keep the smile at bay.

"What did he do, other than the obvious?" she asked.

"It appears the other bedrooms in the house are locked."

"What? No!"

GiGi jiggled the closest door handle. She moved to the next room down the hall and repeated the action, adding a shoulder shove against the wood panel.

He could see the fury bubble up and held up a hand. "Don't cuss him out. You'll lose another article of clothing. Exhibit A." He swept his arm down his torso. Again, her eyes locked on his chest. Her tongue made an appearance as she wet her lips, and Ryker nearly groaned.

He called himself seven kinds of fool for his gentlemanly behav-ior. What was more glorious than his wife without her top? *His wife without a stitch of clothing on.*

"Can you conjure a cot?"

Shaking his head, he replied, "It's doubtful." But, to appease her, he tried.

And promptly failed.

With a dark frown and compressed lips, she charged into the bedroom and came out a moment later with a pillow and a chenille throw. Wordlessly, she handed them to him.

"Let me guess, I'm supposed to sleep on the floor?"

"Or the sofa. Your choice."

The sofa. Right. All the horrible words he wanted to spew to malign the oldest set of Thorne siblings remained locked inside. He'd be running around here bare-ass in less than thirty seconds if he opened his mouth.

The slight smirk twisting her lips told more than words how amusing she found his dilemma.

Screw it. "You know what? You and your damned brother can *bite my ass!*" Whoosh went his pants.

Was there anything more vulnerable than a man without a lick of clothing to protect his junk while a woman laughed? That was the last time he went commando. He wrapped the throw around his hips and headed for the staircase.

Her giggles haunted him his entire descent to the first floor.

ALASTAIR THORNE COVERED HIS WIFE'S DANCING BLUE EYES THE second Ryker's pants disintegrated. He hadn't really believed his friend would say the words to lose his last piece of clothing.

The hilarity of the situation was emphasized by Aurora's belly laugh. Tears of mirth streamed from her eyes, and she wiped them with a shaky hand.

"Her face!" she crowed. "Did you see your sister's face when his pants went bye-bye?"

Alastair chuckled and swiped a hand over the mirrored surface. "I think from here on out we should give them their privacy."

"Watching a naked Ryker storm around his house might be interesting TV, darling. The man has seriously beautiful buttocks."

He snaked an arm around her waist and nuzzled her neck. "Don't make me kill him. He's my best friend."

She bit her lip to suppress her giggles when her clothes disappeared.

"Ryker who?" she asked forty-seven minutes later when they were horizontal and satiated.

$\mathcal{T}$he sofa was roughly two feet too short. The front of the seat also had a tendency to slope toward the ground, so every time Ryker thought he might be besting the beast, the temperamental French P.O.S. dumped him on the floor. Wedging his wrist between the back and the seat, he drew his legs into a ball and clung for dear life.

Until he heard the thud from the room above his.

A litany of curses accompanied the noise, and Ryker was hard-pressed not to run upstairs like his ass was on fire to see if GiGi had lost what remained of her clothing.

He let the fantasy of making love to the incomparable GiGi take up residence in his brain. In less than a minute, he was hard and randy as a teen who just discovered Playboy Magazine. He pictured his wife dressed like one of the Playmates, bunny ears and all. Careful to keep one arm hooked behind the seat back, he rested his heels on the rickety side arm and spread his legs to one-handedly encircle his erection.

He'd only gotten in one good stroke when the not-so-dulcet voice of his irritated wife demanded, *"What the hell are you doing?"*

Ryker's eyes snapped open when he heard her squeak.

Without turning his head, he laughed. It had to be her top that vanished. That was an oh-my-God-my-breasts-are-exposed sound if he'd ever heard one.

He stroked himself again.

"Stop doing that!" She snapped. *"Oh!"*

Yep, she was nearly there. Two more good bursts of temper and she'd be as nude as he was. "If you take off that bra-and-panty set and come here, I wouldn't need to."

Fists on hips, she glared. Through gritted teeth, she counted to ten—backwards.

He laughed again and sat up, keeping his hand on his dick and spreading his legs to give her a view. Another stroke.

GiGi stopped counting around five. The redness in her cheeks was no longer from anger, but from the becoming blush of a woman trying not to let her interest show. They had like ninety-nine problems, but sex wasn't one of them.

"I need you," she whispered huskily.

Hot damn! He came off the couch like his ass was alight.

"There's something wrong with the bed. It keeps collapsing and tilting to the side."

And there he stood, dick in hand and egg on his face. "You only need me to fix the bed?"

"Yes."

"Right." He sighed heavily and wrapped the chenille blanket around his hips. He'd be damned if he'd put his worldly jewels on display if she wasn't going to appreciate them. "Come on."

He trudged up the steps and stopped short in the bedroom entryway.

"Uh, sweetheart." Ryker pointed to the mattress. "Nothing's wrong with the bed."

She ducked under his arm and came up short. Turning back to him, she wore a look of utter confusion. "I swear I'm not lying."

"I believe you." A brief inspection of the bed showed it to be in tip-top shape with no faulty legs or trick springs that might dump its occupant out. "Lie down."

She complied.

He didn't have time to comment on her compliance or savor how lovely she looked reclining on the bed. The edge of the mattress dipped toward the floor. He caught her right before she impacted the ground.

"Another Alastair trick?" she asked. "I can't see the reason behind this one."

"You know, the sofa was doing something similar to me. I assumed it was the design or a faulty leg." He scratched the back of his neck and frowned. "See if you can lie crossways."

She laid flat on her stomach, with her glorious ass facing up.

Ryker paused to admire the view before he lifted his eyes skyward, wondering what he'd done to deserve such torture. He didn't have a minute to see that thought through before the frame pitched and she rolled toward the foot of the bed. Again, he caught her. It was a little harder to release her this time around—especially when she looked so delightfully rumpled and put out. With her body pressed to his, it wouldn't be long before the thin blanket wrapped around his hips would give away his carnal thoughts.

GiGi stared up at him, eyes wide and searching. Her breathlessness came across in light pants, and her mouth fell open enough for Ryker to contemplate the taste of her tongue.

He couldn't keep the heavy desire from his voice when he said, "Don't look at me like that, sweetheart. Bucking bed or not, I'll have you on that mattress faster than you can say yes."

The laugh lines bracketing her eyes deepened, and a soft smile played about her lips. "Duly noted. Now, do you have any ideas about what's causing the bed to actually buck?"

"Obviously, it's magical. Which, if we surmise it has something to do with Alastair's spell, it must mean you cannot sleep in the bed alone."

Her brows collided together, and she looked down at the mattress. "Shall we try it?"

"Dear Goddess, woman. Don't throw suggestions like that

around all willy-nilly, or my willy will be looking to connect with your nilly."

"Maybe this will help you keep your willy to yourself." She waved a hand and, with a shower of twinkling lights, morphed into a tottering old woman with lavender hair, enough wrinkles that, when unfolded, would create two more people, and dentures that slipped when she grinned.

Ryker stared at her in horror, all his passion packing up and heading for the tropics.

Her amused cackle melted the ice he'd used to encase his heart. This was the GiGi Thorne-Gillespie he loved to distraction. The one who delighted in mischief and was quick with a witty comment or action. The one who didn't take life seriously and found joy in the little things.

He wanted to tell her how much he loved her. Wanted it to penetrate her steel-encased heart and revive what they'd once shared.

The laughter left her face in slow increments, and the glamour followed. His serious, distant, soon-to-be-ex wife stared up at him. "Right." She cleared her throat. "We should test your theory."

They both made for the same side of the bed and stopped short.

"This is my side," he said inanely.

"We haven't shared a bed in fifteen years, Ryker. You have no side anymore."

GiGi's underwear stayed securely in place because she hadn't been mean or nasty, just matter of fact. He wanted to roar his denial and tell her he did have a side. Tell her he'd take either side as long as he could always remain next to her.

Stepping around her, he moved to the opposite edge of the mattress. "We both lie down on three?"

She nodded and counted down. Both laid flat on their back, arms folded across their stomach. Not even a slight hiccup came from the bed.

"I guess we found our answer," he muttered.

.   .   .

Inside her mind, GiGi was screaming. How in Hades was she expected to sleep next to a naked Ryker all night long? She'd been hard-pressed not to jump his bones—er, *boner*—downstairs in the living room. Sitting there in all his wondrous nude glory and stroking his erection, he'd tempted her as nothing else had in years. Hell, his chest alone had made the saliva pool in her mouth. His magnificent physique hadn't changed one bit. In fact, GiGi would go so far as to say he'd only gotten better with age.

Suddenly, she couldn't remember why she was holding on to her grudge when all she ever desired sat on the cream upholstered Louis XVI sofa she loved.

"Are you okay?"

His soft voice was sweet and considerate, and GiGi wanted nothing more than to turn to him for comfort. She'd been alone so long.

"I'm fine," she lied. Turning her back to him, she pulled the covers to her chin. "Good night."

"Good night, sweetheart."

Tears threatened, but she ruthlessly blinked them away. How was it possible for the inches between them to feel like a million miles?

After what seemed like hours, but must've been only mere minutes, Ryker rolled toward her. The nerve endings along her spine tingled with awareness.

"GiGi." His voice was raspy and raw, as if he'd swallowed a mouthful of habanero peppers.

"What?" she whispered, not turning. Shifting to face him would force her to see his tortured expression. She didn't have it in her to resist him if she witnessed the stark, aching hunger reflected in his tone. As a natural healer, her instinct was to ease the pain of another. Yet easing his meant betraying herself.

"We never truly talked in detail about what you saw that night."

"And if we had? What would you say? What would you change?"

His "everything" came out breathy and with such raw sincerity that she finally faced him.

"So talk."

"Marg—"

She placed her fingers over his lips. "Don't you dare say her name in our bed."

In the low light, it was hard to make out what he was thinking, but he nodded. The gesture brought her attention to his thick, wavy hair. It was as dark as his midnight-colored eyes. Those luscious locks also begged to be touched, to have her fingers tangle in their silky depths, to caress their roots at his scalp. Because she desperately wanted to keep touching him, she withdrew her hand.

"Go on."

"She-who-shall-not-be-named was in league with Zhu Lin."

"I should have known." She groaned her disgust. "It always comes back to the damned Council's war with the Désorcelers."

Zhu Lin had been head of a large faction devoted to snuffing out witches. The Witches' Council had recruited young, idealistic men like Ryker and had created a spy network to tear apart their enemies from inside their organization. Zhu Lin had been just as bad as his demented warlord father before him, until the day GiGi's niece killed him.

"Yes, it always came back to that damned war," he said heavily.

Her eyes met his.

He'd lost his father in the war, and his sister, Trina, to murder within the next decade. Ryker's mother had never recovered. Losing her husband and daughter broke her spirit and her mind. Five years after Trina's death, Kathryn Gillespie's failing heart removed her from this world.

After losing the last member of his immediate family, Ryker had wallowed in a drunken stupor. Until the day GiGi had shown up and verbally knocked some sense into him. Even though they had been separated at the time, she couldn't stand to see him self-destruct.

"Continue," she urged.

"It was Harold Beecham's idea. He said he had it on good authority there were important documents in the Champeau safe. I was never informed about what those papers contained. I was supposed to do my job like a good little soldier, no matter what, and get them."

"You knew she wanted you. Harold did, too. It's why he suggested you for the job, wasn't it?"

"Yes."

"Were you always meant to seduce her?"

"It's what Harold suggested. I told him it was a one-and-done deal. I'd go there, find a way to trick her, and get the damned correspondence, but in no way did I intend to become her lover."

"And yet you did."

"No, I didn't."

She snorted her disbelief.

He lifted up on his elbow and leaned in, imploring and desperate. "I didn't, GiGi. I swear to you on my family's graves."

Instinct told her he was telling the truth, but she'd seen them half-undressed.

He read her confusion because he said, "My last night there, I was no closer to finding that blasted safe than I was the day I arrived. I didn't know at the time, but it constantly shifted locations to deter theft. No more than four hours in each spot."

Ryker laid his head back on the pillow beside her.

"You said once you were waiting for the drug you'd slipped her to kick in," she said to encourage him to continue.

"Yes. At dinner, I basically roofied her. I was out of options. For the record, she has the constitution of an elephant. It took forever for those damned sleeping pills to kick in. I couldn't magically help the medication along, because she was immune to that type of thing."

The disgust in his voice made her want to smile.

"Like I said, it was my last night, and failure wasn't an option. Or so I believed until the second you showed up. Then I didn't give two shits about the Council or those papers. I only saw the betrayal on your face, and I knew I had to fix things."

She jerked into a sitting position. "Wait! You never got the papers?"

He sat up slowly and wrapped his arms around his drawn-up knees. "No."

"Oh, Ryker!"

To think their marriage had been destroyed and he still hadn't achieved his mission was a sucker punch.

"What happened?" *And why didn't you come after me?* She had wanted to ask that a thousand times over the years, but refrained, as she did now.

"Mar—uh, she-who-shall-not-be-named shot me." He dropped his legs and twisted to show a small round scar below his ribcage. "It's a good thing she was a horrible shot. Or maybe the Zolpidem finally kicked in and she couldn't see straight."

The blood drained from GiGi's face, and she stared at that small puckered mark in sick wonder. "How did I never know this?"

"I'm not sure. I'm surprised neither of your brothers told you." He grimaced and shook his head. "Actually, now that I think about it, I guess I'm not. They both believed I'd cheated and that I'd been shot in a lover's quarrel."

"A lover's quarrel? Let me guess, that's how Beecham decided to spin the situation to cover up his involvement."

"Yes."

"It's a wonder neither of my brothers killed you."

He laughed; his smile a flash of white in the low-lit room. "I believe they thought you should have that honor."

"It's why you never tried to patch up our differences right away," she concluded.

"Yes. I was too ill." He shifted to a reclining position and stared at the ceiling. "By the time I returned home, you had already worked yourself into a state. The doors were locked against me, and you refused to listen." His lips tilted up slightly at the corners. "But damn, sweetheart, you were stunning in your rage. I thought for sure you were going to kill me with that tree."

The tree in question was one she'd practically brained him with in the clearing behind their house on the day he finally arrived to apologize. The tree under which he'd proposed to her and she accepted. He'd caught her out by her garden and attempted to explain what she'd seen at the Champeau Mansion. She hadn't wanted to hear his excuses.

"It wasn't for lack of trying," she muttered.

Again, he laughed. "You were fucking magnificent."

"*Were?* I still am."

His head turned, and even in the low light, she saw the intensity come into his dark gaze. "Yes. You still are."

His fervor came across and made her feel edgy and awkward. A change of subject was required. "Did the bitch ever pay for her crimes?"

"No. No real proof to hold her because I never found the safe that night. The *bitch* walked away scot-free. The Council wouldn't charge her with my shooting. I wasn't supposed to be there to begin with, according to the ruling members. Apparently, this little side mission was all of Beecham's making." He sneered in his anger.

"I met up with her once. A few years after."

His shocked gasp almost made her smile.

"She'd heard through the witchy grapevine you and I weren't together anymore. She told me in great detail all the things you'd done the week you were there. All of them involved the horizontal bop."

"She was lying, GiGi." His tone was dark and dangerous. Murder shone in his eyes.

"I know that now. Maybe even then. She was trying too hard to needle me. She succeeded," GiGi said flatly. His understanding expression was uncomfortable for her, so she looked down at her clasped hands. "The thing that stood out? She continued to walk around free. I told myself, if you were telling the truth, she'd be locked up or banished for her crimes."

"Pretty damning for me."

"Yes."

"What do you believe now?"

Biting her lip, she looked down upon him. He lay sprawled like a fallen angel, arms to his sides and eyes full of trepidation, as if he were worried about his punishment. Perhaps they'd both been punished enough for something out of their control. She didn't know anymore. All she *did* know, was that she was tired of fighting.

"I believe *you*."

He closed his eyes and his mouth tightened. Swallowing hard, he rubbed the heel of his right hand over his heart. "Thank you."

"It doesn't mean I trust you, Ryker. It doesn't mean I've forgiven completely. And it certainly doesn't mean I want to go back to being a naive housewife, always in the dark about your activities."

They remained silent for a short bit, each lost to their own thoughts or concerns.

"Ryker?"

"Mm?"

"Did you ever think about it? About Marg—"

He jackknifed into a sitting position and laid a finger over her lips. "She-who-shall-not-be-named, remember? Not in our bed."

"Not in our bed," she agreed. "Anyway, did you ever think about an affair with her? She has to be the most exquisite female on the planet."

Ryker urged her chin up until she met his serious gaze. "No. Not once. And GiGi, she's not the most exquisite female on the planet. You hold that title."

"She's far more beautiful than I am, Ryker."

"Not to me."

4

*T*heir conversation waned, and they each curled up on their side of the bed, hugging the edge to keep from touching. Their magical bed was having none of it and dipped in toward the middle.

They crashed into each other, GiGi bumping her nose on Ryker's solid chest. "Ouch!"

He chuckled softly as she wiggled her nose. "Come here, sweetheart."

"I—"

"Trust me. We'll fight this bed all night if you don't."

"I'm not having sex with you," she stated primly.

"I wasn't suggesting you do. I intended to hold you while you sleep. It's the only way we are going to get any rest."

As he watched, she seemed to weigh her options. Finally, she nodded and scooted back to allow him to spoon.

After ten minutes, Ryker could hear the subtle shift of GiGi's breathing, indicating she was asleep. He inhaled deeply. Earlier tonight, he'd been furious with Alastair for the trick he'd played. Now, he was feeling a bit more magnanimous. Sure, his marriage issues hadn't all been resolved, but perhaps now he had a chance.

GiGi was receptive in a way she hadn't been since the *unfortunate event*, as he considered it. She had listened without judgment or ridicule. Perhaps it meant she was softening. Or maybe she was well and truly done. If she really intended to move on, she would seek closure. The only way she would achieve it would be to talk the issue through.

Dread curled around his heart and squeezed. His stomach churned at the idea of facing life without her. Sure, they'd been separated for a little over fifteen years, but he'd been able to check up on her. He would have been there for her in an instant should she need him. But if they divorced, he would be on the outside of the Thorne family, no longer welcome or able to call them his.

He was swamped with sadness. A deep melancholy that permeated his bones and made him want to weep. He'd missed so much regarding the family already: the Thorne sisters growing up, meeting their mates. All the years of not being able to make love to GiGi or wake with her in his arms were moments he could never get back.

GiGi wiggled and backed her ass into his groin. He groaned aloud, and she stirred slightly.

"Ryker," she said on an exhale.

Unable to help himself, he placed his arm around her waist and buried his face in her abundance of blonde hair. Again she shifted, pressing back into him. His eyes nearly rolled back in his head, and he prayed to whatever god or goddess would listen that he developed the strength to get through the night. Hiding his hard-on was out of the question, but maybe he wouldn't embarrass himself by begging GiGi for sexual favors.

He must've eventually dozed off because the next thing he became aware of was the sun streaming through the curtains. It lit on his wife's golden head, and the beauty of the moment made him catch his breath in wonder.

Her eyelids fluttered, and in slow increments, she woke. When she focused those devastating violet-blue eyes on him, they softened and she smiled.

"Ryker," she whispered, touching his face.

He shut his eyes and let her fingers wander. As they got to his lips, he gently sucked them into his mouth.

Her light, breathy laugh made him instantly hard.

"Say the word, sweetheart. Please, please, please say the word."

Her hand dropped, and he opened his eyes to stare at her. Gone was the warmth from seconds before, and in its place was cool caution.

"I'm getting out of bed now," she warned.

To say he was disappointed was to put it mildly, but he refused to let it show. "On three?"

She nodded.

He bunched the sheet toga-style around his body and inched toward the edge of the bed. She shifted to the far side, and they rose in unison.

"Look at us, working together," he quipped with a grin.

"Well, thankfully that's over. Let's figure out how to break out of this prison," she said feelingly.

Prison. She would definitely view time with him that way. Ryker looked away and, for the first time, noticed the changes to their bedroom—or her bedroom. Not one item of his remained. His stomach flipped over. Some damned spy he was when he missed the differences the night before.

"I see you've redecorated."

Her eyes traveled the room. "Yes."

"It's nice."

"Thanks."

Because their conversation was turning awkward as hell, he strode to the bathroom.

GiGi appeared in the doorway a few seconds later. "None of your toiletries are here, Ryker."

"I can see that. Do you have a spare toothbrush, or should I conjure my own?"

"In the upper cabinet between the vanities."

They brushed their teeth, each of them at a separate sink. It wasn't lost on him that this was the most marriage-like action they'd had in forever. Still, it was a far cry from their old routine. Once, they would have shared the same sink. They would have exchanged light, flirty kisses throughout the teeth-brushing process.

He'd been a fool to come back here. Each memory was tainted by lies and pain. They were like open, gangrenous sores that would never heal.

"If you don't mind, I need to use the toilet." The light pink flush on her cheeks spoke of her uncomfortableness with the subject.

"Of course," he returned. The politeness between them tickled his gag reflex and made him want to hurl. "I'll go conjure breakfast. Do you prefer coffee or tea?"

"Don't worry about me. I'll fix my own."

Unable to be courteous a second longer and certainly not trusting himself to speak, he left.

In the kitchen, he opened the cupboard to get down a coffee mug only to find it bare. Frowning, he moved to another cabinet. Again, bare. He tried one more before he gave up and moved to the refrigerator. Nothing. He got a sinking feeling that grew exponentially when he found the pantry empty as well.

He was leaning back against the kitchen island when GiGi finally joined him.

"What's wrong?"

"Seems you're out of mugs, plates, and silverware. I didn't bother to check for pots or pans."

As if she didn't believe him, she rushed to the closest cabinet and pulled open the door. She repeated the action for five cabinets. No one could say she wasn't stubborn or determined.

"What the hell?" she demanded. With her fists on hips, she faced him. "Your prank or Alastair's?"

He held up his hands and tried to give the impression of complete innocence. It was hard to do when she glowered there in all her glorious fury and all he wanted to do was leap over the counter to ravish her.

"That rotten bastard," she swore. "I swear to the Goddess, when I see him again, I'm going to rip out his guts and hang them from the nearest flagpole."

They both blinked in wonder as her bra disappeared.

GiGi crossed her arms over her chest. "Oh!"

Ryker was forced to look away from her heaving bosom or show his own flagpole standing at full mast.

She exited the room in a huff, allowing him to breathe a sigh of relief. If left to stare at her mostly naked form, he didn't think he would hold out long. The animal inside was struggling to break free. After such a long hiatus from sex and a night of holding the love of his life within the circle of his arms, Ryker's libido was on a hair-trigger.

A few minutes later, as Ryker was practicing Zen breathing techniques to cool his ardor, GiGi returned with the chenille throw tied like a towel around her torso.

"Have you tried conjuring utensils?" she asked in a controlled tone. Not easy for her to do, he was sure.

Eyes downcast to hide his amusement, he nodded. "Yep."

"Food?"

"Yep."

"Are we expected to starve?"

The shrillness of her tone set his ears to ringing.

"If I had to guess, we need to work together again," he returned.

He was positive he heard her growl out "fine."

She inhaled a deep breath that strained the limits of the valiant lap blanket, and asked, "How do you suggest we go about this?"

"Again with the loaded questions. Obviously it's been too long if you're asking things of that nature."

A short laugh was the reward for his teasing.

"Okay, in all honesty, I'm not sure," he said with a shrug. "I can't conjure food or dishes, so maybe you should try."

Her attempt failed spectacularly. She cast him a worried glance. "Do you think this is an oversight on my brother's part?"

"No. When have you ever known your brother not to think of everything or have a contingency plan?"

"Right. So what's the trick?"

"I'm not sure. Knowing Alastair, it could be anything. He's a sneaky bastard. I can say that now because I have no more clothing to lose."

"Think he'll steal your sheet?" Her eyes lit with laughter and maybe a little interest. The interest was most likely wishful thinking on Ryker's end.

"If he does, try to contain yourself."

"My hysteria or falling on you in a lustful attack?"

He grinned, able to find the humor in the situation, and perhaps because a flirty GiGi always made him smile. "I will not fight off a lustful attack. I may, however, be a little irked if you laugh hysterically at my predicament."

With a prudent change of the subject and a slight smile still remaining, she asked, "When you tried to conjure your food, what did you think about? Or more precisely, did you only think about food for yourself?"

"Yes. You?"

"The same. Perhaps because he intends us to work together for the benefit of the other, I should try to conjure food for you, and you should try for me."

"It's worth a shot. What would you like to eat?"

"I'll take a croissant and a small cup of berries, please."

Sure enough, Ryker was able to produce her breakfast. "Your turn. I'd like an omelet and croissant, please."

Within moments, his piping-hot food was sitting on a plate in front of him.

"Thank you! Is coffee too much to hope for?" Ryker asked as he reached for his French pastry. The plate flew across the counter and came to an abrupt stop in front of GiGi. *What the hell?*

GiGi's wide-eyed gaze locked on the plate. She shoved the dish back toward him. His hand didn't make it halfway to its objective before his food slid back to GiGi.

Ryker picked up his wife's breakfast and walked to her side of the counter to place it there. Sure enough, as she reached for the croissant, it slid out of reach.

"Try to handle my food," he instructed as he reached for hers. "Since I can touch yours, and you can touch mine, but we can't touch our own, what does that tell you?"

"That my brother should die a slow, painful death." Her eyes flared wide, and Ryker suspected she'd lost the last material barrier between her and bare-assed.

He chuckled. "The gods of mischief made off with your panties, did they?"

"I don't suppose we will be able to eat unless we feed one another, will we?" she said with a resigned sigh.

"That appears to be the case."

He ripped off a small piece of her croissant and held it to her mouth. The color flooding her face as she ate the food made him squirm inside. He hated her uncomfortableness. Hated that she was forced to endure his presence when she wanted anything but. Yet when her lips gently closed over his fingers, and her wary gaze met his, there was a deeper emotion hidden within the violet-blue depths.

She duplicated his gesture with his pastry, and Ryker resisted the urge to nip her fingers. On and on the feeding went, each bite more erotic than the last as fingers and lips lingered.

GIGI WASN'T BLIND TO THE SPELL BEING WOVEN AROUND HER AND Ryker. Each touch of his fingers against her lips brought to mind their relationship when things like this were almost a daily occurrence. Neither she nor Ryker had considered feeding the other a strawberry or a bite of toast out of the ordinary. Indeed, it had almost always ended up with the two of them making love.

GiGi also wasn't blind to Ryker's building arousal. It was hard to ignore when he was only covered by a sheet. She suspected he had picked up on her own signs of desire. The most telling of all would be the heat in her cheeks. Resisting those bedroom eyes of his—the ones that saw everything whether she wished them to or not—was next to impossible. A single look was able to singe her. Did she continue to fight the attraction? Why, when she wanted him too?

"One last time," she murmured softly.

"What's that?" He leaned closer to hear.

"You and me. Sex. One last time." The words came out as jumbled as they were in her brain. She frowned when he did. "What's wrong?"

"No, GiGi. I don't think so."

The sadness and resignation on his face disturbed her. "I don't understand. You've been teasing about sex since you returned."

"Not sex, sweetheart. *Making love*. And I don't want one last time. I want *forever*." Ryker dusted his hands of crumbs and left her sitting with her mouth hanging open.

The rejection stung, but she understood his reluctance. It was going to be hard enough to walk away as things already were, but if they complicated the ending with sex—she wouldn't think of it as making love, couldn't really—then their parting was likely to be more difficult still.

With slow precision, she rose and brought the dishes to the sink. As she washed their plates, she wondered how long they'd be forced to endure this exquisite torture. For that's what it was. This game of Alastair's was a constant reminder of times gone by. A time when she and Ryker were hot and crazy for each other. Being trapped here with him was slowly eating away at her determination. All she wanted to do was forgive the past and welcome him back with open arms. Yet, she'd be a fool to do so.

Despite what Ryker said, there was no doubt in GiGi's mind that he would grow bored without danger and intrigue to entertain him. How was she supposed to trust him to put her first? It was all she had ever wanted: to be first. Instead, she had been ever the convenient spouse, available whenever he decided to return home. There were times when she went weeks without hearing from him, and she remained in a constant state of worry until the day he returned. He'd ease her fears, make mad, passionate love to her, then disappear again after a few days.

No, she couldn't do that again. She wasn't cut out to be the wife of a spy. Not for one moment did she believe Ryker could walk away from his career. His identity was wrapped up in what he did. Having lost so many people who mattered to her—most recently her brother Preston—GiGi couldn't take any more death.

5

"*R*eady for lunch?"

GiGi lingered in the doorway, looking like a blonde goddess. She'd found another sheet and created a toga to wrap around her body, draping over one shoulder. Her hair was pulled up into a ponytail with a slight bump at the crown to add a bit of elegance to the hairdo. Makeup flawless, she stole Ryker's breath.

He simply nodded.

What he wanted to do was wail like a toddler with a broken cookie. How was he to get through another meal like their breakfast?

"Are you okay?"

He should've assured her he was, but he really wasn't. What was the point in lying about it? "No."

A deep frown settled between her brows, and she drifted farther into the room.

"What's going on?"

"So many things, GiGi. So damned many things," he said with feeling.

Settling one hip on the edge of his desk, she smoothed a stray lock of hair back from his forehead. "Tell me."

Oh, how he wanted to, but she was half of his problems. Yet the earnestness she exuded begged him to take a chance and spill his guts.

"Beecham. I still can't find a way to prove to the Council he was responsible for Trina's murder. It's been weeks since the truth came to light, and I've been unable to bring him to justice."

"Why do it the legal way?"

"What are you saying?"

Surely she didn't mean he should take the law into his own hands?

"You should kill him."

Okay, maybe she did. Words escaped him.

"Look, we all know he's responsible. Alastair told us Preston revealed as much when he appeared to him at the pond. Why do we need proof?"

Inexplicable rage flooded his being. "Your family's arrogance is what is always getting you all into trouble." Standing, he shoved back his office chair. "You all charge into danger without a thought to who else it might harm. And it does. Each and every time." He drew in a lungful of oxygen and held up his hand when she would've argued. "Don't. You can't justify your excuses. Look at the history, GiGi. Trina, Aurora, Chloe, Dereck, Rafe, Quentin. All injured or, like in my sister's case, murdered. Now one of your own. Why the hell don't any of you think before you act?"

He had rattled off the people closest to her family and had no doubt each name struck GiGi squarely in the chest.

Pale and trembling, she blinked back the tears brightening her eyes. "And you, Ryker? What has been *your* death toll with that damned job? All the people you mentioned? Yeah, it wasn't any one of us seeking trouble. It was trouble seeking *us*. You'd know that if you were around more."

"Don't you dare lay this on my door. I've spent my career as a double agent for your own brother. All in an effort to protect *you*."

"Me? Pfft. You were never *here* to protect me."

"I wasn't far." As quickly as his anger came, it fled. He cupped her devastated face within his palms. "I was never far," he murmured as he lowered his mouth to hers.

Her hands encircled his waist, and she met him halfway. He imagined she'd expected a passionate kiss; however, it was anything but. When his mouth settled on hers, it was for the briefest of seconds. A simple showing of the affection he felt for her.

He drew back a hairsbreadth and whispered, "I will always protect you, GiGi. *Always.*"

While he was fervent in his declaration, he managed to keep the fires within banked. GiGi had made it clear that she'd welcome sex, but Ryker wanted more than an itch scratched. If he couldn't be more than a stud service, then he wouldn't give in to his desires, nor would he satisfy hers.

"I don't need your protection, Ryker. I never did. I needed you to be a husband."

What could he say to that? *Nothing.* He'd already asked for a second chance, and she'd rejected him. No amount of apologies or regrets would turn back the clock on what was gone. It was said Thornes only loved once. His wife might be the exception to the family legend.

"We should go eat," he said in place of all the words struggling to be heard.

RYKER HAD LOCKED HIMSELF IN HIS STUDY DIRECTLY AFTER LUNCH, and GiGi was bored out of her mind. None of her family members had answered any of the texts she'd shot off last night or today. Either all the cell towers in the Leiper's Fork vicinity were suddenly down, or the Thornes were all complicit with the lockdown. She suspected the latter.

Reading wasn't an option because the furniture in the living room and bedroom seemed to have a mind of its own and continuously dumped her out. If she wasn't quick on her feet, her backside would be one solid bruise.

All she had left to do was wander the house and reminisce about the past. It was depressing as hell. She found herself back in the kitchen, staring at the island. A touch of the stone surface proved cool, and she wondered what Ryker had thought upon seeing the redesigned space.

Gone were the mocha-stained shaker cabinets they'd so lovingly decided on together. Gone were the dark granite countertops. The black appliances had been updated to stainless. Now, the upper cabinets were the palest of grays, and the lowers were a deep charcoal. The granite had been replaced with a white quartz flecked with silver, and the backsplash was a white subway pattern that gave the entire space a clean, uniform look.

Even with the changes, the kitchen had been rarely used. Once the heart of the home, now it was just an abandoned space she gave a cursory magical cleaning every few days.

Overcome with the urge to bake, she tried to conjure the items she'd need. Nothing. Damn her brother!

"What if I tell you I'm making a pie for Ryker?" she called out. "Will you provide the stupid ingredients then?"

"You're going to make me a pie?"

GiGi whipped around and found her husband lounging in the doorway, an amused smile tugging at his mouth.

"I will if it gets me the items I need to bake."

"I could try to conjure them for you." He straightened and closed the distance between them. "I can't guarantee you'll be able to touch them, but I'm willing to help if you show me what to do."

Did she want his help? It would mean a close proximity for at least a half hour or more. Every second spent in his company slowly ate away at her anger and determination to be free of him. Dare she risk the thawing of her heart?

"I thought you were working."

"Nothing is pressing, but if it were, it's not like I could accomplish a thing with my chair bucking like a bronco with a burr under the saddle."

The visual made her giggle. "I had a similar experience when I tried to read a book."

"What do you say? Want an assistant baker?"

"If I don't do something, I'll lose my mind and set fire to this place," she groused.

"It might give this space some warmth," he muttered.

"You don't like the new design?"

"It's cold. Almost clinical. There isn't one thing decorating the counters."

Ryker surprised a gasp from her. A quick glance around the room proved him right. "I never noticed."

"You don't spend much time in here?"

What could she tell him? Despite giving the kitchen a facelift, GiGi had been unable to exorcise the ghosts. Everywhere she looked, she saw him whipping up an omelet or pouring a glass of wine. Or worse yet, the two of them making love.

"No. Initially, I would have dinner with Preston and the girls. As they grew older and family dinners became less frequent, I would sometimes go to Nashville for an evening. Mostly, I would magically create what I felt like eating and watch television or read."

"I should never have left you alone."

"It no longer matters." Or so she tried to tell herself.

He opened his mouth as if to form a retort, thought better about what he wanted to say, and shook his head. "What ingredients do we need?"

"What flavor pie would you like?"

"Cherry?"

He was able to produce everything they needed and then some. "I thought we could make cookies while we're at it."

Ryker looked so boyish and earnest, GiGi had to laugh. "Fine. Cookies, too."

Oddly enough, the cookie sheets, pie pan, and large mixer were all present and accounted for. Ryker assigned himself as Mix Master, and GiGi was to measure the ingredients because she was going by her mother's recipe that she'd memorized.

They kept the atmosphere light and playful, neither delving into hurtful topics. It wasn't until he was rolling out the dough and she was dropping spoonfuls of chocolate chip cookie dough on the parchment paper that she brought up the question upmost in her mind.

"Ryker? How long do you think Alastair plans to draw this out?"

He paused for a mere heartbeat or two before he continued the chore she'd given him. "I don't know, sweetheart. I imagine until we reconcile or he's satisfied our marriage is over."

She stopped and studied him. "But our marriage *is* over. You understand that, right?" She was desperate for him to agree with her. The time to move on was now. She *needed* it to be now. No longer could she walk around faithful to a man and a love that was never meant to be.

"I understand you want it to be." Throwing down the rolling pin, he braced his hands on the counter's edge. "Because this is your heartfelt desire, I'm going along with it. But never for one minute believe it's what I wanted. It's not." He went to the sink and washed his hands. "I think you can handle the rest of this on your own. Come find me when you want dinner."

He was gone before she could apologize.

Why was she the one always left feeling like the bad guy? She was the person wronged in this relationship. Why, when all she wanted was to live out her days in relative peace? Maybe she should travel more. Perhaps take the occasional lover here or there. For sure, she would never love again, that was the family curse, but that didn't mean her sexual well should be left to run dry. It had been abandoned for too many years to count, unless one considered her battery-operated boyfriend.

With a resigned sigh, she placed the pans of cookies in the oven to bake and finished making the pie. Maybe she could use it as a peace offering at dinner. Despite what everyone thought about her, she didn't want to fight with Ryker. She just wanted him out of her life.

Her cell buzzed. A quick check of the screen showed a message from Sebastian Drake. She'd met him a few weeks back when she and Aurora were doing what they could to find Aurora's brother, Jace. Sebastian had shown a marked interest in her and went so far as to acquire her phone number.

Still married?

She grimaced and typed, *For another few weeks.*

Her phone pinged.

Want to have dinner with me tonight?

Did she?

Can't. I'm being held prisoner in my own house.

The phone in her hand rang, and Sebastian barely let her get out the "Hello."

"Please tell me you're kidding," he said.

"I'm afraid not."

"Text me your location. I'll come."

"I'm not in danger, Baz. I'm merely unable to leave."

"What's going on, GiGi?"

"My brother thought it would be a brilliant idea to trap me in the house with Ryker until we settled our differences." She heard a choked laugh come across the line and scowled. "Seriously? You think it's funny?"

"A little, but only because your brother is a cunning wanker."

She hit the speaker button so she could continue to prepare the pie. "He is at that. I'm going to murder him."

"I take it you are alone right now?"

"I am. And you?"

"Yes. In my bedroom, fantasizing about a gorgeous blonde I met some time ago."

"Really? Was she hot?"

"Very. What are you wearing?"

GiGi grinned. Men were so easy. "Nothing but a sheet."

"And that dumbass husband of yours hasn't made a move? Trouble with his plumbing?"

A prickle of awareness tickled her spine. Turning, she spied Ryker in the doorway. His arctic stare was felt to the bone. Slowly, with great deliberation, he stalked to where she was rooted to the spot. She was like a damned squirrel in the middle of the road— unable to retreat to save its own life.

"GiGi? You there, love?"

"I... uh, I've got to go," she stammered.

"I think that's a very good idea," Ryker bit out. He reached her phone before she did. "Don't call back until after the divorce if you value your life, Drake."

"I think Gi—"

Ryker disconnected before Sebastian could finish his protest. Without lifting his gaze from the smartphone in his hand, he said, "I came back to try one more time to make you see reason. Imagine my hurt and surprise to find you joking with your new lover about my *plumbing*."

"He isn't. We weren't. Not like that."

The eyes he lifted to her were the eyes of a stranger. A cold, dead-inside stranger. "You succeeded in making me see the truth. Congratulations."

He glanced back at the device in his hand. A quick scroll found him the number he searched for. Ryker left it on speakerphone, and when Alastair's voicemail message echoed in the kitchen, her husband growled, "Game over, Alastair. Remove the spell, or I'll set fire to this fucking house. You have ten minutes."

He hit the disconnect and dropped her phone on top of the pie crust.

"You may want to gather anything you don't want burned to a cinder," he said. All emotion but iciness was gone from his tone.

"Ryker, please."

"I'm done. In ten minutes, you can call Drake back and apologize for my rudeness. I'm sure you'll both have a blast laughing at my expense. Be sure to tell him how pathetic I was to think we could salvage our marriage. That should get a chuckle."

"No, Ryker! It wasn't like that!"

In all the time she'd known him, there was never anything but adoration for her in his expression. Now, seeing his countenance wiped clean of all but dispassion and borderline hatred, she realized what she'd thrown away in her stubbornness.

"I love you," she whispered with dawning horror that she'd truly lost him.

"I don't care."

6

*A*s Ryker thumbed through his papers, deciding what to keep and what could be left behind, GiGi rushed into the room.

"I don't want to be done," she declared.

Snorting his disbelief, he held tight to the fury he'd felt in the kitchen. Hearing her tease and flirt with Sebastian had brought to light their real circumstances.

Truth one: inasmuch as it cut out his heart, Ryker recognized they were done. He could never repair what was broken because she wouldn't let him. She didn't want to bridge the gap. She enjoyed being a free agent.

Truth two: she liked Sebastian Drake for more than friendship. In the minute of conversation Ryker had overheard, he recognized her interest in another man. Maybe that's why his anger had morphed into a living, breathing thing.

"Christ, GiGi! Just accept that you've won. You wanted to crush my heart and pay me back for all the wrongs you think I've committed. You did what you set out to do." He started to blindly fling papers into his briefcase. "Leave me the fuck alone."

"No, I—"

"What will it take? Huh? What?" Ripping the wedding ring from his finger, the band she'd lovingly inscribed, he flung it away. She flinched when it clattered to the floor. "There. Maybe you can melt it down and have it remade for Drake or whomever the hell you want next."

"Ryker, I made a mistake."

"Swap the name from Ryker to GiGi, and you have the same excuse I offered." He looked her in the eye and said the one thing he knew she'd never forgive. "I lied. I did sleep with Marguerite the week I was there. More than once. Just as I'm sure you've slept with Drake."

Her arms folded across her waist, and a harsh sob escaped her lips. "You're just saying that to be cruel. You didn't."

"Do yourself a favor and stop being a delusional fool, sweetheart. Men are bastards who cheat. That's what you tell yourself on those cold, lonely nights, isn't it? If you're with good ol' Sebastian long enough, he'll do the same. Or maybe he won't. Either way, good luck." A sharp snap of the locks, and he lifted the case. He closed his eyes and brought up the image of Alastair's living room. His cells warmed as his magic ramped up, but still he couldn't teleport. *"God-damn him!"*

Drawing on his metal element, he picked up a small steel paper-weight and expanded it to create a baseball-sized sphere and packed it with all the power he possessed. A hard lob at the study window knocked out the frame with its bulletproof glass.

Freedom, at last. As he turned to bid *sayonara* to his soon-to-be-ex wife, the sun glinted off an object the distance.

Intruder? Enemy? Then it clicked—*Sniper!*

Ryker's instincts kicked into overdrive. He dropped his case and lunged for GiGi. *"Get down!"*

His order caused her to jerk, and that small movement, combined with his tug on her hand, was enough to remove her from the bullet's trajectory. The vase, which had been in direct line with her heart, shattered.

"Get to the panic room, GiGi," he ordered briskly.

"What about you?" Her eyes were wild, darting around in an

attempt to find the threat. The ironclad grip she had on his arm was on the verge of painful. "I'm not going without you."

"I'll be right behind you. Now go. I need you to get to safety."

She nodded and crawled for the door. Two more bullets splintered the wood of the doorframe. Freezing in place, she shot him a frantic glance.

"One sec." He kicked the front panel of his desk and exposed a small arsenal of weapons. Checking the safety was off, he handed her a small .32 caliber Beretta. "It's got hollow-point tips. It'll do some damage. Now go."

He didn't bother to watch her leave, instead packing as many weapons as he could carry wrapped in his sheet: four knives, two 9mm guns, a few smoke grenades, and an assault rifle. The Thornes tended to rely on magic, but Ryker found in his line of work there were times he needed something a little more substantial in the event Blockers were present. He didn't care to be caught with his ass out in a fight, but with no clothing to tuck his weapons into, his sheet sling would have to do.

He could hear shouting and the sound of feet pounding the ground. Daring a glance outside, he could see a handful of uniformed men closing in. How they'd discovered where he lived was anyone's guess. Why they had targeted GiGi in the first shooting attempt was a little easier to reason. By taking her life, their assailants believed they could strike at the heart of him. That perhaps he would be so devastated he failed to fight back. But they hadn't counted on the couple in question. Ryker would annihilate anyone who hurt his wife.

Grabbing a roll of clear fishing wire, he quickly rolled out fifteen feet and tied the end to the pin of the smoke grenade. He jammed the panel of his desk in place as the first soldier crested the low stone wall surrounding their garden. Resting the barrel of his gun on the flat surface, he sighted and squeezed off three rounds. Two to the chest to slow the guy's approach and one to the head to take him out. One down, Goddess knew how many more behind him. Concentrating his magic, he lifted the window frame back into place. It wouldn't stop anyone, but it might slow them down when they had to pull it back out from its mooring.

Wasting no time, he wove the wire around the closest chair and across the opening the attackers would need to traverse to get inside the house. It wasn't the best trip wire Ryker had ever rigged up, but it would have to do.

He snatched up his briefcase and took off at a run toward the center of the house. He turned the corner and stopped short in the entry of the panic room. GiGi had her back to the wall and her gun pointed directly at his chest.

"Now's your chance to be rid of me. No one would know it wasn't our attackers."

"Shut up, you damned fool, and get inside." She pointed to the television monitor. "They are coming en masse. I've already placed a call to Alastair, but I got his voicemail."

He heard the fear in her voice. "Call Knox Carlyle. He's closest and the most level-headed. He'll know what to do."

Turning around, he slid the faux-wall panel used to hide the room back to its original position, magically sealing the edge to blend with the existing wall. The long, three-inch-thick metal rods locked into place and secured them inside.

GiGi became more agitated as she failed to reach Knox. "Do you think whoever is behind this has attacked the others first?"

Christ, he hoped not.

"We can't think like that right now, sweetheart. Let's get dressed and use the escape hatch, okay?"

"Dressed?" GiGi wasn't sure she'd heard him correctly. "How the hell can we get dressed when all our clothes disappeared last night?"

Ryker didn't answer but went to a keypad and entered a code. A long, deep drawer popped from the wall. Inside there were two sets of clothing: his and hers.

"Those were here the entire time?"

"Yep."

She felt as if her head was going to explode. For the last eighteen hours, she'd been forced to wear a freaking sheet, and he knew there were clothes stashed in the panic room? In short, jerky motions, she dropped her sheet and pulled on her underwear.

He stopped in the process of dressing to watch her.

"What?" she snapped.

"I like watching the jiggly bits." He smirked, and GiGi fought an answering grin.

"In case you forgot, the enemy is about to penetrate our defenses. How about you hurry it along?"

He tore his hot gaze from her semi-naked body and scrambled into his own clothing. Squatting, he untied his bundle and started hiding weapons on his person. He handed her a knife. "If you're attacked, pretend it's me and go for the jugular."

"Funny," she muttered as she pulled on a pair of combat boots. "How did you know these would fit?"

He lifted a brow as he dragged on his own footwear.

"Never mind. What now?"

"Now we wait. Hopefully, we'll overhear something important or at least be able to tell how many soldiers are out there."

"Soldiers? What makes you think they are military?"

Ryker tapped the closest screen. "See the emblem there? Witches' Council."

Horror flooded her being, and she broke out in a cold sweat. Escaping the Council would become a life-long pursuit. She spun to face him. "Why?"

"Maybe spies aren't allowed to quit." He shrugged. "Or maybe Beecham is behind this. It's possible they aren't truly Council military but are dressed to look like they are. Who knows?"

He slid another drawer open and removed a set of keys, two passports, and money.

"Ryker, couldn't we conjure what we need?"

"I have no idea if Alastair's spell will carry past the boundaries of the walls. I'd rather be safe than sorry."

"Why are you bothering to see to my safety?" she asked quietly.

He froze in tucking the passports into the black duffle he'd dug up. With a snort and a shake of his head, he resumed packing the bag.

She laid a hand on his arm, and he flinched.

"Ryker, look at me. Tell me why you're bothering."

"If you don't know the answer, you're an idiot, GiGi."

"Fifteen minutes ago, you were ready to exit my life for good."

"Yep. But leaving you alive and safe, is a whole helluva lot different than leaving you dead, isn't it?"

She heard the hurt and anger in his voice. By speaking to Sebastian, she'd crossed a line in his book.

"He could never be you," she said softly. "No one could."

He stilled.

For a long moment, she thought he wouldn't say anything, but then he turned burning eyes to her.

"How the hell can you say that to me now? Is this a game to you?"

"No." She shook her head to emphasize her denial. "Never."

Her heartbeat maintained a hard, rapid thudding until he spoke again.

"None of that matters right now. If we get out alive—and that's my fervent hope—*then* we can discuss this."

"No, Ryker. You need to know how much I love you." GiGi clutched his arm, desperate for him to understand. If they didn't make it out of this, she wanted no more lies or regrets. "And I don't care if you… slept with Marg—"

"She-who-shall-not-be-named," he inserted.

"Right. Her. I don't care. It's in the past." Goddess, those words were hard to say. In fact, they felt ripped from her very vocal cords just to voice.

"The past has been our present for a long time. You've made it so. How do you expect to exist without all the crosses you bear?"

A lead weight settled in her stomach, and her mouth dried up along with all the excuses and denials she wanted to hurl in his direction. She dropped her hand to her side.

"I suppose we should go." She forced a small smile.

Ryker stared at her for another long moment, but GiGi couldn't meet his eyes. She sensed his desire to speak, but in the end, he turned away. Squatting, he lifted a trapdoor that had blended so seamlessly with the floor, GiGi had overlooked it.

"Follow the stairs down and pause at the bottom. I'll be down momentarily."

Every few feet a motion-detector picked up her movement and illuminated the tunnel. She was curious where it led but waited for Ryker instead of exploring.

True to his word, he arrived shortly after her.

"Where does this lead?"

"To a hidden garage."

She nearly stumbled. "*The* hidden garage? The one with the Corvette you've always refused to let me drive?"

His lips quirked. "That's the one."

"Ryker? Doesn't it seem odd to you that we can leave now? Or do you think Alastair didn't know to charm this tunnel?"

"This is part of our house, as is the garage. It could be we get there and can't leave."

"Surely, he's set up for some contingency in the event of an emergency." She tried to keep the alarm out of her voice and failed.

"I don't know. I find it odd anyone found our house to begin with, but to break through the wards surrounding the property required strong magic. All things we'll need to take a look at later. My first priority is to get you to safety."

They walked in silence, keeping a brisk pace. It wasn't long before they reached the trapdoor leading to the garage.

"I'll go first. Count to twenty, and if you hear no gunfire, come out. If you do, throw the bolt from the inside and haul ass down the corridor on the left. It leads to the clearing and comes out by the standing stones."

The stones he referred to were the ones hidden deep within the earth surrounding the clearing. When the Thornes needed powerful magic, they were able to call up the formation and altar with an ancient spell. GiGi went there often to meditate and commune with nature. It was one of the only places she could go to exorcise the ghosts of the past and soothe her overactive mind.

"If you have to, hide inside the altar. You can use your magic to create the oxygen you need for a few hours. No one would think to look for you there."

"You're making me nervous."

"I believe in contingency plans, sweetheart. They've kept me alive this long."

He turned to go, and she laid her hand on his arm.

"Ryker."

With a deep sigh, he faced her.

"Please be careful. I…" She faltered. The set look on his face didn't allow for sentiment. The spy had returned, and he was all business.

7

*R*yker did his damnedest to keep his expression emotionless and his hands to himself when what he really wanted to do was crush GiGi to him and assure her everything would be fine. She was feeling sentimental because of their circumstances, that was all. He'd seen it hundreds of times before. Upon embarking on a mission, soldiers would become downright maudlin. They would have their friends promise to take care of this loved one or the other. Those same men would be the first to turn back into hardened assholes when they returned unscathed.

GiGi would rethink her stance when they were safe. She'd throw him right back into the bad guy column and go back to flirting with the likes of Sebastian Drake. Ryker couldn't allow himself to care anymore. If it messed with his head, he'd be vulnerable in the field. He had to shift into complete business mode to survive. Cold and clinical saved the day—always. Emotion had no place in war games.

But dammit if her crestfallen look wasn't getting to him. She lifted her chin and put on a brave face. Her courageous spirit struck right at the heart of him.

"For the record, I've always found she-who-shall-not-be-named repugnant," he said gruffly. Without waiting for a response, he threw open the trapdoor and crawled through.

Ducking low, he ran for the far wall by the entrance and peered out the windows. Careful to keep close to the wall and out of a sniper's line of sight, he checked each of the four directions. Keys in hand, he popped the hood of the 'Vette to do a fast check. Everything seemed to be in working order. No added devices to blow up his car or rig it to breakdown. He quickly scanned under the frame.

The trapdoor opened, and his wife's brilliant blonde head came into view. She scanned the area and entered the garage more fully. "Safe?"

"Seems to be." He tossed her the keys. "I'm going outside to survey the surrounding area. Be ready to drive like a bat out of hell if need be. Careful with her. She's a powerful beast and needs a firm hand." Not unlike GiGi herself. "Take to the road and don't stop for anything or anyone. Don't even dream of going to your family's estate. I'll meet you in two hours at the Carter House in Franklin. I'll call you before then if it's safe to return. Got it?"

"You're not coming with me?" Her hand shook as she unlocked the car and pulled the door open.

"No. I have to clean house and find out who wants us dead."

"Ryker, don't go back. There are too many."

"I have Granny Thorne's cloaking spell and the ability to glamour into one of their own. I'll be fine."

She flung herself into his arms and held tight. Ryker savored holding her one last time. With her wrapped in his embrace, her willowy frame pressed to his, he closed his eyes and breathed deeply of her unique floral scent.

He nuzzled her hair and kissed her temple. "It's going to be all right, sweetheart. I promise."

"Please come with me. I don't want you confronting those men. I couldn't bear it if something happened to you."

"Just promise me you'll have a proper mourning period before you hook up with that toad, Drake."

She snorted a laugh and pulled back to cup his face. "If you run to your death because of some stupid macho need to prove your manhood or worth, you get no mourning period. I'll be too pissed at you."

"Fair enough."

They stared at one another. All the hurt faded away, but they had no time to say the things that needed to be said. Ryker went for the kiss and packed all his love into that one action. She returned his kiss with a passion that rivaled that of their younger years. They broke their embrace to drag oxygen into their lungs. Each stared at the other in wonder.

"I do love you," she whispered.

"The feeling has always been mutual, sweetheart." He smoothed back a wayward lock of her hair. "I'll see you soon. Try to stay out of trouble. Oh, and no picking up admirers along the way."

"I've been such an idiot."

"At times, yes." He grinned. "But exceedingly clever at others. This isn't goodbye, GiGi. I'll meet you in Franklin in two hours."

"Two hours. Don't be late."

He tangled his fingers in the hair at the back of her head and lowered his mouth to hers for a sweet, drawn-out kiss. "I wouldn't dream of it."

Releasing her, he strode out the door to check the surrounding area. He must be a fool to stay behind to deal with the nuisance of the soldiers when he had a warm and willing wife on the other side of that garage wall.

Utilizing the words to the Thorne cloaking spell, he effectively became invisible. As he jogged toward their home, he heard his sports car roar to life. A quick glance over his shoulder showed GiGi easing out of the garage. She cast one last look his way and floored it in the opposite direction. The throaty rumble echoed off the trees along their land and faded in the distance.

Ryker sent a small prayer up for the Goddess to ensure GiGi's protection, then crept through the woods to see what he could find out about their house breakers.

WITH EACH MILE THAT PASSED, GIGI'S ANXIETY GREW. SHE TRIED every phone number in her contact list with no success. Either the entire family had been ordered not to answer if she called, or her family was in dire straits.

Only a short distance outside of town, she pulled to the shoulder of Southall Road and let the Corvette idle. Running away was not an option. She was a Thorne, dammit, and Thornes didn't hide. Of course, she didn't want to appear like one of those too-stupid-to-live characters in a romance novel, who didn't have the sense the Goddess gave a mule and who stormed into trouble at every turn. Ryker would kill her himself if she was captured or injured—especially after telling her to flee.

Her phone rang, and she scrambled to pick up.

"What's happened?" Alastair asked without preamble.

GiGi gave him a rundown, then asked, "Is everyone okay? No one is answering when I call. I'm worried, brother."

"I'm scrying as we speak. Everyone seems to be fine with the exception of your fool husband."

"What?" Her heart stopped, and her stomach rebelled. "What happened to Ryker?"

"I misspoke. I should've asked why that dunderhead is rushing into danger instead of seeing to your safety."

"He did see to my safety, but he insisted on returning to see what he could discover. I'm worried, Alastair."

"Don't be. Head to Thorne Manor. I'll grab my security team and provide backup for your husband."

"Thank you," she said feelingly.

After they disconnected, she drove straight to her family home where two of her nieces were awaiting her outside. She gave Summer and Autumn a brief explanation of the situation.

The three of them loitered on the wide, wraparound porch as they impatiently waited for word from Alastair or Ryker.

"Did it work?" Autumn asked curiously.

GiGi shot her a sharp glance. "Did what work?" It was not a stretch to guess what her niece wanted to know.

"The plan to lock you and Uncle Ryker in." The mischievous look gave Autumn away as did the amused smirk playing about her mouth.

"None of your business. But whose idea was it to steal our clothes?"

Summer gasped and let loose her laughter. "Mama never told us she was adding that little touch," she said when she could finally catch her breath.

Autumn's eyes sparkled with humor. "Oh, to know the details of how you found that out."

If the current circumstances were any less dire, GiGi might have found the whole thing as funny as they did. However, she was too worried about her husband and her brother to join in their amusement.

A shift in the air pressure indicated an incoming witch, and they all remained still in anticipation of an arrival.

Aurora appeared and rushed up the steps to join them. "Alastair wanted me to wait at home, but I couldn't stand to be there with only stoic Alfred for company." She embraced GiGi. "Are you all right?"

"I'm so far from all right, and you are on my shit list. I thought we were friends. How could you pull a trick like this when we have enemies coming out of the damned woodwork?" GiGi's irritation was in direct correlation with her fear for the men. She knew her anger was probably out of proportion, considering she and Ryker were on their way to clearing the air between them.

Aurora's hands dropped to her sides. Remorse coated her words when she said, "I had no idea you'd be attacked, GiGi. None at all. Alastair wove in an escape clause to the spell."

The energy crackled and sparked in the air around them.

"I should be allowed to make my own choices, Rorie. Not be forced into a relationship I didn't want!" she snapped.

The horrified expressions on their faces caused her heart to sink. She spun around. Her timing couldn't have been worse, because with the rise of her emotions and the elements she'd inadvertently summoned, the arrival of her husband and brother was hidden.

"Ryker, it's not like it sounded." She held out a hand, silently beseeching him to understand.

"Do you want it now?" He asked softly.

Tears burned her eyes, and she swallowed back a sob. She nodded.

He handed off his weapon and what looked to be the pie she'd prepped to one of Alastair's security team, then bound up the steps two at a time. Stopping just shy of her, he said, "Prove it."

She flew into his open arms and clung to him, her nose buried against his throat.

"Tell me what I need to do to prove it to you."

He shifted his head until his lips were in line with her ear. "What if I said you had to off Pretty Boy Drake?"

"Consider him dead," she returned.

"You are speaking my love language, sweetheart." He heaved a regretful sigh. "As much as I want to explore the lengths you'd go to in order to make up, we should discuss what happened." He lowered his voice for her ears alone. "Also, when we are alone, I'm going to take great great satisfaction in spanking your delectable ass for not listening when I told you to head to Franklin."

"I'd like to see you try," she retorted.

He barked out a laugh. "There's my girl."

Did she imagine the emphasis on "my"? She hoped not.

8

*H*is timing always seemed to be crap when it came to his wife, but Ryker was learning to obtain all the facts regarding her conversations without overreacting. Twice in a single day he'd walked in on a damning statement. The horror and remorse on her face the last time had made it impossible to turn away. Her pleading eyes had done him in.

Mostly, she wasn't wrong. GiGi should be allowed to make her own choices and not have a relationship forced on her. Which was why, when he was sure they were safe, he'd give her alone time to decide once and for all if she wanted them to reconcile. If, after a quiet interval when emotions weren't as high and life had settled to normal, she still wanted to be with him, he'd be all in. But he didn't want regrets on either side.

"What are you thinking about?" GiGi asked quietly from beside him.

Instinctively, he looked down the length of the dinner table to judge who was paying attention. It was an old habit, one he'd spent years cultivating to maintain privacy during a conversation. With a rueful shake of his head, Ryker focused on his wife. "You."

She questioned him with her soft violet-blue eyes.

"More specifically, *us*," he corrected.

"Are you having second thoughts about what you heard earlier?"

"No. Not in the way you might think." He lifted her hand and bussed her fingertips. "You have the right to determine what you want on your own, without the game-playing."

Her hand tightened beneath his. "Thank you for understanding."

"When everything settles, I'll give you time to decide if it's me you want or if it's the divorce."

She straightened in her seat and tugged her hand away. "What the hell does that mean?" she whispered fiercely. "I told you I loved you and that I'm ready to move beyond what happened."

"People say things in the heat of the moment, sweetheart. Sometimes they don't truly mean it, but they voice the words because they think they are never going to see the other person again," he explained in a calm, matter-of-fact tone. "I don't want you to have regrets."

Her mouth tightened, and she stared down at her plate. Ryker had the feeling he'd made a misstep where she was concerned. What was new? He'd been misstepping their entire relationship.

He sighed heavily and laid a gentle hand on her knee to gain her attention. "GiGi, let's not find a reason to fight tonight. I'm emotionally and physically wrung out. I want to eat my dinner then share a glass of wine with my wife on the porch swing." He leaned closer. "Maybe I'll get to steal a kiss while I'm at it. Please don't be mad at me for trying to give you what you want."

She rose and tossed down her napkin. Wordlessly, she held out her hand, palm down, for him to take. When they were ensconced on the swing, he set it in motion with his toe and cuddled her close.

"Thank you," she said softly. It was odd to hear her voice devoid of rancor or sarcasm. He'd almost forgotten her normal, melodious way of speech.

"For what?"

"For saving my life today. For not having a meltdown that I didn't meet you in Franklin. I couldn't not check on my family."

"As to the first part, I will never not protect you. As for the second, I was a fool to ever think otherwise." He pressed his lips together to hide his amused smile.

She shifted to face him. "About Sebastian, I did enjoy flirting with him. He's made me feel alive in a way I haven't in a very long time. I think he reminds me of you in a way. When you were younger and more carefree."

The struggle to suppress his jealousy was mighty.

"He's good looking, rich, and intelligent. What's not to be attracted to?" He couldn't meet her questioning gaze. "It might just destroy me if you pursue a relationship with him, but if you feel the need..." The remainder of the offer stuck in the back of his throat. No way could he condone an affair, but GiGi had to determine what she desired.

"I don't want him, Ryker." She trailed a finger across his brow and circled it down his cheek to pause at his lips. Her gaze followed the path, and she stared at his mouth with unconcealed hunger. "I only want you."

"Thank the Goddess," he said feelingly.

She straddled his lap and cradled his face.

Taking her time, she traced his features. The smooth softness of her touch as she teased along his lips and through his beard was erotic as hell. She trailed her fingertips over the plane of his cheeks and paused just above his cheekbones to secure his head. All the while he sat immobile and allowed GiGi to explore to her heart's content. Finally, she did what he'd wanted her to do all day; she claimed his mouth in a kiss that shook them both to their cores.

Ryker's hands were everywhere in a flurry of movement. Gripping her neck, dragging her closer, sliding under her top to caress her breasts, locking on her ass. He couldn't decide where he wanted to touch her the most and felt the need to explore everything at once. She was no better. The fingers of one hand dug into his hair while the other hand, of its own accord, roved his shoulder, chest, and throat. Pleasure flooded him. Pleasure from her physical touch, sure, but the enjoyment and gratification of knowing she wanted to touch him, wanted to be with him as his spouse, as his better half, was so much stronger.

GiGi gyrated her pelvis until Ryker gripped her hips and halted her movements. Dragging his lips from hers, he struggled to inhale. "Jesus, sweetheart," he panted out. "I fear if you continue, I'm going to lose control."

"Would that be a bad thing?" She teased.

"It would be if you don't want all hell and back to witness me taking you here and now. There isn't much by way of privacy on this porch."

She released a low, wicked laugh. It deepened when he groaned.

"By the way, I knew it was you down in Grand Cayman, posing as the hired help," she murmured.

She'd been magnificent in her anger, and then later, in her blasé striptease act. He chuckled at the memory and toyed with her erect nipple. "I don't know what you're talking about."

"Are you trying to say, you weren't the hot guy who delivered my bags?"

He paused in the action of worshiping her throat. "*The bellhop?* I was *room service*. You better not have stripped for any other employee."

She giggled and stretched her neck to allow better access.

"GiGi," he growled.

"I didn't. I just wanted you to admit you glamoured into the resort worker."

"There are days I think *you* should have been the secret agent. Your ability to uncover information is frighteningly efficient." He drew back and met her laughing gaze. "How did you know it was me?"

"Like you said, you would never not protect me. Although how you knew where I went so quickly has me curious."

"I may have charmed your wedding ring to track you."

She surprised him when she laughed and glanced down at the jewelry in question. He expected her to have a fit.

"How does it work?" she asked.

"A simple pin on my Google Maps."

"We've been married for longer than Google Maps has been around," she protested.

"True. Prior to the digital age, I used a paper map."

"Clever." She shifted her hips to rub against his straining erection, and he nearly moaned his frustration. "I think we should put the same spell on your ring."

Regret struck, swift and strong. "I didn't pick it up after I threw it earlier."

"I did." The hand she'd tangled in his hair eased, and GiGi drew back slightly to dig around in her pants pocket.

His eyes began to sting, and he closed his lids to ease the burn. Inhaling deeply, he got his wayward emotions under control. "Thank you."

Slipping it on his finger, she raised his hand to place a kiss on the ring. Love shone brightly from her violet-blue eyes. Her irises were lighter than he'd seen in a long time—a witch's tell. It only required one glance to determine the happiness of a Thorne witch. No words were necessary as they shared a moment of understanding. Finally, he cleared his throat of the raw emotion.

"I've never taken it off since the first time you put it on my finger."

She frowned her confusion. "How did you hide it on missions?"

"A simple spell. The magic was so light, most times I avoided detection. The times I didn't, I blamed it on Blockers."

"I'm surprised Zhu Lin let you get away with that."

"He believed me to be a trusted member of his team. Until I gave myself away to save Winnie, he seemed oblivious to my deception."

"I never thanked you for your sacrifice the day she was rescued."

The somber quality of her tone testified to deep feelings in regard to the memories surrounding that incident last year. He'd blown a cover that had taken him years to perfect in order to get Winnie and the men of the family out of Zhu Lin's compound. The Witches' Council chewed his ass and suspended him for a month.

"Speaking of Winnie..." He strove to make the conversation lighter. "I hear she's going to have three babies for you to spoil."

Instead of happiness, GiGi's expression tightened. She nodded and managed a small smile.

"I know sometimes it feels like a lifetime, sweetheart, but that doesn't mean you have to suppress your feelings regarding our own baby. You're allowed to grieve."

She tried to shift away, but he caught her around the waist.

"I think about him too, GiGi."

"It was a long time ago, Ryker."

He drew her closer, urging her head into the crook between his neck and shoulder. "I think about him, too," he repeated. A soft sob escaped her, and he tightened his arms. "I'm sorry I wasn't there. More sorry than you'll ever know."

Hot tears ran down his neck and soaked the collar of his shirt. He allowed his own grief to flow in conjunction with his wife's.

They'd never had a chance to mourn the loss of their stillborn son together. It had coincided with his mission regarding Marguerite Champeau. By the time Ryker had recovered from his gunshot wound and returned home, GiGi had buried their son.

He half suspected her continuing rage had more to do with the loss and his absence than with his alleged affair. Since his wife refused to speak of either, he'd had no way to bridge the distance she'd created between them.

GiGi hadn't spoken of the stillbirth to anyone. Not her brothers, not her nieces, not Ryker. It was as if, when she placed her son in the family crypt, she had sealed it all away. Now, sitting here within the circle of Ryker's arms, the memories sprung free and overwhelmed her, nearly suffocating in their intensity.

"I understand things happen, and just because we're considered Isis's beloved ones, life isn't going to be without its trials, but I'll never understand why the Goddess cursed us with his loss." She finally voiced the one constant, plaguing thought she'd had all these years.

His warm embrace offered her solace and maybe even a smidgeon of his strength. *This* was what she'd missed after the death of her baby. The gentle understanding. The shared pain. The unconditional love.

"I'm sorry we never tried again," he said. "I would have liked to have a houseful of children."

"Do you blame me?" She pushed the question past her dry throat.

Drawing back slightly, Ryker tilted her chin up with a knuckle. She could feel his stare but had a hard time meeting his gaze. When she worked up the courage, the standard adoration was back in addition to a kinder, softer emotion—*compassion*.

"What do *you* think, sweetheart?"

"I don't know why you wouldn't. I took too many risks, trailing you halfway around the world after you asked me not to."

She felt his heavy sigh as she waited for him to respond

"Honestly, I'm surprised you don't blame *me*, but I never once thought it was anything other than ill-luck or the Goddess's will." He shrugged. "You would've been an amazing mother, and I find it difficult to believe you would've done anything to jeopardize our unborn child."

The tightness eased in her chest, and all the self-hate she'd experienced until now left with the whoosh of her relieved exhale. "Thank you."

She snuggled close and placed a soft kiss along his jawline. "For the record, I think you would have been a great dad."

"You're damned tootin'."

Laughter bubbled up. GiGi was surprised she could find amusement so closely on the heels of her remembered grief. They sat in silence, listening to the crickets sing their nightly song.

"I sometimes miss what I don't have," she confessed. "I see other women, other families, dedicated to one another. Mothers snuggling their toddlers close after a tumble make my heart hurt for what can never be."

"You're not too old if you want to try again."

She snorted. "It's ridiculous to have a child at our age."

"No, it might be crazy for a non-magical human without your genetics, but you are essentially like a thirty-nine-year-old woman, GiGi. Any child of ours would be a late-in-life baby, but he or she would be loved all the more for it."

She didn't dare dream that she could have the family she'd always wanted. It felt like pushing fate. And yet, a small kernel of hope popped up. More importantly, she favored the idea of making that baby with her husband after years of a sexual drought.

"Let's get through one dramatic event at a time," she suggested. "When we have slain our enemies and we are settled in our home again, we can discuss the baby-making process."

His hand found its way back under her shirt to cup her breast. "We should probably at least practice the baby-making process."

"Absolutely."

"I think my estranged wife just agreed to make all my fondest wishes come true. If I'm dreaming, don't wake me, okay?"

A happy giggle escaped. "Promise."

9

*R*yker rose and drew GiGi to her feet. Hand in hand, they walked toward the mahogany doors of Thorne Manor. As he reached for the knob, the door swung open to reveal Alastair.

Ryker shook his head. "Don't tell me. I don't want to know. My wife and I were about to reconcile our differences."

She smiled quizzically. "I thought we had."

"Your brother doesn't need to know that. I was hoping to buy us time."

His best friend shot him a dry look and smiled down at GiGi. "It's past time for the two of you to be happy, but we have to discuss what happened today. No one is safe until the threat is neutralized."

Ryker grimaced in response to the truth of Alastair's observations.

GiGi was less pleased.

"Can't it wait until morning, brother? We could both use some rest."

"If I thought you were going to your room to sleep, I might've waited to bring this up. But I have a sneaking suspicion you have other entertaining pursuits in mind." Alastair's knowing smile deepened to a wide, toothy grin.

Ryker never wanted to deck him more.

"I seriously hate you right now." He sighed his disappointment. "I mean, I didn't think I could hate you more than I did last night or this morning for your trick, but this is hitting below the belt."

A bark of laughter escaped Alastair. He moved out of the way to allow them entry, then led the way to the living room, where all the family present sat beaming their pleasure.

Summer jumped up and hugged her aunt. "I'm so happy for you both. I knew, given enough time together, you'd settle your differences."

"It only took locking us in together and stripping us of our clothing, not to mention not answering when we called. At least, you didn't have to resort to drugging us," Ryker said with a glare at Alastair. The heavy sarcasm in his tone didn't go unnoticed, and all around the faces reflected chagrin, except for his best friend. That bastard was too smug for words.

"I tried to tell them. Not everyone likes to be manipulated based on a whim." Winnie's husband, Zane Carlyle, cast his wife a stern look. Having fallen victim to mental machinations by GiGi and Winnie, when the latter decided to wipe clean the memory of their relationship from poor Zane's mind, the guy was still a bit salty about the spell the two women had cast upon him.

A wicked light flared in the chocolate depths of Zane's eyes when he glanced at GiGi. His teasing smile was firmly in place when he said, "I guess turnabout is fair play, Ms. GiGi."

Ryker laughed when his wife narrowed her eyes on the young man.

"Okay, spill, Al. What was so all-fired important that we couldn't go to bed?" Ryker asked.

"We captured one of the soldiers."

Everyone swiveled to face Alastair, mouths agape.

Ryker recovered first. "Where is he?"

"Tied up in a warehouse outside of town." Alastair shrugged. "I didn't want to bring him back here and risk our location becoming known if he had a tracker. Not that I'm sure it matters. Our enemies came close enough by finding you."

"I still can't understand how." Ryker shook his head. "The only things I bring back and forth are my files, and I..." He stopped speaking and glanced around. "My briefcase, GiGi... did you leave it in the 'Vette?"

"Yes."

He all-out ran for the door with Alastair, GiGi, and Zane on his heels. In the distance, they saw the headlights of vehicles. Without ceremony, he conjured a flaming energy ball and firebombed his beloved car.

"Quickly, you need to reinforce the wards," he shouted. "Alastair, get your security team back here, STAT. Zane, come with me." He ran for Summer's old, abandoned animal barn and started tossing hay bales, revealing a line of metal military crates. "There's more there." He nodded with his chin toward a nearby stall. "See that every family member gets a gun then get your wife into the tunnels below the house."

Zane halted his forward movement to stare. "What tunnels, and how do we access them?"

"Jesus! I can't believe Preston and Alastair never told anyone... never mind. Just grab a crate and go! We don't have much time before they arrive."

The younger man stacked two of the containers and waved a hand to lighten the load. He hustled away and was back in seconds for another load. Ryker stacked the crates in Zane's arms and told him not to return to the barn.

From various vantage points, Ryker set up high-powered, long-range rifles. He intended to be the first line of defense in the event the wards disguising the property failed. To the standard eye, the house and surrounding buildings didn't exist. Unless invited to the estate, all a normal individual could see was dense forest. It would take a powerful witch or warlock, perhaps multiple of both, to break the mirage encasing the place. Not that it couldn't be done, but one had to know the exact location of Thorne Manor to breach the old girl's walls.

"Ryker."

He spun, gun at the ready. When he saw his visitor was GiGi, Ryker lowered his weapon. "Dammit, woman! I could've shot you!"

She shrugged and squatted by the chest of weapons. "Could've but wouldn't have. You're too good to make a mistake."

Her words soothed the savage beast within him. Although his first instinct was to rage at her for coming here, he was happy she chose to fight by his side.

"What's the plan?"

GiGi looked so eager to help, denying her was beyond his capability. With a resigned shake of his head, he began handing her weapons. "I'm assuming you showed Zane and the girls the location of the tunnels?" At her nod, he continued, "Do you know how to load a military rifle?"

"Yes. My brothers and father made sure I knew how to defend myself during the war."

"Good. How's your aim?"

"I can hit what I'm aiming at."

"Okay, then I want you up high. I've set rifles in the openings above. Shoot two rounds and move to the next." He produced a piece of paper. "If there are no Blockers present, you can utilize this spell to reload for you. If they are present, you'll need to reload yourself. Never stay in the same spot longer than ten seconds, and don't let anyone see where the shots are coming from. Cloak yourself and pray to the Goddess it works."

"Got it." She gripped his face between her palms. "Be safe," she ordered him. Bringing his head down to hers, she kissed him. A mere clinging of the lips, but it was enough to tell him she'd forgiven him for the past. "I love you, Ryker."

"I love you, too, sweetheart. Now get that fine ass up the ladder to the loft and watch my back if anyone comes through those doors."

"Aye, aye, Captain!"

"This is more of a military op, GiGi, not a ship."

She simply grinned and patted his cheek. "It is what I say it is, babe."

He lightly swatted her backside as she turned away.

"No foreplay," she scolded before she ruined it with a wink. "That's for later."

He couldn't contain his laugh as she teleported to the loft. His GiGi was one helluva woman. Shoving a handgun into the waistband of his cargo pants, Ryker then grabbed a rifle in each hand and ran for the northernmost window.

A pulse of magic, strong enough to rock the building, rode the airwaves.

"What the hell was that?" he shouted to GiGi.

She peered over the side of the loft. "If I had to guess, Alastair's reinforcement of the wards."

"Second guess?"

"I don't have one."

"I'm going to teleport a com unit to the house. Stay hidden, sweetheart."

She nodded and disappeared back into the loft area above. The one great thing about his wife was when she understood the risks, she didn't seek trouble. Not that she wouldn't delve into the action when she saw fit, but she rarely thought to place herself in danger. Perhaps it was witnessing the results of the witches' war years ago. Maybe it was a sense of self-preservation. Either way, Ryker was thrilled she knew when to take precautions.

He grabbed a handful of communication devices from the weapons chest, threw a few bales of hay around it to camouflage the crate, and teleported to the main house. He found Alastair and a few of his security team members in a deep discussion.

"I wasn't sure what you had by way of coms, so I thought I'd bring some for the girls and the Carlyles. Were you the initiator of that pulse?"

"Actually, no. I think Beecham was testing our shields." Alastair's expression was grim. "It may be time to abandon our home."

If Alastair was worried, things were dire. Ryker didn't want to think about what it cost his friend to utter the words. Abandoning Thorne Manor would rip his buddy's heart out.

"Do you think his army is stronger than what we have here?"

"I don't know if we can take the chance with our family, Ryker. If we didn't have the pregnant women present…"

"What about the Carlyle estate? Should Phillip be made aware of the threat?"

"Already done." He looked up from programing a com to his security channel. "Autumn and Keaton left earlier, and Cooper went to warn them along with his parents."

Before anything else could be said, another powerful pulse rocked the house. The people present staggered. A series of small earthquake-like rumbles followed. The tinkling of glass could be heard from the chandelier in the foyer, and the furniture shifted across the wood floors.

"What kind of damned magic can do that?" Ryker demanded.

Frowning, Alastair shook his head. "I have no idea."

The air shifted and crackled around them.

"Incoming!"

The soldiers whipped their weapons up and encircled him and Alastair. Ryker wanted to laugh. It was doubtful anyone had half of the skills he and Al had learned over the years.

Keaton Carlyle arrived, looking harried and panicked. His dark hair was sticking up as if he'd tried to pull it out.

"What is it, boy?" Alastair barked, not allowing time for pleasantries should the young man decide to go that route.

"Autumn's gone into labor. It started right after dinner."

"Fuck! *Achoo!*"

In anticipation of his friend's reaction, Ryker curled his hand into a fist and shot a wave of magic up and out, hoping to stem off the locusts that could decimate the forest around them. Such was Alastair's curse. While he rarely swore, Al had the ability to bring on a plague of insects the likes none had ever seen. The power behind his emotion was what brought the potential destruction. If he was angry or upset enough to swear, the magic he released couldn't be contained without magical intervention, either his own or by one of the family.

"Not only that, she seems to be causing the whole house to shake with each labor pain." Keaton reached up and ran a hand through his mussed hair. "I don't know what to do. We can't move her, and Coop said…" He finally looked around and noticed the soldiers. "Shit!"

"I'll get GiGi. Perhaps she can provide Autumn with something to ease her pain." Ryker started for the door when GiGi appeared in the foyer.

"I don't think the magic pulses are from Beecham. The headlights turned back," she told them.

"It's Autumn. She's in labor."

"Oh, my."

"Is this normal?" Keaton asked with a check of his watch. "I wouldn't think labor pains could rock both estates."

Again, the ground grumbled. Ryker grabbed the banister with one hand and supported GiGi with the other.

"I can't say as I've ever known anything like this to happen." She looked at her brother. "Al?"

Alastair shook his head. "I'll consult with Isis. You and Ryker go with Keaton to see about Autumn." He faced his team. "Martin, I want you to stay here with three others. Guard my family with your life if you have to. I want one of you with Ryker. I'll take one of you with me to the clearing."

They all separated and headed for their destinations. Ryker, GiGi, Keaton, and the guard arrived at the Carlyle estate just as another roll of magic bucked the earth. The terrified cries of the horses at the back of the property could be heard from the front of the house.

"I'll go see what I can do to calm them," Ryker told Keaton. Facing his wife, he said, "If you need me, send Keaton or Coop." To the guard, he merely gestured to the front porch.

GiGi didn't wait a second longer than necessary to run into

the house. She found Autumn writhing on the bed, sweat beading on her forehead and her nightgown wet with sweat.

"Hey, sweet girl. I'm here," she crooned as she brushed back Autumn's damp hair.

"Something's wrong... Aunt G.," she panted. "The pain... the quakes..."

"Could be that you have a tough little earth elemental on your hands who wants to show the world what he can do," GiGi teased. "I'm going to give you something to ease your discomfort then examine you, okay?"

"Okay. Is Mama coming?"

"I'll send Keaton for her now." GiGi nodded to Autumn's husband. "Last time I saw Aurora, she was with Winnie. I'm assuming she's still at Thorne Manor. Also, you may want to get in touch with Knox to help with those horses. Ryker doesn't know the first thing about dealing with animals."

Autumn choked out a laugh that ended with a moan of pain.

Opening her hands palm up, GiGi concentrated on the ingredients she would need to ease the painful contractions for her niece. Once the herbs appeared, she went about crushing them in a small marble mortar and pestle she'd conjured to grind them.

She felt the young presence behind her and turned to welcome Autumn's and Keaton's daughter. "Did we wake you, child?"

"My bed keeps shaking."

"Seems your little brother is ready to raise a ruckus. Care to help me?"

Chloe's eyes rounded with excitement. "What can I do?"

"Conjure a cup of hot water for your mother while I finish mixing these herbs. We're going to make her a tea to drink between contractions." When the girl positioned herself to perform magic, GiGi urged caution. "Wait until after this next wave. You don't want to burn yourself. Find something to hold onto. I think this one might be a doozy, dear."

As soon as the contraction eased and the room settled around them, she gave Chloe the go-ahead.

GiGi helped Autumn into a semi-sitting position and guided the teacup to her lips. "Drink. You'll start feeling better right away." Nodding her head in approval, she conjured a bowl of fresh water to wash her hands. Once she was positioned to examine Autumn, she asked, "What do you plan to name him?"

"Preston Jolyon... Carlyle," Autumn managed between pants.

"Oh!" Caught off guard by the use of her brother's name, GiGi sucked in a breath. "How lovely! My brother would be honored. It's sweet you're using Ryker's middle name, too."

"We'll call him Jolyon. Calling him by Dad's name so soon..." Tears welled in Autumn's large amber eyes.

"I get it, child. I miss him, too." And she did, more than she let on.

Her big brother had always been there for her from day one. Had taught her how to perform magic and to ride a bike. He'd even forced Alastair to let her tag along when Al had been at an age when it was uncool to deal with a younger sister.

GiGi needed to change the subject before they were both blubbering fools. "How are you feeling now, dear? Is the tea helping?"

"Yes. The pain isn't as bad."

She didn't know whether her niece was telling the truth or putting on a good face for Chloe, but the tremors stopped. She'd sent the girl from the room so she could check the dilation. "Jolyon's head is crowning. Are you ready to push?"

"I want Keaton here for this."

"Then he will be. I'll go get him."

As she rose to go in search of Keaton, he arrived, bringing Aurora with him. After a little fawning over her daughter, Rorie took Autumn's hand and ordered her to push at the same time Keaton encouraged and reiterated how much he loved her.

It was a beautiful scene, and one GiGi had missed when her own time had come and gone. Sadness tried its best to swamp her, but she shoved it aside to welcome her grand-nephew to the world. A small magical boost helped Autumn through the worst of it, as did the tea GiGi pressed upon her.

After Jolyon was cleaned and given over to his mother and father, they proceeded to count all ten fingers and ten toes. Keaton proclaimed him perfect.

GiGi stood back and watched the family together. She'd missed all of this. Grief was a strange and complicated beast. When she should be the happiest for her niece, she felt saddened and lost.

Air. She needed air. Spinning about, she would have made good her exit but for Ryker blocking her path. The gentle understanding in his eyes pierced her heart. He must've sensed her need because he opened his arms to her, and she gladly allowed him to swallow her up within his hold.

"Was our baby that beautiful?" he asked for her ears alone.

She nodded, too overcome to speak.

Tightening his arms around her, he lent his silent strength.

"I want to try again," she whispered.

"Then we will," he assured her.

GiGi hated that her pain was on display for the world to see, yet somehow, this time, it wasn't as bad now that Ryker was with her.

10

*R*yker led GiGi outside to the front porch to give the new family time alone. His wife had been exceptionally quiet since the birth of little Jolyon.

"Are you all right, sweetheart?"

"Yes. Of course."

"There's no 'of course' about it, GiGi. This is the first time you've been around a birth since you... since our..." Ryker found himself getting emotional and was unable to continue. He hadn't allowed himself to grieve. If he dug deep enough, he knew the reason was because he couldn't let himself fall apart. If he lost it in the middle of an undercover op, he'd have blown his disguise. Maybe he didn't feel as if he deserved to grieve with all that had happened, all he'd caused with his selfishness. At the time, he told himself he was doing it for the good of the magical community. Now, he wasn't so sure it wasn't just a selfish desire to play action hero.

She rested her hand on his arm. "Ryker, look at me."

He blinked and swallowed a few times before tearing his gaze from the treeline. The compassion and understanding on her face were like a dagger to his gut. His insides clenched, and sweat broke out on his upper lip. With a shake of his head, he inhaled deeply, taking longer to exhale.

"I guess I didn't realize how much it would affect me, too," he told her gruffly.

"I know. I found it difficult to go anywhere there were babies and small children for years afterward." She tucked in against his side and stared out over the property. "We can't replace him, but maybe we can move forward."

"Yes." He rested his cheek atop her head. "That's my fondest wish."

They held each other in silence, wrapped in their own pain, yet able to share in the grief at the same time. Minutes ticked away as the sounds of nighttime played an off-beat tune.

"Why haven't we been attacked by now? They were on the way, and then they weren't?" GiGi's question was whisper-soft.

"I've got Nash and Knox looking into it. I'm waiting for Alastair to check back in."

"Have you heard from him since he went to the clearing?"

He shook his head.

Her body tensed within his embrace. "Let's go."

"GiGi, we can't go off half-cocked."

"He's the last of my immediate family. I'm not going to let anything happen to him," she argued.

When she tried to pull away, he held onto her upper arms. "Think about this. If you go there with Beecham's men present, you put a target on your back."

"I'm not going to stand by and do nothing."

They glared at each other in frustrated silence. As she opened her mouth to argue further, the air around them became charged. Their eyes locked, and they held their collective breath, waiting for the arrival of what would be multiple witches. If it was Beecham's army, then Autumn and her baby were vulnerable to attack.

When Alastair stepped on the porch with a guard at his back, they both released a sigh of relief.

"How's Autumn?" Alastair asked his sister.

"She has a healthy baby boy. Preston Jolyon Carlyle."

Taken aback, Alastair could only stare. Finally, he grinned. "How did you manage to make the cut?" He asked Ryker.

"I'm clearly the cooler uncle."

"Pfft. I rescued her from the dungeon and saved that useless boy she calls a husband," Alastair argued with a twinkle in his eye.

"I provided the key." Ryker shrugged. "What can I say? Jolly Ollie is much more fun than stuffy old Uncle Alastair."

His friend's eyes narrowed, and Ryker grinned in response.

"I'll rectify the matter when I see my grand-nephew," Alastair promised.

"What did you find out about Autumn's labor causing the earthquakes?" GiGi asked.

"The child will be an earth elemental. Apparently, a Thorne and a Carlyle make a very powerful little witch together."

"Wonderful," GiGi muttered. "Let's hope he has a sweet disposition, or he'll destroy all of Leiper's Fork during a temper tantrum one day."

Lifting his hand to reveal a rolled parchment, Alastair smiled. "I have the solution here from the Goddess herself. It's meant to counterbalance his magic in the event he loses control. I'll have both Keaton and Autumn memorize the spell and then put it in their grimoire for safekeeping."

"Is it from the *Book of Thoth*?" Ryker removed the spell from Alastair's hand, unrolled it, and studied what was written there. "Hmm."

"What?" His wife crowded closer to read the words on the scroll.

"Change a few words around, and you could make him even stronger."

"What?" Both Alastair and GiGi stared at him in slack-jawed disbelief.

Alastair was the first to recover. "What do you mean?"

"Here." Ryker pointed. He didn't dare speak the spell aloud because he didn't want to activate it. "Switch moderate with amplify, and you could essentially ramp up his power."

His wife looked like he'd taken a bat to her. "Will the gods and goddesses allow him that much power?"

"Isis gave Knox the power of a God, and Quentin is descended from Zeus." Alastair didn't look worried. "As long as he's as even-tempered as my son-in-law, I don't think we have anything to worry about."

"Jolyon is Autumn's son. He's bound to be testy on occasion," she argued.

Ryker rolled up the scroll and handed it back to Alastair. He faced his wife and pressed his forehead to hers. "Let's not borrow trouble, sweetheart. For now, we give this to Keaton to do with as he sees fit. Then, we find a bed and get some much-needed sleep. It's been an insanely long day."

Alastair snapped his fingers. "I almost forgot." From his pocket, he pulled a small, intricately made piece of jewelry. The size of the chain meant it was made for a baby. "Isis wanted me to gift Autumn's son with this anklet."

Ryker knew the gift was an oddity, but remained silent. The Goddess had reasons for her actions, and to question her motives wouldn't go over well.

"It's lovely," GiGi breathed as she touched the piece. "What are these symbols?"

"That's Spring's department. But if I had to guess, I'd say it's to keep the baby from reducing the estate to rubble if he cries for a bottle," Alastair said with a wry half-smile. "I'll have her decipher them in the morning. In the meantime, you two go get some rest. I'll stay here with David and John to guard the Carlyle estate." He'd indicated his security team with a nod of his head.

"Since we are essentially homeless, we'll head back to Thorne Manor. If you need us, call. I doubt I'll get much sleep tonight," Ryker told him. He shot an inquiring look at his wife. When she nodded, he gathered her close and called his magic to teleport them to her family's home.

As they materialized in the driveway, they paused to look up at the old girl. Ryker had always admired the Victorian architecture of the manor, and with lights pouring from the large windows, it made the place welcoming. Walking into the Thorne house always made him feel like he'd come home.

"What are you thinking?" GiGi asked softly as she rested her head on his shoulder.

"It's good to be welcomed back here." He heard the catch of her breath and reached for her hand. "Let's go to bed and figure out the rest of the world's problems tomorrow, okay?"

She nodded and walked with him toward the large mahogany door, pausing before turning the knob. "You'll always be welcome here, Ryker. You always were, regardless of what went on with us. It's our family, and they love you. You'll never be without them."

His throat worked convulsively as he tried to swallow back his gratitude at her easy acceptance. Except for a few cousins, the Thornes were the only people he considered family. GiGi hit the issue dead center regarding the loss of that connection.

"Thank you, sweetheart," he whispered gruffly. It was all he could manage without bawling like a baby.

Inside, they conversed with Zane and Winnie to make sure all was secure then headed up to a spare bedroom. Once they were alone, uncertainty struck. GiGi avoided eye contact as her hands flitted about.

"GiGi."

She paused what she was doing and glanced back at him.

He strode to her side and caressed her jawline. He could feel the tension along her neck and gently rubbed the tense muscles at its base.

"This is the first time we haven't been at odds in years. Finding a new normal will take time. In the meantime, I'm not going to pounce on you like an animal."

The light frown cleared from her brow when she smiled. "Maybe I'm wondering how to entice you to pounce like an animal," she teased.

"At any other time, you only have to say the word," he assured her. "But at this particular moment, we both need sleep."

"Spoilsport."

"Wake me in two hours. I swear I'll be as animalistic as you can handle."

GiGi laughed at the promise in his low growl. She lifted her fingers and, with a simple wave of her hand, changed into a leopard-print set of pajamas that left little to the imagination. Ryker mentally debated if he was really as exhausted as he'd initially thought.

"Goddess, you know how to tempt a man."

Her self-satisfied smirk nearly did him in. "Come to bed, darling. I want to snuggle close."

"Sounds like my idea of heaven."

As tired as she was, GiGi found it difficult to sleep. Listening to Ryker's steady breathing brought back the memories of their early years together. He used to cuddle her back to his chest with his arms wrapped loosely around her. Tonight, the position was exactly the same, and those strong arms were tighter, as if even in his sleep, he feared she'd leave. But for her, who'd been without anyone in her bed for longer than she cared to think about, it was odd.

He had been correct when he said they needed to find a new normal. She'd been independent far too long. Another thing she'd revisited today was the loss of their child. Holding Autumn's newborn brought back all the love and grief she'd felt for her own baby boy. He'd been perfect just like little Jolyon.

A single tear escaped from the corner of her eye and dropped on the firm, warm arm beneath her cheek.

"Why are you crying?" Ryker's soft, husky question made her jump.

GiGi hastily brushed at her eyes. "The events of today got to me a bit. I'm being a sentimental old fool."

"Jolyon." He stated the name flatly as if it were a forgone conclusion.

Twisting in his embrace, she tried to see his expression in the dark. "It isn't just the baby. I'm finding it difficult to sleep in general tonight. The attack on our homes, the baby, our reconciliation. It's all replaying through my mind." She lightly ran her fingernails through his short beard. "But why are you awake? Surely a single tear didn't pull you from sleep."

"I slept the prerequisite two hours to recharge my body. Making love with you was too good to pass up. Sleep be damned. A promise is a promise."

His sexually charged tone sparked an answering fire within her.

"I love a man of his word," she murmured as she leaned closer to nip his lip.

"Then I'm your man."

"Yes, you are. *My* man. All mine."

He grinned, and GiGi could only assume it was because of her possessiveness. The teasing light dimmed in his eyes, and he rubbed a thumb over her lower lip.

"I don't want to be an insensitive ass here. If you need to talk about anything, I'm happy to listen."

Pure love flooded her entire being. He meant what he said. Despite the fact that they hadn't made love in ages, Ryker would put aside his own wants to ease her mind.

"Nope, I'm good." She pressed a kiss to the pad of his thumb. "Now, how about we get busy? We've waited long enough, don't you think?"

"That right there is why I love you, sweetheart. You are a woman of action."

She released a low, sultry laugh and reached between them to stroke the length of his erection. "Oh, I do love action."

As GiGi encircled and caressed him, slowly running her palm to the tip of his penis and down to the base in a sensual, repetitive move, Ryker moaned her name. She explored his muscular chest with her free hand and placed lingering, loving kisses wherever she touched. Taking the tight bud of his nipple between her teeth, she gently bit down. His body's reaction was swift, and his dick twitched within her grasp.

"Dear Goddess, woman! I forgot how good that felt."

"Mmm. How about how good this feels?" She took him into her mouth, gently sucked, then swirled her tongue over the head.

"Yep," he croaked out. "That, too."

She worked him with her hand and mouth until his hips bucked and he shuddered his release. Ryker panted through his recovery, and GiGi crawled up his body to nuzzle the column of his throat.

"How's that for action?" she teased.

His wide grin spoke for him. "In approximately... one minute... when I... can breathe again,... I'm going to... rock... your... world," he assured her.

"That's what I'm hoping."

She squeaked her surprise when he tumbled her onto her back.

"Start the countdown."

"Sixty... fifty-nine... fifty—oh!" She released a happy sigh when his lips claimed hers. Ryker was the best kisser. The perfect amount of aggression without banging teeth or making her feel as if she were fighting for survival, but with enough passion to steal her wits. Nor was it sloppy wet or clammy, but contained enough slip to make the dance of their tongues effortless and erotic. He always tasted of fresh peppermint. When he pulled away, his lips lingered the perfect amount of time, and the small nip of his teeth on her swollen lip sent a shockwave of lust straight to her lady bits.

His large, warm hand covered her naked breast, and GiGi had the presence of mind to acknowledge he'd magically done away with her clothing.

"Smooth move, babe," she said, voicing her approval.

"Well, as sexy as your sleepwear is, it was getting in my way." His mouth closed over her breast as he kneaded the fullness.

"I'll give you one hour to stop doing that," she moaned.

His husky chuckle added to the wetness at the apex of her thighs. Wicked and knowing, Ryker's light laughter turned her on like nothing else. That sinful sound of amusement promised her all sorts of wonderful pleasure, and her body had a Pavlovian response.

He explored every inch of exposed skin with his hands and mouth, both front and back. Cupping and massaging the muscles of her ass, he teased her core with a thumb or a finger across her clit. The touch was intermittent and pushed her to the limit. She was a moaning, groaning, gooey mass of want, and when he turned her flat on her back and slowly entered her, GiGi wanted to scream her encouragement.

"Please, Ryker," she breathed out. "Please."

The feeling of fullness produced by their joined bodies expanded out and swept her nerve endings. When he would've withdrawn to thrust again, she tightened her thighs around him and held him in place.

"Wait. I want to savor this moment."

Instead of pulling back, he shifted his hips forward. Her name on his lips was like a benediction. A spiritual and near-religious awakening of her soul. Their eyes met and held, and in those heart-melting eyes of his, GiGi saw the depth of his love. She imagined her eyes were the mirror of his, differing only in color.

He began to move again, slowly at first and increasing his pace to match the thrust of her own hips. She looked down to where their bodies became one. What she expected to see, other than the norm, she didn't know, but surely it should have been something more magical than mere body parts for the sensation and pleasure she experienced.

She ran her hands up the sinewy forearms braced on either side of her, and up over the bulkier brawn of Ryker's biceps and triceps to where his shoulder met the column of his throat. She traced the corded muscles there for a second before lacing her fingers in the thick curls at the base of his neck. Digging in, she pulled him down for one of the kisses that never failed to sear her insides.

He bent his arms and rested his weight on her, never losing rhythm. One hand cupped the back of her calf and dragged it above his hip while he fingered her intimately and drove her to the brink. He lifted his head, his lips a mere inch from her ear, and whispered, "Come for me, GiGi."

His softly spoken words were roughened by his desire and sent her straight over the edge. She experienced her most powerful orgasm to date. She flung her arms wide and arched up as the magic from within her cells struggled for release. Light shot from her fingertips and lit the room with a soft rose glow.

Ryker's strong arms held her tightly to his chest as his orgasm followed closely on the heels of hers. She could feel the cool night air pick up speed as the current flowed around them, lifting them both a foot off the bed.

Lamps and vases rocked back and forth on hard surfaces, and the filmy, cream curtains blew parallel to the floor. She may have heard someone outside yell, "What the fuck?" before she got control of her magic and settled them back on the mattress.

"Oops, my bad," she whispered.

She felt Ryker's lips twitch against the skin of her throat and found herself unable to contain a giggle.

"What do you suppose happened out there?"

He chuckled as he rolled onto his back. "A mini tornado?"

She bit her lip to keep the laughter at bay, and when he shifted to his side and rested his head in the palm of his hand to stare down at her, she remembered why this magnificent man was perfect for her. The deviltry in his eyes spoke to her as nothing else ever had.

"I love you, Ryker."

"That's good because I'm not going anywhere ever again, and you're stuck with me."

"Promise?"

"Promise."

"And?"

"And I love you, too, sweetheart."

"Excellent."

11

*M*orning dawned on a beautiful day. The fall temperature was cool without being bone-chilling. GiGi sipped her coffee as she stared out over the Thorne property. Half of the leaves on the trees had changed to a deep red and would shift to burnt orange any day now.

It was her favorite time of year. A time when she could give the air a magical boost and make the dried leaves drift on the wind. She used to do that for her nieces when they were young girls. Their laughter would echo across the yard and trigger a smile from anyone within earshot. She smiled at the memory.

The large mahogany door opened behind her. She didn't have long to wait before a quilt was placed around her shoulders and her husband settled in next to her on the front step with his own morning beverage.

GiGi turned her face up to his, studying him as he now studied her. She noted the fine laugh lines taking root at the corners of his warm eyes. They crinkled as he grinned down at her.

"Morning, sweetheart."

"Morning," she murmured, offering up a soft, sweet kiss which he took full advantage of.

"If I've died and gone to the Otherworld, don't ruin it," Ryker finally said when he came up for air.

Like a young girl, she giggled her response. "Then we've both died happy."

The adoration was back in Ryker's eyes as he wrapped a hand around her waist and tucked her into his side. GiGi rested her head on his shoulder and turned her attention back to making the leaves dance on the wind.

He voiced his approval. "Nice party trick."

"I used to entertain the girls when they were small. Spring would laugh and chase the leaves while Winnie would try to call them to her. Autumn and Summer would stand and let them rain down upon them." She sighed happily. "They were always a joy."

"And now they're having children of their own. It boggles the mind how quickly time speeds by."

"It does. You and I were separated more years than we were together. I think it's why I had a hard time sleeping last night. I'm not used to having another person next to me."

"I know what you mean, and I'm happy that's the case."

Her head came up, and she stared at his profile. "What do you mean?"

"I never wanted you to not be happy, sweetheart. But the idea of you creating a new life with someone else nearly destroyed me. When I heard you on the phone with Sebastian Drake, I wasn't only angry, I was hurt. He's perfect for you, and hearing you tease one another created a knot in my stomach that I'm finding difficult to disperse."

"Oh, Ryker." GiGi twisted to cup his jaw and turn him to fully face her. "He's not perfect for me. You are. It's always been you."

He closed his eyes and rubbed his cheek against her palm. "You don't know how thrilled I am to hear you say that."

Contentment settled into her chest and chased away the last lingering doubts she wasn't aware she had. Leaning forward, she kissed him. In that kiss, she poured all the words she'd never been able to voice. The action was cleansing, wiping away all the hurt, anger, and disappointment of the past.

"I love you, Ryker. Even when I hated you, I loved you."

"Did you hate me so much?" He questioned on an anguished whisper.

"Sometimes." When he closed his eyes, she clarified, "But only because I loved you so much and believed you betrayed that love. After the baby... I wanted you to suffer so badly, the way I was suffering." She choked back a soft sob at the loss. "The past is the past, and it's time to leave it there. I don't hate you now, and I don't blame you."

He swept an arm under her legs and lifted her into his lap. Wrapping the blanket tighter around them, he held her against his chest. "I swear to you here and now, GiGi, I will never give you reason to doubt me again. You are my sole reason for breathing. You always have been. Believe me when I say, I suffered."

GiGi swiped away the tears flooding her eyes. "I want to put it to rest, but I want to do it properly."

"What do you need from me?"

She smiled softly at his willingness to provide what she needed.

"Hold tight." So saying, she allowed the magic to heat her cells. Together with his, the warmth within ramped up to almost burning. Some might find the sensation unpleasant, but not GiGi. She loved witchcraft and everything that came with it.

When she opened her eyes again, they stood outside the family crypt. She held out her hand for his. "Let's say goodbye to him properly."

RYKER STARED AT HIS WIFE'S UPTURNED PALM, HIS HEART THUDDING painfully in his chest. He'd only been here once before, and he'd lacked the courage to walk through the door to see his son's final resting place.

"Ryker?"

Her understanding was in the tone of her voice.

Lifting his head, Ryker grasped her hand and raised it to his lips. "I'm good," he lied.

GiGi's lips twisted in a wry half-smile. The kind that said she knew he fibbed to save face but that she forgave him for it. "We don't have to do this right now. I know I sprung it on you."

"No, we do. I…" He rubbed a hand over his face. "I could never bring myself to visit him. I was too riddled with guilt and feeling savage."

His confession didn't seem to surprise her. In fact, she nodded her head as if she expected as much. "Whenever you're ready. We can wait here as long as you need to."

Compassion shone from her brilliant eyes and gave him the strength he needed. "Let's go say goodbye," he said gruffly.

They worked their way around the crypt, pausing to pay respects to GiGi's parents and to Preston before stopping in front of the marble with their son's name.

Angelus Ryker Gillespie.

"I never told you, but you chose the perfect name." Even though his voice was low, it echoed in the enormous mausoleum.

"He *was* perfect. In every way I could see. He had your dark hair, a full head of it. I knew if he opened his eyes, they'd be yours."

Ryker couldn't ignore the pain in her voice, and it ripped his heart out. He wrapped his arms around her from behind and held her with her back to his chest so they could both see the engraved stone. His thoughts were full of self-recrimination followed by a healthy dose of regret. He imagined hers were the same.

The air around them grew heavy, and a blinding white light lit the corner of the room. It heralded the parting of the veil between this plane of existence and the Otherworld. When the intense light faded and they could open their eyes, Preston Thorne stood before them.

"Hello, sister."

GiGi squealed her surprise and joy, causing Ryker to wince at the loud sound ricocheting off the stone surface surrounding them. She flung herself in her brother's waiting arms.

"How are you here?" she cried.

"You need to ask?" Preston laughed. "Isis wanted me to give you a message. She said your son is ready to return to you." His amber eyes warmed as he smiled. "She feels you are both ready to provide her gift with a stable, loving home."

Preston's message angered Ryker. "We'd have given him a stable, loving home the first time," he snapped. "These fucked up games—"

GiGi clamped a hand over his mouth and frantically shook her head. "Don't question the Goddess's gift, Ryker. Please. Isn't it enough he's returning to us?"

Moving her hand aside, he shook his head. "I'm not questioning the gift. I'm questioning the timing of the gift. Our son's life shouldn't be given or taken on a goddess's whim, GiGi. The pain it caused you… and me…" He shook his head a second time, frustrated at his inability to form the words he needed to express his feelings. He'd always been more action-driven, and finding the proper way to communicate his thoughts wasn't easy.

"We were here to put away the past. Let's appreciate our future."

She was right. He knew she was. Still, it was difficult to not be angry. Because GiGi held hope in her eyes and her heart, Ryker let it go.

She faced her brother again. "Does this mean if we try again, we'll be successful?"

"As it stands right now, yes." Preston's wide grin was infectious, and even Ryker found himself smiling. "Although why you would want that kind of headache at our age, I'll never understand."

"Yes you do, Pres," she said on a laugh. "It's why you had so many little girls."

"They seem to be holding up okay." The question was in his tone.

"They are," Ryker assured him. "You saw Autumn's son? She named him for you."

"I saw. Tell her… tell her that I'm proud of her, won't you?"

"You know I will." Ryker shook his hand and moved away for sister and brother to say their last goodbyes.

As he waited outside the crypt doors, he attempted to get his wayward emotions under control. If he delved deep enough, he'd acknowledge the root of his anger was fear. Discussing parenthood was a whole lot different from actually becoming a father. If GiGi were indeed to become pregnant in the coming months—and Preston had no reason to lie—then Ryker needed to remove the threat of Beecham without delay. He couldn't risk his wife's and child's lives due to that evil fucker.

The problem was lack of evidence. The Council refused to act without more than just Alastair's word via the ghost of his brother. As of yet, no proof could be found. Maybe GiGi was right and Ryker should resort to straight up murder, the way that scum Beecham had when he killed Trina.

Turning on his heel, he reentered the mausoleum. "Preston, can you spare one more minute?"

"Of course."

"Beecham is still free. How do we find the proof to put him away? So far, we've come up empty."

A look of pity settled on Preston's handsome features. "There's no existing proof."

Ryker wanted to swear a blue streak. He could see no way to achieve his goal to bring Beecham to justice.

"What about Trina?"

Both men stared at GiGi in stunned wonder as she shrugged.

"She's the only one who can tell what happened."

"What would it take to call her back from the Otherworld, Pres?" Ryker asked. "Would Isis allow it for a trial?"

"I can't speak for what she may or may not allow." Preston stepped close and lowered his voice to a whisper. "Spring would know since she—" The ground began to tremble, cutting him off mid-sentence.

"What the devil?" Ryker reached for GiGi and ushered her toward the exit. A retinal-searing light illuminated the room just as they ducked outside. The vault door slammed shut, and they were left to assume Preston had been recalled by the Otherside.

"What do you think he was going to say?"

He shook his head and stared at the solid door with its intricate, ancient symbols. "If I had to guess, I'd say he was pointing us in the direction of Spring. The girl is a walking encyclopedia of spells. If anyone can come up with a way to drag my sister into this realm, it would be her."

*T*he next detour for Ryker and GiGi was to Spring's home. They found her and Knox taking breakfast in their extensive gardens. She was quick to jump up and hug them both.

"Aunt GiGi, Uncle Ryker! Is everything okay? We haven't heard anything since late last night."

"We're quite all right, child. Everything seems to have settled down for the moment. But Ryker and I would like to speak with you and Knox if that's okay."

"Pull up a chair. There's more than enough food."

Ryker gave them a quick explanation as to the reason for their visit, while GiGi sipped a cup of tea and mentally marveled over talking to her brother for the first time since his death. Seeing Preston again left her raw and achy. Had he come against the Goddess's wishes? Was that why he'd been recalled with such force? She worried he'd broken a few cosmic rules in suggesting they seek out Spring. GiGi hated to think he would be in trouble with Isis.

"GiGi?" Ryker's voice jolted her out of her musings.

"I'm sorry. I was woolgathering. What did I miss?"

"Uncle Ryker was just saying he thinks my father hinted I might be useful because of my knowledge with spells. It's possible Dad was indicating the *Book of Thoth* as a source of those spells."

The book her niece referenced was one never meant for human hands. Isis had demanded the tome in repayment for her help last year when Spring had gone missing. Only once did the Thornes break trust with the Goddess. It was when they utilized a memorized spell from the book to recall Aurora to the land of the living. Now, they were all hesitant to anger Isis by using the forbidden magic.

GiGi's gaze collided with Ryker's. "He didn't specifically mention that particular book, but yes, that's the impression I got, too."

Despite the seriousness of the conversation, Ryker winked, and GiGi was hard-pressed not to grin in return. Her husband was one cool cat. Very little disturbed his laid-back attitude. The man lived for intrigue.

"Is anyone worried that we might piss the Goddess off so badly this time that she might retaliate? What if she revokes our powers? It could leave us all vulnerable." Although he appeared casual, Knox's anxiety brewed beneath the surface and electrified the air around him. If GiGi understood one thing about the young man sitting across from her, it was that he would stop at nothing to protect Spring. It stood to reason his concern stemmed from the constant threat from Serqet, sister to Isis, who had it in for the couple.

But Knox wasn't wrong about Isis's potential reaction, and the other three shifted uneasily. Finally, Ryker spoke.

"I'll not put our family at risk. For now, I'll continue to see what I can find. But you must know, I strongly feel that yesterday's attack had Beecham's name written all over it. He won't stop."

"I agree." GiGi set down her teacup and shook her head. "I believe he's running scared now that Delphine has been found out. Also, he hates Alastair. He won't quit until one of them is dead." Their cousin Delphine was responsible for Preston's murder. That was one back-stabbing bitch who would never see another sunrise. GiGi had made sure her cousin received her just desserts.

A look of grim determination crossed Spring's perfect features.

"I'll come up with a solution. Perhaps there is something in either the Thorne or Carlyle grimoires to help. If we don't steal from the *Book of Thoth*, Isis can't be cross with us, right?"

"It's worth a shot." Knox joined hands with his beloved, and the love shining from his bright eyes was breathtaking. "We'll both devote time to the search."

GiGi's heart melted when she saw these two together. They'd been to hell and back and deserved every happiness. Not for anything would she allow them to be hurt by any of this, moving forward. "Within limits," she said. "I want neither of you to risk yourselves. You've been through so much. Whatever you may find, leave it to Ryker or Alastair to handle, okay?"

"Of course, Aunt GiGi," Spring said sweetly.

Knox rolled his eyes and snorted. "If you trust that act of innocence, I have a bridge in New York I can sell you."

Spring laughed. "You must like the taste of dirt."

With a low growl in his throat, Knox mock glared at her.

GiGi signaled to Ryker it was time to leave the two of them alone. Things were about to heat up in their little house.

"Thank you both. If you find anything, give me a holler."

"Will do, Aunt GiGi."

"Shall we walk back?" Ryker suggested.

"No. I don't think we should be in the open any more than necessary. I don't trust that Beecham doesn't have spies in the area."

"They'd just see me getting it on with my wife in the clearing," he teased.

"I'd rather not be caught in my birthday suit if the enemy attacks." Still, the idea of making love with Ryker warmed her. GiGi couldn't get enough of touching him after so many years.

His smile flashed even as he tried to hide it. Her husband was the very devil. All games, all the time. Yet he charmed her as no other. Touching her palm to his jaw, she rose on tiptoe to kiss him lightly. "See you back in our bedroom. Last one there is on the bottom."

She teleported to his wicked chuckle, the deep, sinful sound resonating within her long after she arrived home. She wasted no time exchanging her current clothing for sexy, sheer lingerie. Energy sparked the air around her, and his strong, sinewy arm encircled her waist from behind.

Ryker had just dropped a butterfly-soft kiss on her bare shoulder when his phone rang.

They groaned their frustration in unison when they saw the caller ID. With a resigned sigh, GiGi restored her original outfit from earlier.

RYKER ALLOWED HIS DISAPPOINTMENT TO SHOW FOR GIGI BUT KEPT his voice even-toned to answer his cell. "What's up?" Okay, perhaps his brisk tone gave him away somewhat.

"I received word Georgie Sipanil is dead," Alastair said without preamble. "She was tied to a chair and tortured. I'm afraid it's meant to look as if you murdered her."

A long silence dragged on while Ryker wrapped his mind around this new development. Georgie Sipanil had held the high seat on the Witches' Council. She had been an old tyrant but was respected by everyone for her forthright manner and fairness. Ryker had shared the occasional drink with her to ease their mutual loneliness. They'd had long discussions about life and had heated but friendly debates on everything from religion to politics.

"Ryker?"

He glanced down at GiGi's concerned face.

She laid a hand on his free arm. "What's going on?"

Not breaking eye contact, he told Alastair to meet him in the Thorne living room as soon as possible.

"Babe, you're scaring me," GiGi said as he wordlessly gathered her close. "What happened?"

"Georgie Sipanil has been murdered." He didn't tell her the killer intended to pin it on him. There would be time enough.

"Goddess!"

Tears formed behind his closed lids, but he ruthlessly suppressed them. The time was not at hand to grieve his friend. No, avenging her came first. Sorrow could come after.

"I'm going to kill Beecham."

"Not that I'm defending him, but are you sure it's Harold?"

"I can't think of anyone else who would have it in for her."

"Don't do anything reckless. We'll figure this out—together, as a team. You, me, and Alastair. I don't want that sonofabitch slipping through our fingers."

He pulled back enough to gaze down at his wife. Her fierce expression both warmed and terrified him. At least now she was urging caution. There was a time when she'd have been the one going off half-cocked to right a wrong.

As he drew away, she clutched his forearms. "I'm sorry about your friend, Ryker. I know she had to mean something to you for you to react so strongly."

"She was like a second mother to me in many ways," he confessed hoarsely. "I'm going to miss her."

"Let's go meet Alastair."

GiGi tightly gripped his hand in hers, and Ryker wondered if she feared he'd set out to crucify Beecham on the spot. The temptation was strong, but he couldn't risk walking into a potential trap.

Alastair was pacing the living room when they joined him. While Nash was present and sitting down, there was a tension in his frame. His nephew always kept a pulse on the happenings of the Council. His grim expression clearly indicated the direness of the situation.

The energy in the room was thick with worry and laced with a deeper emotion like rage. Ryker suspected that flowed from Alastair. He, too, had admired Georgie. They'd maintained a fun, flirty dance where Alastair skirted the laws of the WC and Georgie scolded him at every turn, all the while protecting him as best she could from her elite position as Head Council.

"Should we bring anyone else into this?" GiGi asked in between hugging her brother and nephew.

"I would suggest Knox Carlyle, since he's the only other one who moonlights for the Council," Nash said. "I can call him if you'd like." At Alastair's nod, he did just that.

"How the hell did he get to her?" Ryker demanded. "Georgie was one of the most heavily guarded individuals on the planet." Due to her station as both Councilwoman and magical royalty, her security detail was greater than that of a U.S. president.

"That's the question of the hour," Nash grunted. "If I had to speculate as to why anyone believes you're behind this, it was your ease of access. She treated you like family, allowing you to come and go."

"What?" GiGi's enraged screech made the men present wince. "Who thinks Ryker is behind it, and why?"

Ryker sat beside her on the settee and gave her a one-armed hug. "We intend to find out, sweetheart. Stay calm." To the others, he said, "Even I had to go through fingerprint and retinal scans to gain access to her home. There were also security cameras everywhere."

Knox, having arrived during this part of the discussion, finally spoke. "Perhaps that's why someone broke into your house yesterday. To obtain evidence to plant in her home." He shrugged. "As to the cameras, they can be altered easily enough."

"Do you think that's the reason Beecham and the Witches' Council army were practically at our doorstep last night?" Zane asked from where he filled the entrance to the room.

"You heard?" Alastair asked.

"Most of it. I came down to get Winnie a bite to eat and stumbled on your little powwow." He moved farther into the room. "Having never dealt with the WC, I'm unsure of their laws, but if I can offer my legal services in any way…"

"Thank you." Ryker nodded to Winnie's husband. Handsome and unassuming, most people overlooked Zane's intelligence, but the young man was bright and could be calculating when necessary. "I'll keep that in mind. But I'm sure if Beecham has his way, I won't make it in front of the tribunal."

GiGi's hand tightened where it rested on his knee, and Ryker covered it with his own. He had no immediate plans to lose what he'd regained only yesterday. If they had to relocate to a remote island in the middle of the Pacific, then that's what they'd do. Parting from GiGi at this point was not going to happen.

Glancing up, he noted Alastair's sharp gaze studying the two of them. A soft light entered his friend's eyes, and Alastair gave him a partial smile. Ryker had no doubt Alastair had honed in on his thoughts. It also gave him a warm feeling to know that his old friend had his back in all things. If it came down to him and GiGi dropping off the Council's radar, then Ryker had no doubt Alastair would make it happen.

"They won't stop looking for you." Nash cut through his thoughts and brought everyone's attention back to the matter at hand. "Not with Beecham driving this train. I expect I'll be suspended pending an investigation based on my relationship with you. If I had to guess, you won't be his only target, Uncle. He'll have tried to set up Alastair and possibly myself as well."

"Christ, this is going to get ugly." Ryker rubbed the spot between his brows. "The only person we had on our side was Sebastian Drake, and I effectively pissed him off yesterday when I went alpha over GiGi."

The expressions on the men's faces ranged from astounded to amused.

"Oh, to be a fly on that wall," Alastair stated with a chuckle.

"I'm surprised you weren't, you prying prick," Ryker retorted.

"Don't be testy. The ends justified the means." His friend gestured to him and GiGi together on the couch. "We're all thrilled you patched things up. Even at the expense of Drake."

"Yeah, well now, I need to call him back to smooth things over."

"I can do that," GiGi offered.

Ryker rounded on her in angry disbelief. "Seriously?"

Her nervous gaze shot around the room and landed back on him. "He'll listen to me. What do you have to lose?" She cupped his cheek. "Let me do this little bit. Sebastian is a good man. He'll understand."

"That gives me an idea." Alastair whipped out his phone and scrolled through his contacts. He held up a hand for silence as he made a call. "Mackenzie? Alastair Thorne. Yes... how are you, child? How's your mother? Yes... Are you still in England?" He paused to listen. "I need you to do me a favor. If I send you coordinates, do you think you can teleport and deliver a message? Wonderful. I won't forget this. Whatever you want, you need only ask." He smiled at whatever was said. "Of course... I'll text you the information... Yes, right away. Thank you, child."

After he hung up, he tapped out a message.

Ryker waited a bit impatiently, knowing Alastair wouldn't reveal his plan before he was good and ready. GiGi was the first to snap.

"Oh, give over, brother. What are you up to?" she growled.

"I'm introducing the lovely Mackenzie to Sebastian Drake. She's stunning enough to divert him from your defection and artful enough to help us obtain all we need to know without breaking a sweat."

GiGi's lips twisted in wry amusement. "You clever beast. It's an added bonus that any calls or texts you make can't be traced to Drake personally. It stops Beecham looking closer in his direction."

"Smart," Ryker added.

"You're welcome."

"I'm lost," Zane confessed.

"Mackenzie is a Thorne. Cousin to your wife. She also happens to be a supermodel. Most don't credit her with much up here." Alastair tapped the side of his head. "They would be wrong. She's as smart and crafty as they come. Think Spring, Winnie, and Autumn rolled into one."

Zane chuckled with evil glee. "Yep, Sebastian Drake doesn't stand a chance."

"No, he truly does not."

Ryker studied GiGi for any sign she was upset by Alastair's machinations. When she turned sparkling eyes upon him, he breathed a sigh of relief. A small part of him was still hurt by her phone call with Drake yesterday. Her lack of jealousy for this new match by her brother went a long way to soothing Ryker's insecurities.

He leaned close to whisper into her ear. "As beautiful as

Mackenzie is, she doesn't hold a candle to you. I hope Drake isn't terribly disappointed he lost out."

Her lips curled in a mischievous smile. "Something tells me he'll enjoy drowning his sorrows by flirting with Mackenzie."

"My guess is that he'll arrive at my mountain estate within the hour," Alastair said. "Zane, you'll want to get your wife that food now. In the meantime, the five of us will head to my place to antici-pate Drake's arrival. We'll fill you in as soon as we know anything. Have Winnie keep a close eye on her scrying mirror. At the first sign of danger, the two of you get to my estate." He clapped Zane on the back. "Tell your cousins to do the same. I'll inform my daughter Holly and her husband to remain on guard. I'll also leave you two of my team for backup."

13

Can you believe you're already at this point in the book? As usual, this chapter has been omitted to preserve the tradition associated with the Thorne Witches series.

Now, back to your regularly scheduled reading!

14

Sebastian Drake surprised Ryker when he pulled him aside. "Inasmuch as I admire your wife, I'm delighted to see you've patched things up. No hard feelings?"

"Only marginally," Ryker responded. "For the record, unless I am six-feet under, my wife will always be off-limits to you. Even then, I want at least a two-year moratorium on any relationship."

Drake laughed and slapped him on the back. "I'll agree to a one-year mourning period, but then all bets are off."

"Eighteen months is my final offer, or I haunt you from the beyond."

"Agreed."

The two men shook hands and headed for the drink tray.

GiGi materialized at Ryker's side, causing Sebastian to swear. Hands on hips, she glared at the two of them. "Were you seriously just bargaining over my future affections?"

While poor Drake froze like an animal down the barrel of a rifle, Ryker laughed and drew her close for a slow, satisfying kiss. When they came up for air, he said, "Yes. Yes, we were."

With an air of complete indifference, his wife patted her hair and smoothed her dress. "All right then. But I shan't mourn you for longer than fourteen months. A woman has needs." So saying, she sashayed off, both men observing the seductive sway of her hips.

"You are one lucky bloke, Gillespie," Sebastian said on a heartfelt sigh. "Now, I suppose we should discuss this new turn of events with Beecham and poor Georgie."

Grief swept Ryker, and he gave a single, solemn nod. "I want to tear Beecham apart more than ever. No doubt he covered up this atrocity with black magic, just as he did my sister's murder and probably countless others before and since." He met the other man's watchful gaze. "I loved Georgie like she was my own mother. I would never—"

Sebastian held up a hand. "I know, Ryker. I've spoken with her in the past. She returned your affection and respected you above all others. She was truly a lovely woman. Anything I can do to bring her killer to justice, I will."

"Thank you."

They didn't have long to wait before Alastair directed them all to be seated at the dining table. By silent agreement, those present waited until lunch was served before launching into the discussion of Georgie's untimely demise. Ideas for outing Beecham were thrown about and systematically rejected.

"GiGi and I spoke with Preston this morning," Ryker revealed.

All the silverware around them clattered to the table with the exception of Knox's and Alastair's. Knox, of course, had been informed earlier so the topic of Preston came as no surprise.

Alastair, on the other hand, carefully set his fork and knife against his plate then wiped his hands on a linen napkin. "Did I hear you correctly? You spoke with my brother?" His voice held only the slightest tremor.

GiGi explained their visit to the crypt, with Ryker inserting extra explanations here or there.

"Afterwards, we visited Spring, hoping she might remember any spells from the *Book of Thoth* to recall Trina to this plane from the Otherworld. If she eventually finds one, perhaps we can bring Georgie back the same way to testify for a tribunal." Ryker met the thoughtful gazes of every person at the table. "I'm willing to do whatever it takes to bring Beecham down. But that means avoiding detection from the Witches' Council. Possibly going into hiding. I don't expect anyone here to keep my secrets because I don't want any of you to get on their bad side. It's not worth the risk to what you hold dear." He faced GiGi. "That means you too, sweetheart. I want you to stay here with Alastair and Rorie until this is all resolved."

"No." Her chin went up, and steely determination entered her eyes.

"GiGi, be reasonable. Do you know what it would do to all of us if a stray bullet found its way to you?"

"I said *no*, Ryker." She closed her eyes and shook her head.

Sitting next to her, Ryker could feel the dark emotion brewing within her. "GiGi."

She pinned him with a look. "We're not doing this again. I won't sit idly by while you go chasing the bad guys. We do this together, or we don't do it at all."

"I work better alone." He didn't mean the words to come out as hard or as cutting as they did. Her wince made him squirm inside. Yet he couldn't back down. Couldn't allow her to get involved to the degree it could cost her life. He softened enough to say, "Beecham regards women as collateral damage. Look at Trina. Look at Georgie. I couldn't bear if he hurt you too, sweetheart. I just couldn't."

"You either take me with you or say goodbye to me forever, Ryker. I'm done sitting on the sidelines." There were no hysterics, simply a matter-of-fact statement. She rose and, with careful precision, placed her napkin beside her plate without looking at him. "I'll give you one hour to decide."

She left the men gawking in her wake.

GiGi's heart was practically pounding out of her chest as she exited the dining hall. There was little doubt Ryker would go off on his own and come crawling back for forgiveness. It was his M.O.

But she meant what she said. If her husband couldn't see they worked better as a team, if he insisted on the lone-wolf routine, they had no future.

She understood the stakes were higher than they'd ever been, but she had plenty to contribute, whether he chose to see it or not. Shoving aside the kernel of hurt trying to pop into a bigger feeling of betrayal, she walked the gardens at the back of her brother's estate.

"Men always think women are weak, don't they?"

The soft voice jerked her out of her musings. GiGi spun to face the garden's other visitor. The woman elegantly shifted from her reclining position on a two-person lounger. Her long, toned legs unfolded as she stood. Topping GiGi's height by a good six inches, the sultry redhead seemed to tower over her, helped along by the four-inch stilettos she wore.

"Hello, Mackenzie."

"Hello, GiGi."

The two women embraced.

"How do you know I'm upset by a man?"

A thumb gesture over Mackenzie's shoulder directed GiGi's eyes to the small compact mirror on a glass table.

"Spying. How positively sneaky of you!" GiGi laughed.

"You taught me well."

"I'm glad to see my life lessons were effective."

Mackenzie's smile was enough to equal the sun in its brilliance. "Without a doubt. And they've seen me through some trying times. I can never repay you."

"Tell me, dear. What do you think of the delicious Sebastian Drake?" GiGi teased. "I mean, you do realize my brother has it in mind to match the two of you?"

"The man is positively yummy, but I'll make both Alastair and Sebastian believe I'm indifferent." With an elegant shrug typical of a Thorne, Mackenzie picked up her compact and slipped it into her purse. "It will gain me the upper hand."

"That's my girl," GiGi cheered. She checked her watch. "I have about twenty-five more minutes to kill before Ryker tries to convince me to reconsider my stance. Tell me all about what's happening in your world."

The women conjured wine and strolled the grounds. Her cousin was a great distraction from the thoughts wresting around GiGi's brain. Or at least she believed it was so until Mackenzie nudged her, and GiGi realized she hadn't responded.

"I'm sorry. I'm poor company at best."

"You have a lot on your mind. It's understandable." Taking her arm, Mackenzie guided her to a stone bench. "Do you want to talk about it?"

"The idea of being left behind yet again…" GiGi shrugged and sipped her drink, trying to form the words.

"I only want to keep you safe, sweetheart." Ryker's gravelly voice came from behind them.

Mackenzie patted her wrist and rose. "I'll leave you to work this out."

Ryker took her cousin's place on the bench. He shifted sideways, bending one knee and hooking a foot behind his other leg as he silently studied GiGi.

She looked anywhere but at him. She knew what she'd see—the standard adoration peppered with frustration and a beseeching expression. Afraid she'd give in, she sipped her wine and avoided his searching gaze.

"Are you not going to give me the courtesy of looking at me?" Irritation laced his tone.

"I can't," she confessed on a whisper. "If I do, I take the risk of caving to your demands, and I want our marriage built on more than that, Ryker."

"I'd never forgive myself if something happened to you."

"And I'd never forgive you if you went off and got yourself killed."

He gave a short, hard laugh. "Such faith in my abilities."

Finally, she faced him. "I do have faith in your abilities. I also know Beecham is out for blood and willing to use black magic to do it. We've lost a lot to him, Ryker. But we're stronger together, whether you choose to believe it or not. Look what we did to take down Delphine when she attacked our family."

His eyes skimmed over her face and settled on her lips. He groaned and kissed her lightly. "Fine. You go with me."

Had she heard right? "What did you say?"

"You heard me." His lips curled in a wry half-smile.

Unable to resist the urge to tease him, she said, "The only way you can make this moment better is if you say 'GiGi, you were right and I was wrong.'"

He barked out a laugh and pressed his forehead to hers.

"Come on, Ryker. You have it in you."

"GiGi, you were right and I was wrong," he said on a chuckle.

"You do realize this means you're stuck with me forever. Leaving me here to traipse about the world would have given you your freedom."

"I don't consider being tied to you for the remainder of my life any type of punishment. In fact, it's a reward of the highest magnitude."

"Oh damn, babe. You say the sweetest things." She swiped at a renegade tear.

"It's all in an effort to get laid by my wife."

She climbed onto his lap, straddling him and cupping his head between her palms. "Oh, you'll definitely get laid with that silver tongue." She captured his mouth and savored the feelings the brush of his tongue against hers brought. When Ryker gripped her hips and deepened the kiss, GiGi felt as if he truly had come home for good. In her heart, she sensed everything would be okay. The Goddess couldn't be so cruel as to allow another separation between them.

Ryker drew back and smoothed her hair behind her shoulders. "We should go back inside and see if anyone has come up with a way to best Beecham."

"Thank you," she said softly.

"I just hope I don't regret it. Like I said, if anything happened to you..." He shook his head as if he couldn't bear to voice his concerns again.

"It won't."

"You can't know that, GiGi, and I don't have a great track record with my loved ones surviving my enemies."

Seeing Ryker's side of the situation wasn't difficult. Yet there were no guarantees. All she knew was that if Harold Beecham succeeded in laying the blame of Georgie Sipanil's death at Ryker's door, she'd lose him to the Council's standard punishment of death. And if she didn't do all she could to prevent that from happening, she'd never be whole again. She'd be a broken shell of who she had originally been.

"Have faith, my love. I do," she assured him. She only wished she could convince herself as easily as she seemed to convince Ryker.

15

*R*yker was still doubting his sanity as they rejoined the group in the dining room.

"We may have figured out a plan," Alastair told him as soon as he sat down.

"I'm waiting with bated breath."

His friend shot him a dry look and refrained from a sarcastic comment. "Spring called and said she found a spell in the Carlyle grimoire. It will take blood magic, but she thinks it might do the trick to recall Trina for a tribunal. As far as Georgie, there's no way to bring her back."

Nash leaned forward, a deep frown playing between his brows. He met Ryker's eyes across the distance of the table. Blood magic meant extracting it from one or both of them since they shared a high concentration of her DNA.

"She stated it would take three sources," Alastair continued, expression grim.

"What does that mean?" Ryker didn't mind letting blood to bring his sister's murderer to justice.

"You and Nash are related to Trina, but as far as I know, there are no others."

"I could try to round up a distant relation," Nash offered.

Alastair shook his head. "Too diluted. It needs to be an immediate connection like a parent, sibling, or child." His phone buzzed on the table in front of him. "Excuse me."

He stepped from the room, and the remaining occupants sat in silence, each still at a loss as to how to proceed.

"How much blood do you suppose you would need?" Sebastian Drake asked.

Ryker twisted to see him. "Why?"

"I had the idea we might obtain her blood-stained clothing from the evidence locker at the Council Center. Perhaps we could find a magical means to separate the blood from the material."

He nodded slowly. Drake's idea had merit. After Trina's body was found, the Witches' Council swept in and confiscated anything related to her murder. As far as Ryker knew, they still held all the items in a cold-case storeroom. "It's worth a try. But I can't stroll in to retrieve it, and Nash's on suspension, pending my arrest."

"I have no such restrictions." Sebastian grinned. In that wicked smile, Ryker saw how he, himself, must've been in his youth—carefree and craving excitement. No wonder GiGi had found the young Brit attractive.

"I don't need to caution you about getting caught, Drake. If Beecham suspects you're involved with us for even one minute, he could target both you and your sister."

"I know." Drake's face lost his devil-may-care expression, and he sat straighter. "But it goes against my nature to allow that evil wanker to continue in this vein. If I can help prevent another untimely death, I most assuredly will."

"Well, all that's left to figure out is how to prove your innocence regarding Georgie," GiGi said. "You were with me practically every minute of the last two days." She addressed her next questions to Sebastian. "Do you have a time of death? And will the Council take my word for an alibi?"

"The crime was within the last forty-eight hours. As far as an alibi, I don't know. It's worth a try. But we would have to find out who on the Council isn't in Beecham's pocket or under his thumb. I have the feeling his reach is longer than any of us expect."

Ryker nodded. "I agree. How else did he command the army to attack our home?"

Knox, having remained quiet for the entire meeting, chose that moment to speak. "Do you have video footage from your security cameras? If the date can be verified, you may be able to provide a digital backup to second your alibi."

"As far as I know, they never breached our panic room. I can take a trip back and see what I can dig up."

"Not you," Sebastian said. "They're likely lying in wait for you to return."

Ryker cast GiGi a conspiratorial look.

Sebastian glanced between them. "What am I missing?"

"Let's just say we won't walk through the front door," GiGi told him.

"It's risky for either of you to return," Nash cut in. He looked at Knox, who nodded in return. "Knox and I will head over. Tell us everything you can about how to get through your system."

Ryker gave the two men a rundown of the security and the tunnel's location.

"You should know, even with all this evidence to the contrary, the doctored video in the Council's possession is damning. It shows you entered Georgie's compound and exited again during the time of the murder. Your fingerprints were found on multiple surfaces," Sebastian warned.

"You'd think that damned council would know I'm a much better agent than that. All the years I've worked for them without ever getting caught or leaving a trace, and they think I'd be this sloppy?" Ryker rose to pace off his anger. "Not to mention I visited Georgie often. It stands to reason my fingerprints would be inside her house."

GiGi joined him, stopping his continuous movement. Placing her palm on his chest, she turned confident, trusting eyes up to him. "It's going to be all right, Ryker. Once we prove Harold Beecham killed Trina, the Council will be more open to listen in regards to Georgie.

And if they aren't, they'll have the entire Thorne and Carlyle clan to deal with. Not to mention your cousins. I doubt any of the remaining Gillespie clan would allow this injustice. That is a helluva lot of unrest in the magical community for the Council to handle."

He nibbled the delicate skin of her wrist. "Thank you, sweetheart," he said softly. Her faith in him was humbling, considering all he'd put her through in the past. "I needed to hear that right now."

Her blossoming smile warmed his heart and gave him hope. His GiGi would decimate the entire Council if she had to. He grinned his response. They were on the same page in this. He'd destroy anyone who tried to frame her or hurt her in any way.

She slid into his embrace. He couldn't resist the urge to check Sebastian's reaction over GiGi's head. Drake's expression held a wistfulness that was almost painful to witness. The other man gave him a nod as if to say he understood the way of it.

Ryker's gaze traveled to Mackenzie, who sat as if pleased with their affection. He shot her a wink. He hadn't failed to see her interest in Drake when she thought no one was paying attention.

Finally, he settled his attention on Nash, who sat fidgeting with his phone. "Is it going to be too painful for you to call your mother forward?"

Seemingly surprised by the question, Nash rose and walked to where Ryker still held GiGi. "Do we have a choice, Uncle? There is no hard proof other than my mother." He kissed GiGi's smooth cheek. "I'm going to the standing stones after your place to consult with the Goddess. With any luck, she'll be forthcoming with information or, at the very least, look favorably on what we intend to do."

"Good plan," Ryker agreed. "Thank you."

"I'm only doing it in part for you. The bigger reason is justice for my mother."

"Understood."

"Tell the sperm donor where we've gone and to buzz me if he needs me."

Nash teleported away with barely a disturbance in the air. Knox was close on his heels.

"Our nephew is gifted," GiGi said softly. "I'm just sorry he's had such a tough life until now. It makes him harder than most."

"He's got a good heart."

"He does."

Spring arrived shortly after the men left. In her arms, she cradled a small box. Setting it on the table, she nodded a greeting to Mackenzie. "Welcome to the madness, cousin." She turned her curious jade eyes on Sebastian Drake. As with all the other women who happened upon him, GiGi noticed Spring was helpless not to undress him with her eyes. The man was insanely good looking, and the kilt he wore stirred women's fantasies.

Sebastian lifted Spring's hand to brush a kiss upon her knuckles.

"You should know she's living with Knox. That's a tree I wouldn't piss on. The man has the power of a God," Ryker informed him, much to both GiGi's and Spring's amusement.

"Duly noted," Sebastian replied smoothly.

Mackenzie sauntered around the table and stopped in front of Spring. "Family rumor has it you lost your memory, little cousin. Have you fully recovered?"

A slight grimace passed over Spring's features. "For all intents and purposes, yes. I remember we met when I was a young teen."

"Yes, you were eager for me to meet Knox. I must say, he's filled out quite nicely. You make a stunning couple." Mackenzie hugged her. "I'm happy for you."

Spring graced her with a beatific smile. "He's amazing, and he loves me. Can you believe it?"

"What's not to love?" GiGi quipped. Her niece was beauty personified. "What do you have for us, darling girl?"

The intelligent light in Spring's green eyes flared brighter. "I found a spell that could work in conjunction with one I remember from the *Book of Thoth*." She faced Ryker. "As you know, the aim was only to bring Trina to a tribunal. We never had the option to pull Georgie with her because the lack of relatives necessary for blood magic." She dug into the box and removed a rolled-up piece of parchment. "Another concern I have is the amount of time Trina has been in the Otherworld. It might be tricky to bring her to this plane, and if she does, she could have amnesia about the incident." She held up a hand to stem off his objection. "*But*, what if we brought the Council to *her*? Her memories should still exist or be easy to recall with the help of Isis."

"The last time we used a forbidden spell to revive Rorie, we fell out of favor," GiGi reminded her.

"Yes. However, we will only steal a portion of a *Thoth* spell for this, *and* we'll ask permission first. Uncle Alastair is still her favorite. I'm sure she would help him."

Ryker tugged a lock of her coppery tresses. "I love your optimism." He squinted slightly at Sebastian in contemplation. "Do you think it's possible to round up all the Council members under the pretext of an emergency meeting?"

Sebastian nodded slowly. "It's possible. First, let me see if I can manage to smuggle out any evidence they currently have for Trina. If so, we'll take the next step in your plan."

"I appreciate anything you are willing to do, Drake."

"Call me Baz. All my friends do."

"Baz it is." Ryker shook his hand. "I'm honored to be considered your friend."

It thrilled GiGi to see the two of them working together. While she found much to admire about Sebastian, her heart belonged to Ryker, and she didn't care who knew it. Her fervent hope was that these two get along so they could remove the threat of Harold Beecham.

"I think you should bring Arabella here, Baz," GiGi told him. "If Harold suspects for one second you might be playing him false, he'll do what he can to hurt you. She'll be safe here under Alastair's protection."

A deep frown marred the perfection of his face. "I can't say she'll willingly come, but I can try."

"She enjoyed Rorie's company when we visited you a few weeks back. I'm sure she won't mind a couple of days until we can clear this up."

"A couple of days?" Ryker snorted. "You are being overly optimistic, sweetheart."

"No. I'm simply determined to end this once and for all. I'm tired of that troll Harold Beecham playing fast and loose with my family."

"Remind me to never get on your bad side," Mackenzie said with a laugh.

"You couldn't if you tried, dear. Now, let's look at this spell."

As far as magical spells went, this one was fairly straightforward if a little tricky. It required blood magic, as suggested earlier, but the twist was in the wording. As always, Spring's interpretation of the grimoire and *Book of Thoth* was impeccable. A more brilliant, gifted witch, GiGi had yet to meet.

"I believe this will work. We should run it by Alastair and Nash to see if there is anything in the wording that might backfire, but I think this could be the perfect combination of magic we need to pull this off." She sent her niece an approving glance. "Well, done."

"While you double-check this with Alastair, I'll retrieve my sister. I shouldn't be longer than an hour. If I am, I'll send you a text." Sebastian addressed Ryker. "If you don't hear from me within two hours at the maximum, it will be cause for concern. I prefer you don't do anything foolish in the meantime." He bent over GiGi's hand, spared a lingering glance for Mackenzie, and teleported away.

Spring fanned her face. "Don't any of you dare tell Knox I said this, but that man—" As if her words had conjured him, Knox appeared.

"What has you hot and bothered? Or do I need to even guess?" GiGi heard him tease Spring in a low voice.

"I was picturing how hot you'd look in a kilt," Spring replied pertly.

"Mmhmm."

The dry, knowing look he gave Spring tickled GiGi. These two youngsters were a match made by the Gods. A truer love she'd never witnessed, with the exception of Alastair and Rorie, and perhaps her feelings for Ryker. She cast a side glance at him only to find he was watching her, a soft look in his eyes. She'd never tire of that expression.

"Where's Nash?" Ryker asked Knox. "Did he head straight to the clearing?"

"No. He said he needed a reference book from his library. He decided to consult with Alastair and Spring before making a formal request to Isis, so he should be here momentarily."

Spring directed him to the parchment she'd uncovered. She explained the theory behind her plan. "What are your thoughts?"

Knox nodded and bussed her temple. "I think you're exceedingly clever. Let's find out what your equally smart cousin and uncle have to say, but I can't see where this wouldn't work. No major red flags from my perspective."

Alastair joined their group. "Show me what you've discovered."

"I believe we can put the entire tribunal group to sleep and transport them as a whole to the Otherworld. From there, they will be able to conduct an interview with both Trina and Georgie," Spring explained and handed him the parchment. "This is an ancient spell from the Carlyles' book. It's never been tested, but I believe, with the modification here and here..." She pointed out the lines she referred to. "...using what I remember from the BOT, it quite probably will do what we need it to."

"What's the bot?" Alastair asked.

"Not bot, Uncle. B... O... T... *Book of Thoth*."

His lips twitched. "Is there any way we can avoid using the... BOT?"

"We could, but then we could only transport Trina to our time. We would still have a problem proving Uncle Ryker didn't murder Georgie if we go that route."

"Fair enough. Next question, what magic do you suggest we use to put a roomful of Council members to sleep and contain Beecham in the process?"

"I was hoping you'd ask." Her green eyes twinkled with mischief, and she withdrew a vial of clear liquid. "A few drops of this, and they will all enjoy a nice nap while we put the Thorne magic to good use."

"How do we get everyone to consume it at once?" Knox asked.

"We don't. We convert it to a gas." Mackenzie grinned when everyone's attention turned on her. "What? You think my only super-power is my beauty? I majored in chemical nanoscience."

"Of course you did," GiGi laughed. "Brilliance runs in our family. We are putting you and your cousins in charge of this little science project while the rest of us figure out how to gather the Council without raising suspicion."

As the younger generation converged around the table to discuss science and all things foreign to GiGi, she pulled her brother aside. "Would you like to tell us about your phone call, Al? It had to be important to pull you away."

"I've investigators searching for Leonie."

"Delphine's daughter?" GiGi's stomach dropped. "Why on earth would you wish to find her, other than to send her by way of her mother?"

"Beecham never released her after Delphine's death. I don't know what he's holding her for, or if she's even still alive, but Leonie's son, Armand, has been left without a mother. I mean to rectify that wrong."

"We owe that branch of the family nothing. Not after what she did to our brother."

"This isn't for Delphine. This is so we don't raise another genera-tion of enemies."

She rubbed her temples. As usual, Alastair had thought of all the angles. He was ten steps ahead of her on any given day. Never had she seen anyone predict the future with such accuracy and not have metaphysical power. He'd been gifted with an empathic ability— most water elementals had it to a certain degree—yet Alastair had it in spades. It allowed him to get a good bead on the emotions of those in his immediate sphere. However, his uncanny ability to see into the future had nothing to do with premonition and everything to do with his diabolical thought process.

"Where is he now?" Ryker asked.

"Nash tasked Liz Thorne with his care until we can find his mother. Should that prove impossible, we'll figure out a long-term solution. Perhaps binding his powers and giving him into the care of a family who would love him."

"Do you intend to wipe his memories?"

"If I need to, but my main hope is to find Leonie alive and well."

GiGi shared a concerned look with her husband. "What's to stop Leonie from seeking revenge for her mother's death, Al?"

"Nothing."

*L*eonie Foucher had waited patiently for her chance to escape Harold Beecham's clutches every day for the five months he'd held her captive. Less than a month ago, he'd brought her news of her mother's death at the hands of her cousins, and the grief nearly sent her over the edge into madness. If she hadn't suspected it was his intent all along—to hone her into a grief-stricken, vengeful weapon to use against Alastair—she might have been easier to manipulate. As it was, she was fairly certain Alastair Thorne had had no choice. He didn't strike her as a man who would kill indiscriminately.

She remembered him as a kind man. Granted, one who didn't suffer fools lightly, but in all the times he visited her mother in the past, he'd shown nothing but affection for their small family. His visits were less frequent since Aurora Fennell-Thorne had fallen into her stasis. He'd once explained to Leonie he felt the need for hands-on care. He didn't like to leave his Rorie alone for long periods of time. This, she understood. When Armand had fallen ill the one and only time in his young life, she never left his side except to sleep, and only then because her mother was there to care for him in her stead. No, Alastair wasn't cruel, and he wouldn't have killed or had Delphine killed for no reason.

Armand. Her boy. How she missed him! Without her mother, Leonie feared he'd been thrust into a foster care system. Small for his age, he might suffer at the hands of bullies and the like. Mother had parted ways with her sister, Rachelle, early on in life. Leonie was doubtful anyone would know to contact her aunt to help with Armand. Her heart ached for her son.

The door cracked open, and one of the night guards entered. Matthew. Tension eased from her shoulders as he smiled her way. Tall, he had the muscular makeup of a bodybuilder. With his mussed blond hair and his carefree smile, he'd found a place in her heart. Not that she'd ever let him know because she couldn't be certain this wasn't another ploy of Harold's to get her to do what he wanted.

Matt paused in front of her, a dinner tray in his hands. "You look sad."

"Nothing like stating the obvious." She shrugged and shifted to take the food. "I miss my son. I don't know what's happened to him since Mother's… death." Clearing her throat, she set the metal tray on the table. "Anyway, thank you for dinner. You may go."

She felt more than heard his approach. Her nerve endings became live wires.

"Do you want me to see what I can find out?"

Boy, did she ever. Again, she gave a delicate shrug. "What can either of us really do for Armand while I'm here? I don't know if it would torture me more to know if he was handed over to the State or not."

"Leonie, look at me."

Unable to comply with his request, she removed the tops to the dishes then replaced them. Perhaps she could eat later, when she wasn't so upset.

"Tell me how to help you," he whispered achingly.

Anger rolled through her. Spinning to face him, she snapped, "You can release me."

"Beecham would kill us both." His left eye twitched. "I won't go against my employer."

"Then you can't help me, can you?"

They stared at one another, and in his blue eyes, she saw frustration. What she couldn't tell was whether that frustration was born from her rejection of his affection or from his inability to manipulate her. At this point, she didn't dare trust anyone.

His frown dropped away, and a cool, indifferent mask replaced his expression. Turning his back to the south side of the room, he looked around. His lips scarcely moved when he lowered his voice and said, "Be ready to go at midnight tomorrow."

Hope flared to life within. Did he mean what she thought he meant? Would he help her escape?

Casually, she presented her back and toyed with a lid again. He moved to the table and began laying out the silverware, his back to the camera in the corner of the room. "If I don't arrive by fifteen past the hour, I'm not coming," he said, whisper-soft. "Who can I contact on the outside to help you?"

"Alastair Thorne."

He rolled his eyes. "Could you pick someone a little more accessible?"

She lifted the lid as if to sniff the contents. It blocked the lower half of her face from the camera. "He has a son, Nash Thorne. He's in charge of Thorne Industries. I imagine getting a message to him might be easier. You could also try my cousin, Preston Thorne. He runs an antique shop in Leiper's Fork, Tennessee."

Matt twitched slightly. "Preston Thorne is dead."

She tried not to react badly to the news. Placing the lid to the side, she eased into a chair. Matt's body now blocked the camera.

"How? How did he die?" Preston had seemed invincible to her as a child. How anyone could hurt someone so large and vital was beyond her comprehension.

Concern and discomfort warred on Matt's features.

"Matt. *How?*"

"He was shot and dumped in the woods of Leiper's Fork."

As she processed the information, tears came unbidden and slid down her cheeks. Ducking her head, she used the linen napkin to wipe them away. "My mother and Beecham were responsible, weren't they? It's the only reason Alastair would end her life or allow anyone else to."

"I can't begin to speculate. I only know the Thornes are a little harder to get to now. They've closed ranks."

"Try Nash. If you can't reach him, it's likely I'm screwed and on my own."

"No, you aren't. I won't let you be. Whatever happens, you and I are out of here tomorrow night."

She wanted to grab his hand and offer up her thanks, but Beecham would have his security team watching her closely. Instead, she picked up her fork and pushed around the mashed potatoes.

Because he could no longer delay or account for the time in her room, Matt moved toward the door. It was the same whenever he was on duty. The brief minutes he visited with her at dinner were all the stolen moments they dared. He was almost to the door when she spoke.

"Matt? Thank you... for dinner."

"You're welcome, Leonie. I'll be back to remove the trays in an hour."

After he left, she was careful to keep her expression bland, as she had every day since she'd been here. To allow even a glimmer of excitement or hope, was to alert Harold of a potential escape plan. She prayed to the Goddess that Matt wasn't playing her false.

JUST AS NASH WAS GEARING UP TO RETURN TO HIS FATHER'S ESTATE, the main line for his office rang. Normally, he'd let his assistant answer or let it go to the after-hours service, but the second the light flashed on his main number, a sense of importance rippled through him.

"Hello?"

The person on the other end of the line cleared their throat and spoke low into the phone. "Hi, I need to get in touch with Nash Thorne. It's urgent I speak with him."

"Who's calling?" Before he confirmed or denied his presence at the office, he wanted to be sure he wasn't being set up.

The man on the other end of the line cleared his throat a second time. Although his voice was still laced with tension, irritation replaced the uncertainty. "Look, I don't have much time. My name is Matt Turner, and I'm calling about his cousin. Is it possible to speak with him or not?"

Nash channeled and processed the energy of his caller. The man was on the level as far as he could tell. "This is Nash. Which cousin are you referring to? I happen to have quite a few."

"Oh, yeah, sorry. Her name is Leonie Foucher. She's being held against her will by my employer." A gusty exhale came across the line. "If we're being honest, man, I am worried for her safety. She seems to think you can be trusted to help her."

"I can. Is it safe for you to talk now?"

"As safe as it ever will be. My co-workers think I'm out for a smoke."

"Okay. Tell me what you know."

Nash listened as Matt explained where Leonie was being held. Other than a location and the identity of his employer, the man was clueless as to why she was a prisoner to begin with. Matt continued on to say he'd promised to get her out the next evening, whether Nash would help or not.

"I could use an assist. If Beecham even suspects, I doubt my life would be worth anything. He's a bad seed, man."

"Can you memorize these coordinates?"

When he agreed, Nash gave him the location of a downtown warehouse owned by a corporation under the umbrella of Thorne Industries.

"If I can determine you aren't setting me up, I'll be there to get you and Leonie to safety."

"One more thing, Mr. Thorne. Leonie's son, Armand—is he okay? She's supremely worried about his welfare."

"Tell her not to worry. Armand is receiving the best possible care."

"Thank you. She'll be relieved." He swore softly. "Gotta go. Tomorrow night. Don't fuck us over."

The line went dead. Nash hoped to hell Matt hadn't been discovered. If he was, there would be no doubt the man's corpse would turn up somewhere in the next few weeks. The other concern would be what Matt spilled if he was tortured by Beecham's elite security team.

He replaced the receiver in the cradle and picked up the book he'd stopped for, then teleported back to Alastair's estate.

"I had the most interesting phone call," he told the group without preamble. He went on to detail the conversation. "I think Matt Turner is on the up and up."

"I'll run a background check," Ryker offered.

Nash stopped him with a hand on his forearm. "I don't think that's a good idea. It's possible it could electronically trigger an alert to Beecham. Oddly, I trust the guy I spoke with."

His father nodded. "I agree. If you feel we can trust him, then we will." He checked his watch. "There's plenty of time to send a team to fortify the warehouse. I'll have Alfred assign a group of ten men to stage the rescue and another three to watch the location Mr. Turner gave you. No Thorne sets foot near that building until we can determine it's safe. No exceptions. I won't lose another family member to Beecham."

"Understood."

When Alastair left to inform Alfred of his wishes, Nash glanced around, his attention stopping on Spring. He grinned. "If you're here, you've come up with something exceptional, cousin."

"I don't know about exceptional," she objected good-naturedly with a twinkle in her eye.

"Right. Tell me." After she explained, he gave her a one-armed hug. "Like I said, exceptional."

Hearing her light laughter, he smiled. He'd become close with his cousins over the last year, and his respect for Spring's intelligence was through the roof. She not only had a photographic memory, she somehow catalogued the contents of both the Thorne and Carlyle grimoires in her mind. If she needed, she could draw forth a spell at a moment's notice. When Spring claimed she was "checking" the books, she made sure she had the most minute detail of a spell written down for whomever she might be obtaining it for. It had nothing to do with her ability to recall what she'd read. At times like these, when she mixed and matched the magic, she left the others shaking their heads in awed wonder.

Handing her the book he'd brought, he asked, "What do you make of this to extract the blood from my mother's clothing?"

She opened the tome to the bookmarked section. A quick skim of the page caused her to nod. "This is perfect."

"All we need is for Sebastian Drake to retrieve the evidence related to Trina's death, and we can get started," Ryker added.

Alastair returned, and Nash pulled him aside. "What do you mean to do with Leonie after we meet her?"

"You and I are going to evaluate her mental health and determine if we can get a sense of her intentions toward anyone involved in her mother's death. If we suspect for even one second she might want revenge, she'll trade one prison for another." His father's expression hardened. "As I said, I won't lose another family member."

The hair on Nash's arms rose, and a chill chased along his spine. There was no doubt in his mind that Alastair would do what he thought was necessary, even to the point of murder should the need arise. Nash rested a hand on his father's shoulder. "You'll get no argument from me, Sperm Donor. Let's try to gain permission from Isis. I'd like to clear Uncle Ryker and bury Beecham in the process, if we can."

*R*yker and GiGi left Alastair's living room and headed to the garden to walk off some of their building tension. They had another thirty minutes before they agreed they should be concerned about Sebastian and Arabella.

"I was happy to see you and Baz getting along," GiGi said as she tucked her arm through his.

"I won the girl." His tone and expression were smug, causing her to bite back a smile.

"Hmm, you make this sound like a contest. Did you only want me because—" She didn't have time to finish the thought before he swung her around to kiss her.

As their tongues tasted and teased one another, GiGi practically purred her enjoyment. His hand slid down her backside to cup her buttocks and draw her closer. Ryker worshiped her with his mouth, taking all she offered and more. *This* was what she'd missed all those years, what she craved on a daily basis. His simplest touch drugged her and made her weak at the knees, at the same time, firing up her blood.

When he drew back, an intense, ready-to-ravish gleam was in his eyes. She leaned into him for a second helping.

"While I'd hoped we could get back here, I never dared dream." With his index finger, he smoothed back the wind-blown locks from her face. "I fear for you, sweetheart."

"I've survived this long, babe. It will take someone a helluva lot tougher than ol' Harold to take me down."

His frown showed he wasn't going to be easily teased out of his concerns.

"Ryker. I'm going to be fine. I swear I won't take unnecessary chances with either of our lives."

"I'll hold you to that." His mouth eased into a slight smile. "Now, tell me how much more handsome I am than Sebastian Drake."

"He's standing right behind me, isn't he?"

Ryker's grin gave him away.

"You are so obvious, husband."

"Isn't he, though?" Sebastian laughed.

As one, they faced the siblings.

"Arabella," GiGi greeted. "You are looking well. Thank you for accommodating us. I know it couldn't have been easy to upend your evening to sit around this place."

The dark-haired woman cast a cursory look around and smiled tightly. "It won't be a hardship. However, I am concerned for Baz. The idea of him sneaking out Council evidence disturbs me on every level."

Ryker stepped forward and offered his hand to shake. "Your brother is doing me the greatest of favors. If there is any way I can repay you both for the sacrifice, all you have to do is say the word."

GiGi almost laughed when Arabella's strikingly handsome face softened. "Baz lives for intrigue."

"Just like someone else I know," GiGi muttered.

Ryker lightly side-checked her with an elbow. "The intelligence games are now for the young."

"Just keep it that way."

"I'll take Baz inside and check what the gang has come up with. I'll leave you ladies to talk."

After the men had gone, Arabella turned to GiGi. "My brother is disappointed."

"I can't help that."

"No, I don't suppose you could. I must say, I'm a bit disappointed myself. I like you, GiGi. It would be wonderful to be part of such a large and loving family."

In an impulsive move, GiGi gave the other woman a hug. "You and your brother are now honorary Thornes. We'll always support you both." She laced her arm through Arabella's and guided her down the stone path. "Besides, my brother has plans for Baz and my cousin Mackenzie. She's a doll, and you're going to adore her as much as we do."

"I know it's wrong of me, but I want a woman who will give him a difficult time."

"Mackenzie is your woman."

"Brilliant."

"She's that, too," GiGi quipped.

Laughing, the two of them headed toward the house to join the others.

Inside, plans were underway to gather the members of the Witches' Council.

Sebastian decided to contact the one other leader Georgie Sipanil had previously indicated she trusted. "I'll pop over to Councilman Stanley Smythe's house tonight and explain the circumstances. Perhaps he can call a meeting to order."

"Don't give anyone notice of your intentions, son," Alastair warned. "Go and come right back. Be sure you don't touch a thing. I wouldn't put it past Beecham to have his finger on the pulse of all that is happening. We don't need another one of our group framed for a crime."

"You think he'd risk another strike against a council member this soon?"

"Based on what we've discovered about Beecham's plans to start a second war, I'm left with little doubt."

"Valid point."

"Just be careful, please."

"Why, Alastair Thorne! If I didn't know any better, I'd believe you actually like me."

GiGi laughed when her brother rolled his eyes. From her angle, she could tell he fought a smile. Without a doubt, Sebastian Drake was a charming devil.

Alastair tugged on his cuffs and straightened his tie. "On that note, dinner will be ready. Alfred should be arriving any moment to inform us to take our seats."

Sure enough, Alastair's prediction proved true, and for the second time that day, GiGi was awed by his uncanny ability to *know* things.

The family and two guests meandered to the dining hall and took their seats. It wasn't lost on her that this might be the last meal they shared if Harold Beecham succeeded with his scheming. As she glanced from beloved face to beloved face, she was filled with a deep sense of fear. She never wanted to lose a single one. They were all essential to her peace of mind.

Ryker placed an arm along the back of her chair and leaned close to ask, "Are you all right, sweetheart?" His voice was low and for her ears alone, yet her brother looked up from his salad to meet her worried gaze over the table's distance. One of his arrogant blond brows lifted in question.

"I love you, brother," she mouthed.

"I love you, too," he mouthed in return.

She ducked her head to hide her emotional response, appreciating her husband's supportive hand as he caressed her neck.

"You have no need to fear for Al, GiGi," Ryker murmured. "Your brother leads a charmed life. He's practically indestructible."

She couldn't disagree. Alastair had survived more than most. "Preston's death is still raw," she said. "I couldn't bear it if I lost Alastair, too."

"That's what this is all about. Beecham and Victor Salinger need to be taken off the playing field. In that order. Then our family should be safe."

She loved that he said "our family." With a light squeeze of his knee, she focused on her meal.

RYKER UNDERSTOOD GIGI'S FEARS WITHOUT NEEDING HER TO elaborate. He'd lost his beloved sister to a monster, just as she'd lost her brother. Now, his own neck was on the line. If they couldn't prove he didn't kill Georgie, there would be no place he could hide. There was no need to point out the ramifications of failure. The severity of the punishment would be enough when the time came. Not that he was ready to call it quits or die for a crime he didn't commit, but he had to be realistic. He had a short window to make all this go away, or he was royally fucked.

His dinner companions all seemed to be of the same somber mind, shooting the occasional disquieted glance his way. Never had he wanted to yell as much as he did now. He wouldn't. He'd been trained to keep cool at all times, and he would. Hotheads never lasted long in the field.

What would have happened had Beecham murdered Trina and let his anger die with her? How many lives would've been spared in the interim between then and this moment? Had Beecham sent him to Marguerite knowing she would play the black widow in Harold's web of lies, ready to kill Ryker after her attempted seduction?

"You're awfully quiet, babe."

He grimaced. "I guess I'm feeling what everyone else is: a heavy dose of worry."

"Understandable. But we will win."

"GiGi, you do realize there is nowhere for me to run should this go south, right?"

"You won't need to. Let them come."

Her steely determination made him chuckle. "I'm glad you weren't as angry with me as you pretended to be in the past, sweet-heart. If you'd truly hated me, I would be a pile of ash somewhere." Casually, he took a sip of wine.

"Then I suppose you're lucky I don't carry a grudge."

He sputtered his drink, much to his wife's amusement. As he

mopped up his chin and chest, he caught Alastair's self-satisfied expression. Yeah, old Al had a lot to be pleased about. His dirty trick to lock him and GiGi inside their house had worked exceedingly well.

"What did you come up with to protect the girls, brother?" GiGi asked.

"I have a bevy of guards at both the Carlyle estate and Thorne Manor. They all know they better protect Rorie and her daughters or die in the process. If they don't, they'll face my wrath."

Sebastian sent him a wry look. "I'm glad I chose to make nice rather than gain an enemy in you, Thorne. You are one scary sonofabitch."

"You chose wisely, Drake."

Everyone at the table laughed, and the somber mood was broken. They spent the remainder of the dinner socializing. A few hours into the evening, Ryker and GiGi made their excuses.

"We'll be down at first light. If anything drastic happens in the meantime, you know where to find us."

Ryker led GiGi to his room. She stopped just outside the door and laughed.

"What's so funny?"

"On the rare occasions when I've stayed here to look after Rorie while Al was on some trip or another, I used this room. I suspect this has always been *your* room when you stayed over." She patted him on the chest and entered. "Do you suppose he was trying to get us back together even then? Maybe he thought if one of us showed up while the other just happened to be asleep in this bed…?" She trailed off with a naughty look.

"Remind me to kiss that crafty bastard in the morning for having my back."

"Too bad our timing was terrible," she teased.

"Well, we're both here now. No reason we can't make up for lost time."

Laughing, she drew him farther into the room and flicked a hand to magically shut the door.

18

*T*he next morning was an exercise in patience. Something Ryker knew GiGi found difficult. She fiddled where she was normally casual or serene, and she seemed a little irritable and snappish to the others at the breakfast table.

As she lifted her knife only to put it back down for the third time, Ryker captured her hand and kissed her palm. "You'd think after last night, you'd be nicer to everyone around you," he teased.

She looked startled, but her standard humor returned in a flash. "True." She did a quick scan of the table and returned her attention to him. "They are all going to believe you are leaving me dissatisfied with your lovemaking."

"Hardly that." He nipped her fingertips and grinned when she laughed. Picking up his own silverware, he divided and buttered the blueberry muffin on his plate then handed half to her. "You still have that satisfied glow."

A light blush tinged her cheeks, and the loving smile she now sported was certain to match his. She nibbled her half-muffin then set it down.

"I can't get rid of this feeling of impending doom," she confessed.

All the Thornes were intuitive to a large degree. GiGi fell only a step below Alastair in her ability to pick up on the vibrations around her. The siblings were naturally skilled like no one Ryker had ever encountered before. Added to that was keen intelligence. He'd learned a long time ago to trust their instincts.

"So what do you want to do?" he asked in a low voice.

She seemed surprised he'd posed the question to her. Shaking her head, she squeezed his fingers. "I don't know. I'm sure I'll feel better when Baz returns with Trina's clothing, along with the assurance he's gathered the Council."

"I know. It goes against my nature not to act, especially on my own behalf." He gave her hand a return squeeze then drew back to dig into his meal. "But we need to bide our time and try not to irritate everyone around us in the process." He winked in the face of her scowl. "If it helps, I'll let you do that thing you did last night again right after breakfast."

She snorted her laughter, drawing the attention of their dining companions. A quick glance showed everyone smiling indulgently and perhaps on Alastair's part, a little smugly. Ryker met his best friend's direct gaze and silently conveyed his thanks. Al nodded in return. There was no need for words between the two men. They'd been friends many years and, for the most part, were able to read each other with a simple look.

"I intend to drop in this morning and check on Autumn," GiGi announced. "Al, do you want to go with me to visit Rorie?"

"Absolutely."

She faced Ryker. "Stay out of trouble until I return?"

"You're cracked in the head if you believe I'm letting you out of my sight until Beecham is six feet under, sweetheart."

"It's only to see family, Ryker. I have no intention of knocking on Harold's door."

"Right," he snort-laughed. When she stared him down, he shook his head and sighed. "It goes against my better nature to let you run around brewing up trouble, sweetheart."

"Don't be overbearing, babe. It doesn't suit you." She leaned down and placed her lips on his. "I have phone calls to make."

Although he was curious, he refrained from asking about her plans. She'd tell him when she was good and ready and not a second before.

After she left the room, Ryker addressed Alastair. "She won't handle it well if we can't convince the WC of my innocence."

"None of us will. If I know my sister, her 'phone call' will be to buy an island in the Pacific as a backup plan."

"If the worst should happen, don't let her do anything foolish or impulsive, Al. Please."

"I can't promise that, my friend. We are both likely to act in conjunction. If you are found guilty, it will be both GiGi's and my first priority to remove you from harm. Anything less is an unacceptable outcome."

Ryker sighed his frustration with the siblings and turned his attention to a watchful Nash. "What about you?"

"This might shock a few of you, but I'm in one-hundred percent agreement with the sperm donor. We will do what is necessary to save you."

Fear and irritation at their stubbornness manifested into a sharp anger. "You are a damned stubborn lot, you know that? Damn the torpedoes, full speed ahead. *That* should be on the Thorne family crest."

Nash's jade green eyes lit with laughter although his expression remained impassive. "I'll have new banners made up."

"You remind me of your mom at times, Nash. I miss her. But I'd also be doing her a disservice if I let you cross the Council for my benefit." Nostalgia and regret bubbled up. "She'd want you safe."

"She'd want me to be a free thinker and to stand by my family. I've read her journals. Loyalty was important to her."

Alastair's head whipped around to stare at Nash. "Journals?"

"*Of course!* Let me see what I can find."

Within seconds, Nash had vanished.

"Do you all share one collective brain wave?" Arabella asked curiously from her seat midway down the table. "I swear, since I've been observing you all, it's as if you interact without needing to say a word."

"You have no idea. They're all a trial," Mackenzie stated from beside her, as she casually scooped out a bit of her soft-boiled egg. The twinkle in her eye belied the put-out quality in her tone.

In a spontaneous, astonishing move, Alastair tossed a balled-up napkin at the oh-so-prim Mackenzie, hitting her in the center of her forehead. She sputtered out her egg and turned incredulous blue eyes on the patriarch of the Thorne clan.

With a simple snap of her fingers, she flung egg in his direction. Already anticipating her response, he teleported, appearing directly behind her. He leaned in to kiss the crown of her head. "You'll have to be faster than that, child. I was the initial instigator of family food fights."

His deep laughter echoed about the dining hall even after he left.

"That's a side of Alastair Thorne you never see," Arabella said in awe.

"You're family now, dearest." Mackenzie patted her hand. "You'll see more of his playful side going forward."

"The whole lot of you are uncivilized, aren't you?"

Ryker laughed and pushed away from the table. "You have no idea."

GiGi MADE THE ROUNDS THROUGH THE FAMILY. SHE EXPLAINED what Ryker intended to do with the blood magic and how he hoped to be able to clear his name. She also explained her contingency plan. If things went wrong, she had every intention of getting Ryker out of the country and off the Witches' Council's radar. If it meant fleeing, her contact with family would be curtailed to emergencies only. The risk to those she loved would be too great if she and Ryker became outcasts in the magical community.

The last call she made was to her coven. She was the only

Thorne who still subscribed to quarterly gatherings with other witches. Mostly, the practice of rituals had fallen out over the last twenty years or so. At three p.m., her group of friends met at a pub they frequented, roughly twenty miles from the Fairy Pools on the Isle of Skye in Scotland. All but one showed up.

"Where's Tildie?" she asked no one in particular.

"She'll na' be coming, GiGi." Bridget O'Malley said with her lilting accent. She was beautiful in her own right and came from hearty Irish stock. Quick with a quip or a laugh, she always spoke in a matter-of-fact manner. Of all the coven, she was the only witch without any true power of her own. It wasn't to say she didn't possess magic, but due to a family curse, she couldn't tap into that magic. GiGi was determined to help her break the spell one day soon.

"I'm sorry, but her da's on the Council, and she'll na' go against his wishes. Thornes are to be avoided," Bridget went on to say, clearly irritated with Tildie's defection.

"I see." Disappointment rode her hard. Tildie was a skilled witch, and until this moment, GiGi had considered her one of her closest friends. But times change and allegiances faltered. "How many of you feel this way?"

Jill Burns offered her a hard hug. "We're here, aren't we?" Jill was a compact dynamo with bright red hair and an engaging grin. They'd been friends since childhood. "You can't get rid of us that easily."

Bittersweet emotions wrapped up in a thick blanket of worry nearly suffocated GiGi. "I don't want to put you in harm's way. You all mean too much to me."

Becca Calhoun placed a hand on her arm. A sweet Southern Belle of a woman, Becca had the ability to soothe. Calm replaced GiGi's anxiety from moments before. Such was the power of Becca's gift.

"We are with you one-hundred percent, hon. We know how to take care of ourselves."

"Thank you." GiGi looked into the serene, moss-green gaze and smiled. "You are all true friends."

"What are ye needing from us, GiGi?" Bridget asked.

With a simple wave of her hand and a two-line phrase, GiGi muffled their conversation, making their actual words indistinguishable to anyone who might overhear them. Facing her three steadfast friends, she smiled. "Are you up for a little intrigue and mischief?"

A wicked gleam entered Bridget's bright green eyes. "Aye. I thought ye'd never get around to askin'."

"You are an adventurer at heart, Bridg."

The feisty woman's husky laughter turned male heads. "Stop stalling. What will ye have of us?"

"Sebastian Drake is rounding up the Council for an emergency meeting. He's doing it under the pretext of worry."

"For what the Thornes will do to protect one of their own?" Bridget surmised.

"Yes. I'm sure by now, you all know my husband is suspected of killing Georgie Sipanil." She met each woman's gaze squarely. "I'm telling you the Goddess's honest truth; he was with me that night." She went on to explain the details of the attack on their home by Beecham the following afternoon. "So you see, Ryker has an airtight alibi. Any video footage of him entering Georgie's home is doctored."

Becca leaned in to ask, "You want each of us to appeal to the council on your behalf? A divide and conquer?"

GiGi laughed. "Oh, no. I want you to fuel the fire."

"I don't understand."

Bridget, however, did. "You want us to assist Sebastian Drake. Make our complaints about the Thornes known."

"Yes. Buy us time to gather them in one place." GiGi explained about the gas Mackenzie was creating and how they would need time for it to take effect. If her three friends could rally witches to appear as an angry mob, then the community at large would be transported to the Otherworld to witness Trina's testimony. "The Council will be forced to turn on Beecham." She then explained Harold's desire to start another witch war.

Her three friends each sat straighter. "Count us in," Jill said grimly. "That rat bastard isn't getting away with his vicious scheming. The first war cost too many too much."

"Be prepared by tomorrow morning. I may also need you to help me break the wards protecting the Council chamber."

GiGi felt their intrigued looks were a good sign.

THE LONG WAIT WAS DRIVING LEONIE MAD. MATT HADN'T SAID anything more to her other than to assure her Armand was receiving the best possible care.

Once again, he angled his body to block the camera and gestured to the tray. Under her dinner plate, she found a note explaining he'd come for her at precisely ten minutes after midnight. She was to dress for bed and shut out all the lights by ten, as if she were following her standard routine.

Matt would bring the guy manning the security cameras a drug-laced coffee and engage him in conversation. Minus the drug, it was their regular nightly habit. After the guard passed out, Matt would come for her.

She slipped him the paper to destroy and finished her meal. Hope blossomed in her chest. Soon, if the Goddess was kind, Leonie would see her son again.

THE ANTIQUE GEBRUDER WALL CLOCK STRUCK MIDNIGHT.

"It's time to go," Nash told Alastair and Ryker where they hovered in front of a large computer monitor, watching the live video footage from the team they'd sent to secure the warehouse. "Matt will have Leonie there within the next ten minutes."

"Our entire team is in place. We'll observe from here until we are sure everything is going to plan," Alastair informed his son. "When they arrive, we'll teleport, and not a moment before."

"You think this is a setup?" Ryker asked.

"No, but neither do I believe that it isn't." Alastair straightened his tie and readjusted his cuff links. A sure sign he wasn't as calm as he appeared. "Trusting that girl's mother proved fatal to my brother. I won't make that mistake again."

Ryker understood his caution. Alastair's belief that Delphine was loyal to the Thorne's might have cost Aurora her life had his brother not recognized the smell of the poisoned tea Delphine had gifted her. No, Al was wise to urge caution. Preston's death had cast a dark pall over the Thorne family.

The minutes ticked by with nothing but the sound of the soldiers' even breathing coming through their body cameras. Finally, at eleven minutes after midnight, the cameras flickered, indicating an electrical disturbance. When the picture came back into focus, Leonie Foucher stood in the center of the warehouse, with a large blond male beside her. Her eyes flittered wildly about, as if she was tallying enemies and allies. Giving her companion's arm one last squeeze, she released him and stepped forward to call out, "Alastair? Are you here?"

Thirty seconds elapsed. Alastair gave a short nod and disappeared, only to reappear on screen. Ryker and Nash were both hot on his heels.

"Hello, child."

Tears filled Leonie's golden eyes. "Thank you for coming for me."

"You can thank your friend. But for now, we will need to separate the two of you."

The large man stepped forward to encircle her waist. "Why?" he barked out the question.

Ryker placed himself between Alastair and the man they all assumed was Matt Turner. "Precautions. You will both be scanned for tracking devices, but not here and not now." He gestured to the soldiers around them, and the men closed ranks around the couple. "We need to get out of here ASAP in case Beecham has you magically marked."

"Christ, I didn't know that was possible." Matt's face paled. "How can he do that?"

"He's into the black arts, boy, and he'd dare anything," Alastair stated grimly. "Let's move. Leonie, come with me now, child."

She cast one last, longing look in Matt's direction and moved to take Alastair's hand. "Thank you, Matt. I'll never forget what you've done for me."

His face softened enough to smile. "Take care of yourself, Leonie. Hug that boy of yours tight."

"Let's go," Ryker said. He gripped Matt's arm and teleported to a second warehouse, just one block closer to the river than the first building, and waited for the others to join him.

Confusion was written all over Matt's countenance when he glanced out the floor to ceiling windows of the top floor. "We didn't go far."

"No. The water can be a conductor, but it can also mute a magical signal," Ryker explained. "If Beecham intends to use a supernatural means to find you, he will only be able to get a general locale. Our hope is that he winds up at the first warehouse. We're close enough to stage a counterattack."

"Why are you trusting me with this information?" Matt asked curiously.

Ryker slapped him on the back and laughed. "You passed the initial Alastair Thorne test."

"I don't know what that means."

Nash chuckled and stepped closer. "My father, like me, is an empath. He can feel intent. You have none that either of us can detect. Your concern for Leonie was evident, and although there was a hint of unease when you saw our team, you express no evilness that we can sense."

"Yeah, just a basic half-breed witch here, man. Mom was a non-magical. Dad had powers but essentially lived a basic existence. Pretty much what you see is what you get." Matt scrubbed his face with his hands. "What's next? A debrief? I can't tell you much about Harold Beecham's organization, but I can tell you some."

Ryker gestured to a table and chair in the corner of the warehouse office. "Have a seat."

Matt complied and faced the camera sitting on the tripod.

"A team member will scan you while you tell us what you know," Nash told him.

"Will Leonie be okay? She seemed worried about how your family would treat her because of her mother."

Nash and Ryker exchanged a long look. They both knew her life was worthless if Alastair caught wind of any deception. Nash sat across from Matt to tell him this. Although Beecham's ex-guard paled under his tan, he nodded his understanding.

"I don't think she has any hidden agendas. Not that I could tell. She was just scared and lonely. Concerned for Armand, ya know?"

"Does she know my wife shot her mother?" Ryker asked, studying him carefully.

"She knows a Thorne is responsible, either in actual deed or to have someone take action against Delphine. I don't think she blames any of you." Matt scratched the stubble along his jaw. "It's not like either of us could have long conversations. She was always watched. I suspect I was, too."

"Fair enough." Ryker crossed to the door. "Tell Nash everything you know that may be relevant to us. Start at the beginning. If you can think of anything criminal you've witnessed, we could use that to sway the Witches' Council."

When the guard standing behind Matt nodded the all clear, Ryker left Matt and Nash alone to talk.

*R*yker kept an eye on the laptop monitor as he conferred with Alastair's head of security. "Martin, have the wards been strengthened now that we've returned?"

"Yes, sir. We've added a little something we hope will guard against Beecham's special brand of evilness."

With a laugh and a clap on Martin's shoulder, Ryker removed his cell phone from the inside pocket of his jacket and called his wife. When she answered, pert and sassy as always, he smiled. "Hey, sweetheart. It's me."

"I figured as much when the caller ID showed your name," she said dryly. Her voice softened. "How did it go?"

"So far, so good. Knock wood. Nash is questioning Matt, and Al has shuffled Leonie off to another location. Presumably to tell her about her mother."

"Any sign of Harold?"

"Not yet. Either he was clueless as to all of this, or he has his own reasons for letting these two go. I hope it's the former." He sighed and scrubbed a hand along his jaw. "I want us to catch a break where this fucker is concerned."

"Maybe we have. Let's hope the Goddess is on our side in this."

"Yeah. Everything okay back there? Nothing out of the ordinary?"

"So far, so good. Knock wood," she repeated his earlier statement.

He grinned. "I love you, GiGi."

"I love you, too."

"We should clear this up in about an hour. Then we can make our next move."

"Be careful."

"Always."

"Uh huh."

He chuckled as he disconnected the call.

Martin cleared his throat. "If I may say, sir, we're all thrilled you and Ms. GiGi have patched up your relationship."

"Thank you. It's only about fifteen years overdue."

"Better late than never."

"Let me ask you, Martin. If you were Harold Beecham, why would you let these two go? What motive would you have to release them at all?"

"To cause havoc or let them lead me to my intended target."

Ryker nodded. He'd have done the same. "Double the guards around Alastair and make sure someone is with him at all times."

"That leaves you and Nash vulnerable, and Mr. Thorne would have my ass."

"I've got a bad feeling, Martin. This was way too easy."

The words were hardly out of his mouth when an explosion rocked the far end of the building. "Get Nash and get out," he ordered as he ran toward the commotion.

"Cloak!" He heard Martin shout. As he tore up the ground, he muttered the words to hide his presence and palmed a weapon in each hand: a knife in his right, and a Sig .40 caliber in the other. Before he reached his destination, Alastair appeared directly in front of him. Ryker skidded to a stop and cursed.

"Expando!"

The cloaking spell now extended to cover both him and Alastair, allowing his friend to see him in an instant.

"What the devil do you think you're doing, Al? Get the hell out of here!"

"Not without you. I'm not facing my sister should something happen to you."

Calm and droll as ever, Alastair seemed unruffled by the shouts and gunfire sounds from the first level.

"I've said this before, Al, and I'll say it again. You're. *Crazy.*" Ryker punctuated his words with a glare. "Crazy."

To his surprise, Al grinned and wrapped an arm around his neck. "Come on, the sooner we are out of here, the sooner my men can teleport to safety."

"I want to put a bullet between that sonofabitch's eyes."

"I know, and you will. Just not right now. *After* a tribunal. I want your name cleared with no lingering suspicion hanging over your head."

He heaved a frustrated sigh but jogged back the way he came, his friend at his side. Martin waited, his pistol pressed to a kneeling Matt's head.

"Ostende." Their invisible shield fell away.

"Is he responsible?" Alastair asked sharply.

"Not that I can tell. No tracker on him either. I've given him an herbal truth serum. He hasn't told Beecham a thing. Even Leonie didn't know where they were headed."

"Release him and then head back to my estate with the others."

"I'm not leaving you, sir," Martin stated firmly as he helped Matt to stand.

"You'll do as I say if you want to keep your position on my staff," Alastair warned.

Martin shrugged. "Sorry, sir, but I'm more afraid of Alfred than you."

Ryker laughed and nudged Alastair with his shoulder. "You've lost this battle, my friend. Let's get the hell out of here." To Matt, he said. "You're on your own, kid. My suggestion would be to do what is unpredictable. Don't go to family or friends for help. You know how to contact Nash. Hide out for a bit and contact us in two days' time."

With a nod, Matt disappeared.

The shouts now sounded from the second-floor landing down the corridor.

Ryker faced Alastair. "Your place?"

"No." A deep frown settled on his features. "I think it would be better to head to your panic room. Martin, tell the others to go, right now. You are coming with us." Alastair clasped Martin's wrist in one hand and Ryker's in the other. With a nod, he said, "Take us there, Ryker."

Envisioning his empty security center, Ryker pulled the magic from his cells and transported the three of them in seconds.

"Nice setup," murmured Martin as he looked around.

"Why did we come here, Al?" Ryker asked, ignoring the guard.

"I suspect I know how Beecham keeps showing up uninvited to the party. Do you have a scrying mirror in here?"

Ryker opened a drawer and extracted a two-feet-by-two-feet, silver-framed mirror.

Without fanfare, Alastair swiped a hand over the surface. At first, the image was of the warehouse, but faded as if a cloud obscured their vision.

"Bloody black magic," Al muttered. "Give me your knife."

Because he didn't seem to direct his command to either man in particular, they were both quick to whip out their weapon. Alastair grabbed the closest one from Ryker's hand. Taking an amulet from his neck, he placed it flat on the top right of the mirrored surface, then scored the flesh of his index finger. He let the blood run over the amulet and onto the mirror as he spoke.

"Goddess hear my plea,
Assist me in this time of need."

His next word was foreign to Ryker, and apparently to Martin also, since astonishment lit the other man's face.

"Dezvalui."

The fog lifted to reveal Beecham as he shoved one of the soldiers he employed. "What do you mean he's not here? Find him!"

"He's not here, sir. We've—"

The soldier's words were severed as a wicked six-inch blade slashed across his neck. Within seconds, Beecham held a small bowl to the man's throat and caught the spurting blood. "Get me a scrying mirror."

Ryker shot a quick glance toward Martin. "Be glad Al used his own blood."

"I am. Exceedingly so."

Alastair shot them a glare and returned to the scene unfolding in the mirror. Beecham's reveal spell was a little more complex and took longer to activate.

Ryker assumed it was because the man didn't possess half the natural magical talent as Alastair. "Is that a creole spell?" he asked.

"Yes." Alastair's answer was abrupt, and his eyes connected with Harold Beecham's as their faces appeared in the other man's mirror. Beecham swore when Alastair held up his middle finger and swiped a hand over the glass. *"Occaeco."*

They could still see Harold, but now the mirror he held was useless. His face turned the shade of a ripe beet. He swore long and loud as he smashed the mirror on the floor.

"Looks like his favorite toy was taken away," Martin muttered.

"Yeah, he's a real fucking peach," Ryker returned.

"If I'm correct, he'll be here in a few minutes." Alastair swept his arm in a wide circle. Seven crimson candles appeared in a perfect circle surrounding a pentagram now etched in the wood floor.

"No amount of sanding is going to take that out," Ryker quipped.

"Will you be serious for two minutes? We need to sever his connection to you."

"Say what?" Surely he hadn't heard correctly. Either that, or Alastair had finally gone over the deep end.

"He arrived here, Thorne Manor, and then at the warehouse without ever going to the first building Matt and Leonie teleported to. He's not tracking them, Ryker. He's tracking you."

"How the hell would he do that?"

"Trina's blood."

Ryker's stomach dropped, and his insides went cold. If that was true, he couldn't be anywhere near GiGi without endangering her. Hell, he already had.

"Al, it's not a simple matter to remove a spell of that magnitude. If you do this, we can kiss any chance of using blood magic to bring the Council to the Otherworld."

This whole thing could backfire, and the ramifications didn't bear thinking about.

"What do you suggest?"

"I keep moving until you and Spring have everything in place for the transference."

"And if he catches you? The whole thing is a bust."

Ryker's mind raced frantically, searching for a solution. It was Martin who solved their dilemma.

"Turn yourself in to the Witches' Council."

Both he and Alastair stared at Martin.

"Elaborate," Al barked.

"They have to hold you until trial. You can insist Harold Beecham not be allowed access to you and that a few of Mr. Thorne's guards be on hand for your protection round the clock as a condition of your surrender. It would make it harder for Beecham to target you." Martin shrugged. "As soon as the tribunal is set up, we spring you for whatever plan you all have up your sleeve."

A slow, pleased smile came over Alastair's countenance. "Remind me to give you a raise, Martin."

A slight flush dusted the other man's cheeks. "You pay me plenty, Mr. Thorne."

"A bonus then." Alastair turned his attention back to the scrying mirror. "Beecham is gathering his army to come here. Call Drake and have him set something up with Stanley Smythe. We need to get you to safety."

Ryker placed the call.

20

"*What do you mean, he's in the custody of the Council?*" GiGi screeched.

The three men standing in front of her winced. Martin looked a lot less thrilled to be confronting her with the news than either Nash or Alastair.

A boiling rage mixed with mind-numbing fear set her off, and in doing so, created a maelstrom of emotions she found difficult to control. The windows slammed open, threatening to shatter the glass, and wind whipped into the room. Vases rattled on their shelves, and stray papers began to swirl in the air around them. They crinkled as they whipped past.

"I should have known better than to trust him in your care," she snarled at Alastair. "How could you?" She lifted up her hands and blasted him with icy air.

Although he grunted and skidded a foot, her brother remained standing. "He's going to be fine."

"You can't promise that, Al!" She threw her arms wide, and dining chairs toppled. If she were a bystander, she'd be impressed by the power behind the tantrum. As it was, her heart was in her throat and her stomach was tied in knots. All she wanted to do was destroy anyone responsible for Ryker's capture.

"He knew you'd react like this and told me to tell you, he'd see you soon and 'no hooking up with Sebastian Drake in the meantime.'"

GiGi stared at Alastair, and all the fight died. The windows slid back into their original position, and the handful of papers settled on the floor. "He can't protect himself from Beecham in a jail cell, Al. He can't."

They all knew what imprisonment by the Council meant. Ryker's powers would be bound, and he'd be thrown in a room designed to make the use of magic impossible.

"If Harold Beecham decides to stroll in and use his abilities against Ryker then he'd be as powerless as a newborn babe." She sent her brother a beseeching look. "You have to get him out of there."

"Harold can't get to him. We've made sure of that."

Alastair gently embraced her, and she fought against the mind-numbing terror threatening to take her since the second he had told her Ryker was now a prisoner.

"What if they bypass a tribunal?" she whispered fearfully. Her heart spasmed at the thought.

"They won't. No matter what the crime, a tribunal is standard procedure."

"I couldn't bear it if something happened to him. Not now. Not after resolving our differences."

"It won't, sister. I promise."

"You can't promise that, Al," she said again, softer this time, but with no less angst.

"I will tear that institution to the ground before I let them execute him. I imagine every Thorne in existence will stand beside us to do it."

She pulled back to gaze up at him. The harsh lines of his face were sharpened by the determination in his sapphire eyes. "Okay."

She borrowed from his steely resolve and inhaled a fortifying breath. "Tell me the entire plan and leave nothing out."

Alastair had just finished explaining the steps they intended to take, when Sebastian Drake arrived. He looked as grim as GiGi had ever seen him.

"What is it? What's happened to Ryker?" she demanded.

"They've set a time for the tribunal. Tonight at nine," Sebastian stated.

"What? Is that normal? So soon? How can they not let him mount a defense?" All the questions tumbling around her brain came pouring out of her mouth. Dear Goddess! That gave them only eighteen hours to figure out their next step.

"It's not normal, but they fear Alastair. They believe if they limit his window of opportunity..." Sebastian trailed off, the reasoning implied.

"They should fear him—along with the rest of us," Nash replied, anger tinging his words. "I'll call Spring and Knox. Drake, will you go wake Mackenzie and tell her we need her keen scientific mind? First room down the hall on the left." He faced Alastair. "We're on."

"Go make your calls. I have a few of my own." Alastair glanced down at GiGi. "Are you going to be all right for a few minutes?"

"Yes. Go. Do what you need to."

When all the men left the room, GiGi closed her eyes and envisioned her niece's home. Within seconds, she approached Holly's and Quentin's front porch. The guards on duty recognized her and admitted her through the front door. She found Quentin sprawled half asleep on the sofa with his infant daughter resting on his bare chest.

"Ms. GiGi," he murmured. A warm, lopsided grin graced his jaw-droppingly handsome face. "Here to finally run away with me?"

For once, she couldn't find it within her to tease him in return. "I need your help."

"Let me wake Holly to care for Frankie." Immediately, he became alert, all semblance of sleepiness gone.

Within moments, Holly was downstairs and seated beside GiGi

as she explained the circumstances to the couple. "I'd like Quentin to assist me with my backup plan."

Although she paled, Holly nodded her agreement.

Quentin squatted in front of his wife and cupped her lovely face within his large palms. "I'll move heaven and earth to return to you and Frankie. I've done it before. Don't worry."

"That's like telling the grass not to be green, you tool."

"I adore you, my prickly pear." His grin was wider and much more impactful than the lazy smile he'd cast GiGi's way upon her arrival.

GiGi rose and shifted away when he swooped in to kiss Holly. Based on the seductive look in his eye, it would be a steamy one. Holly's soft sigh brought a small smile to GiGi's lips. These two were perfect for each other in every way. Where Holly's temperament was indeed "prickly," Quentin's was laid back and playful. They balanced each other marvelously well.

"I'll see you in the morning. Try to get some sleep, love."

"Like that is going to happen," Holly retorted.

GiGi placed a hand on her niece's shoulder. "Perhaps you should go to your father's with Frankie until we return."

Quentin nodded his assent.

Holly searched her husband's face. For what, GiGi didn't know. Reassurance that all would be well?

Finally, Holly nodded. "All right. Let me gather a few things, and I'll follow you over. Am I to assume you don't want my father to know of your intentions?"

"I don't care if he knows or not. I'll do what is necessary to protect my husband."

"Spoken like a true Thorne!" Quentin laughed. "Come, let's go have some fun."

And for him, it probably was. GiGi, on the other hand, found it difficult to keep fear from clawing a hole through her throat.

"Harold Beecham is dangerous and not to be underestimated, my boy," she warned with a hand on his arm.

"Understood. Lead the way, Ms. GiGi."

RYKER LOUNGED ON THE UNCOMFORTABLE TWIN-SIZED MATTRESS IN his ten-by-ten cell and stared at the white cinder block wall. How the hell had he let Alastair and Martin talk him into this stupid-ass idea? He was claustrophobic. On his best day, he could scarcely tolerate a space like this: basically a box with a twin bed, a sink, and a tiny one-person table with matching chair. On his worst? Yeah, he would go out of his freaking mind. Although he didn't have too many days to stress it. According to Sebastian Drake, an emergency hearing would take place tonight.

He snorted his disbelief. The entire WC had to believe he was guilty as sin. Although he was a bit surprised they hadn't given him time to mount a defense. If Al and Nash couldn't rally the rest of the Thornes in time to create a mass drugging of the Council, Ryker was as good as dead.

Regrets poured in, nearly drowning him, as he thought of his wife. Without a doubt, GiGi would be raging about now. He grinned. He'd be surprised if she hadn't blasted Alastair to hell when he broke the news. Hopefully, she wouldn't do anything impulsive to put herself in danger. There was no telling with GiGi.

He ran a hand through his hair and blew out a sigh of frustration. The end had never seemed more eminent before. Well, maybe once when Marguerite Champeau shot him, but never since.

The clank of the outer door opening caught his attention, and he lifted enough to rest on one elbow to face the opening. There was no need for actual doors for the cells because all prisoners had their magic bound and an electrical forcefield protected the cell entrance. A hole widened large enough for the attendant on duty to pass a tray through.

As if he'd conjured her, Marguerite posed dramatically on the other side of the doorway. She hadn't aged a day in the fifteen years since he'd last seen her. Still lovely as ever. Ryker could only imagine the inside had withered and blackened through and through.

"To what do I owe this *non*-pleasure?"

Her lips tightened, and her aquamarine eyes hardened. "No more playing the charming rogue, Ryker?"

"It was all an act, Marguerite. There is no way on earth I could be attracted to a succubus like you."

"Tomorrow you will be put to death. I thought I'd extend you the chance to apologize."

He laughed. A deep, loud belly laugh that echoed off the block walls around him. "For what?" he managed.

"You used me."

"No, darlin'. Beecham did that, and you let him. Did you ever consider what would happen if I'd have died the day you shot me?" He studied her frowning face. "No, I can see you didn't, or not fully anyway." Slowly, he sat up and placed his feet on the floor. "Beecham would have seen you were put to death for the murder of a Witches' Council agent. You were a patsy to him. Nothing more."

Though her face paled, she remained silent.

Rising, he strolled to stand on the other side of the opening. He folded his arms across his chest and stared down into her comely face. "Beecham is the spider, and the rest of us are flies in his web, Marguerite. He is a master game player. All he ever wanted was to tear apart anyone who stood in his way. Alastair, me, you, Georgie, my sister, and everyone else whose life he's destroyed along the way. He leaves a path of murder and destruction in his wake."

Her frown deepened.

He gave her a wry half-smile. "I'm sorry if you felt used. I was only ever doing my job, just as I'm sure you were doing yours. Without a doubt, we were at crossed purposes." He rubbed the back of his neck, suddenly weary of this whole mess. "Watch your back, okay?"

Her mouth tightened in a silent, little mew. She stared at him a moment longer, then turned on her heel to leave. She made it five steps before turning back. "Ryker?"

"Yeah?"

"I'm sorry, too. For you and GiGi and... your baby."

Emotion clogged his throat and made it hard for him to swallow.

It was the odd moments when the loss of his child snuck up and hit him with a two-by-four across the back of the head. Incapable of speech, he merely nodded.

She approached him again and softened her voice to say, "For what it's worth, I don't think you murdered Georgie. Deep down, you have a moral compass that most of us don't."

"Thank you." He took a step closer and lowered his own voice. "Get as far away from this mess as you can, Marguerite. Get off Beecham's radar and find someone to make you happy."

"I always wanted that man to be you." The smile she flashed him was bittersweet. "I thought maybe once, when we were young, long before the war, before you and GiGi got together, we might have had a chance. I suppose the disappointment of failure is what made me so easy to manipulate." She sighed and swiped the moisture from the corner of her sad eyes. "I couldn't let you die without saying goodbye."

"Goodbye, Marguerite."

Tears burned brightly in her exquisite eyes. Placing her fingertips to her lips, she spun away and rushed from the holding area.

Ryker sighed heavily. He'd had no idea she carried any type of unrequited feelings for him, but it wouldn't have mattered. The moment he'd set eyes on GiGi he was a goner.

Moving to the sink, he stared at the man in the mirror. How many times over the years had he studied his own reflection, wishing he could be worthy? Worthy of his deceased family. Worthy of GiGi. Worthy of the friendships he'd cultivated over the years, like the ones with Alastair and Georgie. He owed it to all of them to come through this unscathed, or if not, then at least to take out Harold Beecham in the process.

The outer door clanked again, and with a resigned sigh, Ryker turned around. It seemed whichever enemy he happened to think about coincidentally strolled through those doors.

No one would believe the pudgy, unkempt, balding man standing on the other side of the cell opening was a murdering sociopath. With his round, pink cheeks and perpetual smile, he looked as jolly as old St. Nick.

Ryker leaned back against the white porcelain sink and folded his arms over his chest. Crossing his ankles, he perfected a careless pose he knew would get under Beecham's pale skin. The man firmly believed he deserved the devotion of everyone he came in contact with. He wouldn't get it from Ryker.

"Why did you do it, Gillespie? Why did you murder Georgie?"

He wasn't sure what game the councilman was playing, but he refused to participate other than to claim his innocence. "I didn't. I loved her like a mother, and that's all I'm going to say about it until the tribunal."

A crafty expression flashed so swiftly across Beecham's face, Ryker almost believed he imagined it. Harold effected a sorrowful look. "She was like a mother to us all. How you could do something so heinous to that poor woman... tsk, tsk."

In an effort not to grind his teeth to the pulp, Ryker unclenched his jaw and dropped his arms to his sides. He wouldn't be baited. Georgie would have urged caution. And where the devil were Alastair's guards? Beecham should have never been allowed into the holding area.

"What do you want, Harold?" Ryker demanded when he'd had enough.

"To let you know I'll be happy to comfort your widow after you're gone."

If the invisible electrical beam across the opening wouldn't send Ryker into cardiac arrest, he'd have been through it in a second just to rip that rotten fucker's head from his shoulders. As it was, trying to keep a tight rein on his temper was proving near impossible.

"She can have any man she wants to keep her company should I be found guilty. Trust me, she'll never fall for a smarmy shithead like you."

"Ah, ah, ah!" Beecham waved a finger back and forth. "Temper, temper, Gillespie. Keep it up, and the Council will see exactly how volatile you can be."

Harold didn't know it, but his words were precisely what Ryker needed to calm down. The video cameras had to show him in control at all times. He gripped the edge of the sink and offered up a chilly smile. "If you don't mind, I'm going to turn in and get some sleep until the trial. You can show yourself out, I'm sure."

It gave him a little thrill to know Beecham would chafe under the dismissal.

"All of this could've been avoided if you'd have just turned Alastair over to me when you had the chance," Harold snapped. The real reason for his visit becoming clearer.

Harold had approached him, proclaiming he was certain Alastair was behind some shady dealings. He'd offered Ryker two-hundred thousand dollars to betray his best friend. Ryker declined. He'd been paying for it in small ways here or there ever since.

After Trina's murder, Beecham came to him again with some lame story about Alastair's involvement in her death. Ryker shut him down for the second and final time.

"You know better than to believe I'd betray Alastair Thorne for some trumped-up charge and pocket change."

"Pocket change? That type of money sets some people up for life."

"Like the real murderer of Georgie Sipanil?" Ryker countered, unable to help himself.

A dark rage clouded Beecham's face. "You've sealed your fate. You'll also go to your death knowing you couldn't protect the Thorne family. They will all perish one way or another."

"Aren't you worried about how much you're revealing to the security cameras?" Ryker taunted with a tilt of his head toward the corner of the room.

"Not when I control who monitors them."

"Right."

Long after his nemesis had left, Ryker stared at the spot where Beecham had been. One thing was for certain, Spring's idea had to work, or the lives of the Thorne family wouldn't be worth a spit.

"'ll see my no-good excuse of a husband, or I'll burn this fucking place to the ground. *How about that?*"

"Ah, the dulcet tones of my beloved," Ryker called out, a wide grin on his face. "What took you so long, sweetheart?"

GiGi's head popped around the corner a second before the rest of her. She sashayed straight for the opening, but Ryker held up a hand before she got close. "The space is magically wired to electrocute anyone crossing through."

A dark cloud of anger settled across her exquisite features. She studied him across the distance and finally shook her head.

"What kind of bonehead turns himself in for murder when he's supposed to be finding evidence to the contrary?"

"Your faith in me is astounding."

She waved an impatient hand and checked over her shoulder.

Despite his dire circumstances, Ryker was hard-pressed not to laugh at her obvious pique.

"It's going to be all right, GiGi. And if, by some horrific turn of events, it isn't, I give you permission to shorten the mourning period. You can make it a year before hooking up with that English playboy."

"How did you manage that without choking?" she asked dryly.

"It wasn't easy."

She dropped any pretense of teasing. "Are you all right? Are they treating you okay?"

"Mostly. They keep letting in unsavory characters."

"Hey!" she objected with a hand on her hip.

"Not you, sweetheart. Beecham and She-Who-Shall-Not-Be-Mentioned. Although, she did come to apologize for her part in shooting me and for our loss."

"Did you believe her?"

GiGi's head was cocked slightly, her expression was curious. No trace of jealousy could be found, so he answered honestly. "Yes."

She nodded and remained silent.

"Beecham, on the other hand, came to rile me about Georgie. He all but admitted he had the camera operators in his pocket."

Her concerned gaze snapped to his. "That's not good. It means he's getting reckless." She glanced around a second time. "Where are Alastair's guards?"

"No clue," he said grimly.

"Step as close to the opening as possible, babe." She crooked her finger.

He did, and she followed suit. She didn't bother to look toward the lens monitoring their every move. Lowering her voice, she said, "When I go to leave, cause a distraction and get the cameras on you, okay?"

"What are you planning?" he whispered fiercely, struggling to keep his expression bland.

She winked. That was it. No explanation, no warning, just a damned wink. That gesture had trouble written all over it—as was the GiGi Thorne-Gillespie way.

He swore low and long.

"I'm going to cause a fight now, Ryker. Time to prepare to draw attention to yourself."

"Be careful of Beecham, GiGi. He was here, taunting me, not fifteen minutes before you arrived."

A minuscule nod was her answer. She raised her voice to yell, "You and your jealousy! I can't take it anymore."

"My jealousy! Boy, are you the pot calling the kettle black, *sweetheart*," he sneered. *"Fifteen years, GiGi!* Fifteen fucking years of your emotional bullshit!"

She looked like he'd just slapped her, and it hurt his heart.

"When they fry your ass, I'll dance on your grave, you toad!" she shouted.

Lifting her hands, she directed a blast of cold air his way. It crackled along the energy barrier and lit up the blue beams previously hidden by magic.

"It's a good thing you're protected by that damned ward, you pathetic excuse for a man. Otherwise, I'd—"

The sound of rubber soles slapping the shiny terrazzo floor echoed down the corridor.

GiGi shot another blast of air, and a shower of sparks peppered the ground. Ryker caught her eye. If the force of her small surges of power could cause that effect, could she take down the entire power grid with another witch if necessary? Based on her slight smile, she'd had the same thought.

"Ma'am, we're going to have to ask you to leave."

A hulking male security officer placed a hand on GiGi's arm, and Ryker lost all ability to reason.

"Get your goddammed hands off my wife!" he snarled.

The other man look startled at his reaction. "I'm not... I mean, I didn't..."

GiGi backed into the wall and placed her hands behind her back. Instinctively, Ryker knew it was his signal to create a scene.

"Yes, you damned well did!" He reached for a side chair to smash against the barrier. Just shy of touching the electric fence, he released the metal chair and stepped back. Another shower of sparks lit the room.

From the corner of his eye, he noticed GiGi's lips moving although any words were drowned out by his "temper tantrum."

Ryker then slammed his hands down on the table, gripping the edges to fling it across the room. Two more security guards joined the first.

"Gillespie, if you don't calm down, we'll release a gas to calm you down."

He froze in place. He wondered if GiGi had picked up on the revelation. If they already had a system in place to distribute gas, Mackenzie might find her job a lot easier than expected.

"Fine. Fine," he muttered as he bent to reposition the table. There was nothing he could do about the chair because he refused to be burnt to a crisp. "I'm calm, okay? Just get that wench out of here."

As one, the security team turned to face GiGi, who sported the perfect horrified expression. "Yes," she breathed. A light flutter of her lashes softened the expressions of the two men. A female officer narrowed her eyes. Not to be faulted for her acting skills, GiGi produced a tear or two to soften the other woman. "Won't one of you escort me out?"

"I will!" Both men answered at once as they surged forward to help this gorgeous damsel in distress.

Ryker nearly snorted his disbelief at their gullibility, but it would have given the game away. Instead, he yelled "Hag!" at her retreating back. GiGi stiffened and sent a narrow-eyed glare over her shoulder.

"Gentlemen, will you wait for me here? I have one more thing to say to my troll of a spouse."

As if they were puppets, they nodded in unison and waited with their arms down by their sides, or as near as they were able with their bulging biceps. Ryker wondered if the WC shot these guys up with steroids.

While passing the female guard, GiGi patted her hand and said, "I promise not to cause another problem. If you need to get back to your station, I understand. I have these two strong men to protect me if need be."

With a slight frown of confusion, the other woman exited the room.

"Nicely done, sweetheart. I hope you achieved what you set out to do."

"I did. But if you ever call me a hag again, you'll rue the day you were born."

He scrubbed his hands over his face to hide his laughter.

"If you think you may be in danger between now and tonight's trial, holler Quentin's name."

"Quentin's?"

"The mirror is hidden but spelled to respond should you need it to. He'll be monitoring it until you head to the council chamber."

"Do I say 'mirror, mirror on the wall…'?"

"Funny," she said in a tone that was anything but amused. She gave a toss of her hair and glared at him to carry on the ruse. "It was nice knowing you," she said loudly with smug satisfaction as she spun away.

"I don't know why I ever thought I loved you, you hagasaurus!" he yelled across the distance.

The two male guards struggled to school their features, but their shaking shoulders showed their laughter. The violet-blue eyes GiGi turned on him were as bright as he'd ever seen.

"You'll pay for that!"

"I've no doubt," he assured her.

GiGi teleported into a room filled with laughter. She caught Alastair's amused attention first.

"Hagasaurus?" he crowed.

"He's nothing if not original," she laughed. "I really will make him pay for that one."

"I think the Council hired the wrong person as their spy. You're a natural."

"Ryker said something similar recently." She hugged her brother and turned serious. "Please tell me this is going to work."

"It is. Did you catch the comment about the gas?"

"I did. I wonder if there's any way to tell if that gas line runs to the main council chamber?"

"We need to bribe a maintenance worker or two."

"Think we can? It looks like security is tight around Ryker."

Alastair gave her a slow, confident smile.

"Forget I asked, brother. I can see you already have a plan."

"I do. Now, tell me. What was the comment about Quentin?"

GiGi shrugged and twirled a tanzanite bangle around her wrist. "Never you mind. I have my own backup plan should I need it."

Alastair's eyes lit on the motion and the circle of stones within the silver. Ever so slowly, he raised his speculative gaze to stare at her. "A hotline to the powerful warlock able to alter time?"

"Perhaps."

He laughed and gave her a one-armed hug. "Keep your secrets, sister."

"I'm assuming you heard what Ryker said about Beecham, Al?" At his nod, she continued. "I'm frightened for him."

"He's been in worse situations before, and he's always managed to return home in one piece."

"Except for the time Marguerite shot him."

He grimaced. "Yes, well, he did manage to survive that little incident. The man is like a cat with nine lives. He's only used up one, so he should have plenty more."

GiGi smiled in the face of her brother's positive prediction. "Thank you, Al."

"You're welcome, sister." He tugged his cuffs and cleared his throat. "Now, let's see who we have to bribe to find out about those gas lines."

As she watched Alastair walk away, GiGi smiled. If it was in her brother's power, he wouldn't allow anything to happen to Ryker. The two men were as close as two people could be. True best friends. As far as she knew, they'd always had each other's backs and were always there for one another, with the exception of the time when Ryker had been shot by Marguerite. Even then, GiGi had to believe Alastair would have dropped what he was doing to help him.

"Al?" she called. He faced her and lifted a brow. "When Ryker was shot by Marguerite, was it you who helped him?"

His brows clashed together. "No. It was Delphine."

They both registered the danger at the same time. GiGi could feel the blood drain from her face.

"Beecham may have his blood," she whispered in horror. "If he does…"

Alastair sighed and strode back to her side. "We assumed he was using Trina's for tracking. It could be he's using Ryker's."

"What do you mean you assumed he was using Trina's to track him?"

"Beecham's little army showed up everywhere Ryker was over the last few days. It wasn't coincidence." He shook his head in frustration. "It's why he turned himself in, GiGi. To remove you from Beecham's reach."

"That stubborn fool! Ryker should have let him come. It was easy enough to set a trap."

Alastair let loose a deep, booming belly laugh, and anyone still remaining in the room turned to stare at this rare phenomenon.

"What's so funny?" GiGi demanded.

"You may be even more ruthless than I am."

A grin tugged at her mouth. "Never doubt it, brother. At the very least, I'm more persistent than you."

"Pfft. That was never in any question." The look they shared said it all. It spoke of affection and respect. "Go rest if you intend to, sister. The tribunal starts in less than seven hours."

Didn't she know it! She'd been watching the clock since the moment Sebastian told them the hearing would be that night. "I'll try to take a nap. I can't imagine I'll manage any sleep, though." She squeezed her brother's forearm and headed to the room she shared with Ryker.

As she curled up on the mattress, his unique smell drifted over her. The subtle scent of sandalwood and new leather teased all her senses and filled her with longing. What would she do if this whole thing went belly up? How was she expected to survive a second parting from him? The first time was difficult enough when she believed he was safe and secure. There was nothing more permanent a separation than death. Burying her face in his pillow, she prayed as she never had before. Perhaps the Goddess would take pity on them and help them get through this mess unscathed.

GiGi must've dozed because the next thing she knew, a gentle hand was shaking her awake. Slowly she sat up, blinking to clear her head and clear her vision of sleep.

"Spring? Is it time?"

"Soon. Uncle Alastair thought you might want to get a bite to eat before heading to the Witches' Council headquarters."

"Did he find someone to provide the information on the gas lines and if they run into the main chamber?"

"Better than that. He found someone to hook up our canisters." The underlying excitement in Spring's voice almost made GiGi laugh. To look at her niece, one would believe she was all sweet innocence. They would be wrong. She was clever to the extreme and full of mischief, a female version of Alastair when he was her age.

"I'm expected to be there, along with Alastair. I'm not sure we should look as if we are descending en masse. But, should any of you wish to be there in support, I would suggest concealing yourselves in some way. You're more than welcome to utilize my elderly lady disguise."

"Yes!" Spring did a fist pump. "I've always wanted to try that one on."

With a laugh and a hug for her darling niece, GiGi headed to the bathroom for a quick shower. "Remember, the key is to let your dentures slip and affect a cranky attitude. Will you tell Al I'll be out for dinner in about twenty minutes, please?"

"Will do, Aunt G. Oh, and dinner is at Thorne Manor."

It struck her as odd that a casual dinner would take place at the Thorne estate when it could just as easily be held here. She could only assume Alastair was hosting it at their old family home for his own purposes.

NINETEEN MINUTES LATER, GIGI SAILED THROUGH THE DINING ROOM doors to join her family. Alastair sat at the head of the table with Aurora to his right. Autumn, looking hale and hearty after childbirth, sat on his left with her husband, Keaton, beside her. The only thing separating the two of them was a small bassinet pulled close to the table. It appeared as if GiGi's entire immediate family had turned out: Winnie and Zane, Summer and Coop, Spring and Knox, Mackenzie, Nash, and even Leonie with her son, Armand.

Now she understood. Alastair would remain cautious of Leonie until he discovered any hidden secrets. He wouldn't take the risk of revealing his own home, but he knew, as well as GiGi, that Leonie had been at Thorne Manor and could pinpoint its location.

"Before dinner starts, may I have a word with Leonie?" she asked. She owed it to her young cousin to explain the circumstances surrounding her mother's death, to explain she was the one to have pulled the trigger that ended Delphine's life.

She led Leonie out on the porch and gestured to one of the wicker sofas, but before she could say a word, Leonie held up a hand.

"I know."

Tears burned behind GiGi's lids. There, in Leonie's golden eyes, so like her mother's, there was understanding and forgiveness.

"All of it?"

"Yes. Alastair told me at the warehouse. I know you were the one who shot Mother. I also know you didn't have a choice."

"But I did. I could have found a way to bind her powers. I could have—"

"No, GiGi, you couldn't have. Voodoo mixed with black magic and a Thorne's natural ability is powerful stuff. Harold tried to get me to turn to the darker arts for his benefit. I refused. It's why he kept me locked up and preyed on my mother. She'd have done anything to save me." Leonie shook her dark head and swiped at a stray tear. "I'm sorry for the grief she caused you. I'm sorry about Preston. He was truly an admirable man."

"Two wrongs don't make a right. We all know that, and still, I wanted revenge for what she'd done. Yes, my primary goal was to stop her from hurting anyone else in our family again, but I had hate in my heart. I can't ignore or deny that, child."

"Do you hate me for what she's done?" Leonie asked quietly. It was as if everything was hanging on GiGi's response.

The question brought her up short. She studied her feelings on the entire matter and found she couldn't visit the sins of the mother on the daughter. "No. No, I don't hate you. I feel horrible that your life will be tainted by her actions—and by mine. I only wish for your happiness, dear girl."

"May I hug you?" Leonie's tentativeness brought a swell of regret. There was a day when this young woman had run into GiGi's arms with unrestrained joy as a small child.

"You never have to ask, Leonie," she choked out, opening her arms to the beautiful soul standing in front of her. They embraced and cried for the past.

After a few minutes, they got their emotions under control.

"Well, that was a hen-fest! Who knew we had all those bottled-up tears?" Leonie exclaimed.

"I should thank you. That's the most cleansing cry I've had in ages."

Leonie laughed and linked arms with her. "Let's go enjoy some good ol' home-cooked dinner."

"You mean home-conjured. Except for pastries, this crew doesn't make anything from scratch," GiGi said dryly.

22

"*I*t's time."

Alastair's voice broke GiGi's meditation and went straight through her. The words started a ball of dread rolling downhill at a far greater speed than she'd experienced when she found out Ryker had turned himself in. Part of her wanted to avoid the tribunal all together. Another, larger part wanted to be front and center to protect her husband.

Rising, she walked toward where Alastair lounged against the doorframe of the attic room where the Thornes kept their family grimoire. She stopped in front of him and stared up into his handsome face. Alastair seemed ageless. If one looked close enough, his stunning sapphire eyes revealed so much of what he was thinking. Or perhaps it was only to her because they were siblings and because they had known each other the better part of a century. Maybe others looked at a face that was perpetually thirty-five years old and saw an impassive mask or a threatening countenance. They found it difficult to see the softer side of this man, the side his family and close friends were privy to.

"Don't worry, little sister," he said softly, tapping her nose as he'd done when she was a small child. "Ryker won't die today."

She desperately fought the wave of threatening tears. "Oh, Al. I'm so scared."

"I know. But come hell or high water, Ryker leaves with us tonight."

"I love you, brother. I know there was a short time there when things were rocky between us. Most of it was my fault, but I've always had a special place in my heart reserved just for you. For the day we would patch things up and be friends once again."

His smile was bright with a hint of mischief. "I know that, too. Don't think your posturing when I came for Morty last year scared me in the least. You're a big softie, sister-mine."

"Pfft." She rolled her eyes, but his teasing did the trick and helped her firm her backbone for the trial ahead.

They took their time descending the stairs to the main level, tortured with thoughts of "what if." If GiGi was thinking or feeling it, odds were her empath brother was too.

"Am I making it too difficult for you to be around me?" she asked in concern.

Surprise filled his face when he looked up. "No. Your worry is obvious, but so is your determination. One tempers the other." He clasped her hand and give it a firm squeeze. "Neither Harold Beecham nor the Witches' Council stands a chance against you, GiGi."

She grinned. "They don't, do they?"

Twenty minutes later, GiGi along with Alastair, Leonie, and Nash were seated behind the defendant's chair. The council members filed in and called a moment of silence for the deceased Georgie Sipanil.

Harold Beecham registered surprise when he saw Leonie sitting beside Alastair. Hatred flared in his eyes as he met Alastair's cold stare across the distance. No doubt, these two would have it out very shortly.

A side door opened, and a pale Ryker was led to the defendant's table. He swayed slightly before sitting.

Something was off.

GiGi could feel it in her bones. She'd only left him a few hours before, and he had looked hale and hearty, if a little tired and world-weary. Currently, he was a bit gray around the gills. Her heart began to hammer in her chest, and she sat forward in her chair to study him closer. A glance to her left showed Alastair had noticed the change in Ryker as well. He looked as worried as she felt.

Behind her, the main doors to the chamber opened, admitting Sebastian Drake. He looked breathtaking and regal in his official council robes. GiGi frowned at the yellow sash draped around his shoulders. He met her confusion with a half-smile and a wink then joined Ryker at the table.

Leaning in, she lowered her voice to ask Alastair, "Did you know he intended to represent Ryker?"

"I had a good idea," he murmured in return. He gestured with a slight tilt of his head toward the long, curled table at the far side of the room. "I don't think Beecham did, nor is he thrilled at the prospect."

Sebastian popped the locks on his briefcase, took out a thick file, and closed the lid, but not without GiGi catching a glimpse of the items for their upcoming ceremony. He'd agreed to smuggle the needed tools into the hearing, knowing the wards on the room would make it impossible to conjure what they needed. Sebastian had chosen a case deep enough to hold the candles, herbs, and spell book they needed. Also visible had been a blood-stained dress. Trina's dress unless GiGi missed her guess. She noted he didn't lock the case again and sighed her relief. The items they would utilize would be easy to get to when the time came.

Next, her coven sisters entered. She was surprised to see Tildie amongst their small number. Across the distance, their eyes connected. Apology was in Tildie's soft brown eyes. GiGi smiled her understanding and forgiveness. The presence of these four women meant they would have her back if push came to shove tonight.

A last-minute commotion sounded behind her, and GiGi shifted to look over her shoulder. Suppressing a bubble of inappropriate laughter, she stared on in admiration of Spring's use of the decrepit-old-lady disguise GiGi had used on more than one occasion. Spring's new form was less than five-feet tall, with mismatched, thick knitted socks sagging just below her mid-calf-length floral dress. She looked wider than she was tall, and her faux, enormous breasts looked unbound and hanging close to her waistline. Her lavender hair was styled short and stuck up in tuffs as if she'd just woken up. Based on the wrinkled dress, that might have been the look her niece was striving for. Her handbag was a throwback to the last century and looked to weigh as much as Spring. Currently, she used it to swat at a guard trying to hurry her and her veiled companion to their seats.

"Back off," Spring snapped in a crotchety voice, allowing the dentures to slip and slide around her mouth. "You damned young people! Always pushing, always prodding. I'll stick my size-eight shoe right up your one-oh-five if you touch me once more, young man!"

Swat! Spring swung her purse and nailed the man in the stomach, causing him to grunt. "Now back the hell off before I sic my sister Gertie on you." She nodded to the black-veiled figure beside her. "You don't want none of *that!*"

The lace material was so thick, it was impossible to distinguish a face.

"She's in mourning, the poor dear," Spring declared to no one in particular. "Let us pass."

Not a soul stood in their way, and one gentleman in the front abandoned his seat for the two elderly women.

GiGi bit her lip and squeezed her brother's hand in order to contain her laughter.

"She's given you a run for your money with that disguise. Who do you suppose *Gertie* is?" he murmured the question in her ear.

"If I had to guess, Summer, but really, I'm clueless."

"No, not my daughter. I'd know if it were her. I don't think it's a Thorne at all."

She cut him a sharp glance. "What do you mean?"

"The energy is different."

They didn't have time to converse longer as the hearing was called to order and the trial began.

Beecham stood and sneered at Ryker. "Ryker Gillespie, you've been charged with the murder of Councilwoman Georgie Sipanil. How do you plead?"

"Go fuck yourself," Ryker responded in a calm but unsteady voice.

The courtroom exploded in outraged cries and appalled gasps.

Councilman Smythe slammed his gavel to restore order.

"Ryker's sick," GiGi whispered to her brother. "Look at the sweat coating his forehead."

She made to stand, but Alastair placed a restraining hand on her arm.

"Wait."

Leonie leaned around Alastair to address her. "Dark magic."

Two words GiGi dreaded above all others.

Nash entwined his fingers with hers. "Stay calm, Aunt GiGi."

"Calm?" Disbelief dripped from that one word as gently as water over the edge of Niagara Falls—*not at all*. In fact, her response was just shy of a shriek.

Ryker twisted to face her. His weary smile tried to relay he was okay, but she knew his struggle to keep from passing out was real.

Pressing a balled fist against her lips, she nodded her understanding. Remaining seated when all she wanted to do was rush to his side was the hardest thing she'd done to date.

"I love you," she mouthed.

He grinned, and for a second or two, he looked less haggard. "Hagasaurus," he mouthed back with a wink.

It was enough for her to steel her spine, as she imagined he intended.

Sebastian stood, commanding everyone's attention.

"Dear Councilmen and Councilwomen, what Mr. Gillespie means is 'not guilty.'" He looked down at the handwritten note Ryker had just handed him and smirked. "Not guilty, but Harold Beecham can still go fuck himself."

Laughter rippled through the room, ranging from titters to all-out guffaws—the latter being Alastair. GiGi herself found it difficult not to laugh. The profanity from the proper Sebastian Drake was amusing.

Beecham slapped his hands on the wooden surface in front of him and snarled his fury.

"I will not be disrespected in my courtroom!" Harold raged.

"*Your* courtroom?" Councilman Smythe questioned the outburst with raised brows and gestured down to the purple sash he wore. As acting head of the Witches' Council, he was clearly in charge. "I believe this is the *entire* council's legal chambers, Councilman Beecham. I suggest you control yourself so we might proceed with the hearing."

GiGi touched the tanzanite stone on her wrist, and Quentin's telepathic response was immediate.

"You summoned me, my glorious queen?"

She nearly rolled her eyes at this flirting.

"As you young uns say, shit is getting real here in the chambers. Ryker looks as if he's been poisoned. Will you have my medical bag ready?"

"I'm on it. Has the gas been released?"

GiGi glanced at the wall clock above the curved table.

"Three minutes and counting."

"I'm prepared, and your plan B is in place."

"I saw the coven arrive. Thank you, dear boy."

"I'll always have your back, Ms. GiGi."

The warmth of his response moderated the chill that had set up residence in her soul upon first seeing Ryker's overall gray aura.

"Councilmen and Councilwomen, we intend to prove to you that Mr. Gillespie is not only innocent of the crime of murdering Georgie Sipanil, but that one of your own members is directly responsible in not only *her* death but in that of Trina Gillespie. This person was behind the kidnapping of a young witch and exploited her mother's magic to use against a well-respected and powerful family of our community."

Speculation ran rampant in the frantic murmurs of the observers.

All eyes turned to the Thornes, who had all remained silent and watchful.

GiGi didn't imagine Harold's loss of color, and she reveled in his nervousness. Across the distance, she met his hostile glare with one of her own.

"This is ridiculous!" he blustered. "They are going to try to turn this farce on me."

"I don't believe anyone mentioned your name, Councilman Beecham," Sebastian said dryly. "With the exception of Mr. Gillespie telling you to go fuck yourself."

Ryker looked directly at her. He pointed behind his hand to Sebastian. In a loud stage-whisper, he said, "I like him."

GiGi bit the inside of her cheek to prevent her giggle.

"We'd like to present our first evidence," Sebastian continued. He reached into his briefcase and withdrew five gas masks. Handing one each to Alastair, GiGi, Leonie, and Nash, he then put one on. He looked at Ryker, anticipating his question. "It's better if you're out for this next part."

From the corner of her eye, GiGi saw Spring place a cloth to her nose and mouth. She nudged the person next to her to do the same. The hiss of the gas coming through the air vents was distinct. Looks of panic crossed the faces of those around them, and a few quick-thinking individuals raced for the exit. Since the room was warded against teleportation, they knew the main double doors were their only means of escape. Except, those double doors were locked from the outside by Knox Carlyle. They were well and truly trapped.

With the exception of the four coven members who had brought their own masks thanks to GiGi's warning, the courtroom visitors dropped where they stood. GiGi winced as some fell harder than others. She, along with Alastair, Nash, and her friends, rushed to magically heal any head wounds or scrapes. At most, their fellow witches would wake to a slight headache from the gas hangover.

She crossed to where Ryker was slouched, fast asleep in his chair.

"I think he's been poisoned," Sebastian said softly, concern and indecision weighing heavily in his tone. "I'm not sure if his blood will work for this spell now."

"I can separate the poison from the blood when it's extracted from him," Leonie told them. "I just need a few things from my mother's shop."

"Please hurry. We only have about fifteen minutes to pull this off," GiGi encouraged.

Leonie raced for the door with Nash hot on her heels. They rapped on the door in a pattern of short and long knocks. Knox responded immediately and disengaged the locks.

GiGi cradled Ryker's head to her breast and stroked his thick, dark hair. "If you die on me, babe, I'm not honoring your no-dating moratorium. I'll start dating right away."

She didn't realize she was crying until Sebastian gently brushed the moisture from her cheeks.

"He's not going anywhere, GiGi. I promise."

The sincerity in his eyes made GiGi feel marginally better.

"Thank you, Baz."

Dropping a kiss on Ryker's forehead, she moved away for Alastair and Sebastian to position him on the ground. She had to look away when her brother drew a long, wicked-looking knife from the briefcase.

"Can't I just plunge this in Beecham's heart and be done with this mess?"

"I'll pretend I didn't hear that, Alastair Thorne," a shaky voice spoke from the gallery.

They all stared in astonishment when Georgie Sipanil removed the black veil from her person. Spring grinned, and the slipping dentures broke their immobility.

GiGi rushed to the frail older woman. "We thought you were dead! The video... the trial..." She shook her head as she trailed off.

"It will take more than Harold Beecham's thugs to do me in, young lady."

She smiled at Georgie's use of "young lady." It had been many years since she could claim that status.

"How is my boy?" Georgie asked as she limped to where Ryker rested.

"Why didn't you come forward and spare everyone this mess?" Sebastian demanded, ignoring her concern for Ryker's condition.

"Would you like to answer that, Miss Thorne?"

Spring shrugged. "Previous to Ms. Georgie's attack, she had contacted Knox. She told him she was worried about Harold and had asked if he would come round to see her that day. I decided to go with him to finally meet the legendary Georgie Sipanil. When we showed up, Harold's men were following through on their orders." She shrugged. "We were able to subdue them all. That's when Ms. Georgie came up with the idea to fake her death. It was to see exactly who was behind her attack."

"That's why I couldn't reach either of you the night Beecham sent his little army after Ryker and me," GiGi deduced as she checked Ryker's pulse.

"We weren't purposely ignoring you. We were just otherwise occupied." Spring smiled and shoved the dentures back in her mouth.

"Oh, for goodness' sake!" Georgie slapped Spring on the shoulder. "Get rid of that horrid disguise already."

"How did you get Beecham's men to go along with this plan?" Alastair asked after he stopped laughing.

"Hypnosis," Georgie said simply. "I come from a long line of skilled mesmerists. Now, enough of the explanations for the present. What's happened to him?" She pointed to Ryker. "He didn't look well when he entered, and he looks more ghastly with each passing second."

Alastair's expression was dark and forbidding. "Our cousin, Leonie, believes it is black magic on Beecham's part."

"Harrumph! Perhaps I *should* let you stab that rotten S.O.B. and be done with it," Georgie muttered. "Miss Thorne told me you initially intended to bring the entire council and these horrid spectators to the Otherworld to speak with both Trina Gillespie and myself. It will be a lot safer to bring Trina here since I'm not deceased."

"Isis has granted us permission to do what we need. She's claimed Beecham is upsetting the balance."

Georgie grimaced in Alastair's direction. "Then explain to me why she doesn't smite him already?"

"You know that as well as I do, dear Georgie. She won't go against Fate's design." He clasped her hand and guided her to a seat. "Tell me true, how bad are your injuries?"

She waved him away with an affectionate smile. "At my age, it will take a little longer to heal, but I'll survive." The older woman lifted her brows in stern warning. "And don't even think to ask me my age."

"I wouldn't dream of it." He tugged up his slacks and squatted in front of the pint-sized witch. "For what it's worth, we all mourned your 'death.' Ryker was beside himself. He views you as family."

Her severe expression softened, and her eyes flitted to Ryker's face. "He holds a piece of my heart." She patted Alastair's cheek as if he were a small boy. "As do you, and as did your brother, Preston. Rascals, the lot of you. I didn't get a chance to express my condolences for your loss."

"Thank you, Ms. Georgie." He held her hand and placed it over his heart. After a silent communication between the two of them, he rose and moved to Ryker. "We still need his blood to summon Trina here. Where the devil are Leonie and Nash?"

"Don't fret, boy. They'll return."

GiGi, Sebastian, and Spring all gawked at Georgie Sipanil calling Alastair a boy. To their surprise, he took it in stride and grinned.

"I have no choice but to trust your wise counsel." He bowed low, then checked Ryker's pulse. "His pulse is weak. I'm worried if we extract his blood now, we could put him at risk."

"Do it," GiGi croaked. "He'd want you to. For justice... for Trina."

2 3

*L*eonie and Nash rushed back into the room with a box of supplies.

"I'm sorry we're late," Leonie gushed. "My mother's shop has been ransacked and…" Tears filled her gold cat-like eyes. "I'm sorry."

Nash took the box from her hands and nudged her shoulder. "No one here is judging you, cuz. Let's set up." He turned around and came up short. "Ms. Georgie!"

"Hello, dear boy."

"I… I…" He stopped trying to speak and shook his head. Setting the box on the desk beside her, he took her hand and brought it up to his lips. "I'm thrilled you're still with us."

"Like father, like son," muttered Sebastian with a shake of his head. "I don't know how you Thornes charm others with such ease, but if we could bottle it, I'd make millions."

"It would be a fifty-fifty risk on investment. Our particular brand of 'charm' also causes an intense hatred from the other half of the population," GiGi inserted dryly with a quick squeeze of his forearm.

She walked around the desk to where Harold Beecham was

sprawled on the floor. Drawing back her foot, she kicked him in the balls. Other than a slight moan, he remained motionless.

"You're savage!"

She glanced up from her study of Harold. "No, Baz. Just testing to see how much pain can be felt in this sleep state before anyone cuts on my husband." She kicked the unconscious man again, this time in the ribs. No sound emerged. "I figure ol' Harold makes the perfect test subject."

GiGi knelt beside Ryker and stroked his bearded jaw. "This may hurt a little, babe, but we need to get the blood you promised us." She nodded to Alastair, unable to cut Ryker herself. "Do it."

Her brother drew on a pair of nitrile gloves after he handed her a second set and a bowl. Without hesitation, he scored Ryker's palm.

"How much do we need for this spell?" she asked. Queasiness assailed her as she witnessed Ryker's blood drip into the porcelain bowl.

Sebastian glanced over from where he was distributing the candles in a circle. "You should have enough. I don't think we'll get more than that from Trina's dress."

"Do you want mine in the same bowl?" Nash asked Alastair as he accepted the cleaned knife from his father.

"No. Use another until Leonie can withdraw the poison from Ryker's."

Spring laid Trina's bloodied dress on the prosecutor's table. From the oversized bag she used to badger the security guard, she pulled a spray bottle and misted the fabric.

"How is that going to help?" Leonie asked.

"Watch this, cousin dear." Spring grinned and lifted her hands, palm up. *"Seiungo!"*

Droplet by droplet, the dried blood turned the deep red of fresh blood and lifted from the material to hang in the air. When the separation was complete, Nash set the bowl under the dark ruby cloud. Spring shifted her hand so they resembled a bowl and lowered them slowly toward the table. All the particles in the air drifted down to land without even a splash to join the blood taken from Nash.

"Incredible." Georgie thunked her cane on the floor in appreciation. "You are one of the most naturally talented witches I've ever come across, Miss Thorne."

"Thank you, Ms. Georgie," Spring said primly. The twinkle in her eye belied her butter-wouldn't-melt-in-her-mouth tone.

"Leonie, you're up, child," Alastair said gently.

From the box, she withdrew a few jars filled with herbs and removed the lids. One smelled distinctly like the tea given to Aurora the day Preston died a few weeks before.

"What do you intend to do with that herb?" GiGi asked sharply.

"When mixed with the charcoal, plantain, and mugwort, it will reverse any poison in Ryker's system. This is for you to give him when he wakes," Leonie explained patiently. The understanding in her wide eyes caused a moment of shame for GiGi. "This would have been the herb my mother tried to poison Aurora with. I get you have concerns, GiGi, but I promise you, on my soul and that of my son's, I am trying to help."

GiGi accepted the medicine. "What do I do with it?"

Leonie removed a bottle of water and a mug from her store of supplies. "Boil the water and create a tea for him to ingest. He needs to drink the entire mug."

She withdrew a black silk robe, the dried tail of a rattlesnake, a small vial of oil, ivory dice, what looked to be an ostrich egg, and a staff. Tied on a single leather strap hanging from the staff was a small skull, various colored stones, black feathers, and cowries.

First, she anointed herself with oil and donned the robe. What followed was an intricate magical dance with words only Leonie understood. She swayed and chanted over the bowl for endless minutes. Just as GiGi was worried they'd run out of time, Leonie threw a handful of herbs into the mixture, causing sparks to explode from the dish in front of her.

After what GiGi assumed was the equivalent of closing a circle, Leonie handed her the bowl.

"It's done. You can now use this for your ceremony."

"Thank you, child."

She combined Ryker's blood with that of Nash and Trina and handed it off to her brother. "How long can we hold Trina here with your spell?"

"Until she reveals what Beecham did."

"Fair enough. Let's get started. I can't wait to see Harold's face when he wakes to find Trina standing over him."

GiGi gestured to Bridget O'Malley to gather their coven into a circle. The four women worked to bring down the courtroom wards.

The Thornes created a circle within the candles Sebastian had set. They all joined hands and began the ceremony. Once the call to the Goddess was made, GiGi's cells ramped up and her magic connected to that of those around her.

"Wow!" Sebastian exclaimed. It wasn't hard to tell he'd been startled by the sheer force of the power they wielded.

Alastair, being the arrogant ass he could be, smirked and lifted a brow in Sebastian's direction. "Now you know why people fear us, son."

"I'm just glad I'm on your side. If I'd suspected this, I might have had second thoughts about trying to cross you last year." He referred to his aspiration to turn Alastair over to the Witches' Council at the behest of Harold Beecham. Unbeknownst to Sebastian, Harold was plotting to start a second war among their kind.

"All's forgiven. Start the spell."

"Right." Calling on the Goddess and their elemental powers, Sebastian read from the page Spring had marked in the Thorne grimoire. He finished with "Bring forth Trina Gillespie, to speak her truth."

A rumble shook the floor, and bursts of light exploded around the chamber.

"She can't break through the wards!" Sebastian exclaimed.

"Try again," Georgie ordered from her seat at the defendant table.

This time, Alastair and GiGi joined their voice to his. Still with the same effect.

"Try again!" Georgie shouted over the rumbling.

Nash shifted to link Leonie's hand with GiGi's, then he stepped to the center of the circle and lifted the athame Alastair had set there earlier. He nodded to his father to repeat the spell. This time, as the words were spoken, he scored his palm and added more blood to the bowl. "Mother, please," he beseeched Trina. "I need you now. Uncle Ryker needs you now."

The lights dancing above them flared brighter, but still, Trina didn't appear.

"We need a seventh person, and we're out of time." Alastair gestured toward where some of the council were starting to slowly wake.

Georgie Sipanil rose and limped into their circle. "Try again."

"Georgie, you're recovering. This might take too much from you," GiGi objected.

"Or your magic flowing through me just might heal me faster. Stop pussyfooting around and get this spell done."

Alastair tried to hide his grin and failed spectacularly. "Yes, ma'am."

The addition of the seventh witch did the trick, in conjunction with the breaking of the wards by the coven members. The dancing overhead lights came together to form Trina Gillespie. She was backlight by her white aura which, in addition to her white gossamer gown, gave her the look of a celestial angel.

Her eyes were immediately drawn to their circle, and more specifically to her son kneeling in the center with a knife in one hand and his other curled into a fist to stem the blood flow. Nash rose as she approached, and their circle of witches parted to allow him to exit.

"Mother," he breathed in wonder.

Her tear-brightened mocha eyes devoured his face as she reached out to smooth his hair from his eyes. "My beautiful boy."

Nash dropped the knife and clung to Trina as silent sobs shook his body.

GiGi hadn't been aware she was crying until Georgie handed her a handkerchief.

"Harold Beecham will pay for his crimes, or I'm not a Sipanil," the older woman vowed, her voice shaking with her own strong emotions.

"He'd better," GiGi practically growled in return. "He's hurt my family for the last time." She stepped from the protection of the circle, trusting Alastair and Sebastian to do what they needed to close their ring of magic.

Ryker's eyes fluttered as she knelt beside him, and he cradled his bandaged hand.

"Welcome back, babe." She smiled down into his beloved face and stroked his dark hair. "Trina's decided to join us."

"You didn't heal me," he observed with a study of his bound palm.

"I couldn't. I think Harold's poisoned you in some way." She heated the water in the mug and the herbs. When she was satisfied the contents were seeped enough, she urged him to drink by lifting the mug of tea to his lips. "Leonie created this for you. She thinks it may help draw out any toxins."

He swallowed a few sips. "It's not poison. I haven't consumed anything since I've been in custody. I think he's done something magically to me."

GiGi's heart sank to her stomach, and she cast a glance toward Harold, who was currently stirring.

"We'll figure this out," she said, trying to portray a confidence she didn't feel. "Can you stand? I think Trina will want to say hi."

His expression shifted to guilt, and he closed his eyes.

"Ryker?"

"I failed her, GiGi. On so many levels, I failed her."

"No, you didn't. You couldn't predict what happened. You're not psychic, Ryker."

He focused tortured eyes on her. "Still—"

Placing her fingertips over his lips to cut off his self-recriminations, she shook her head. "No. You are blameless."

"Completely blameless," Trina agreed from over her shoulder.

. . .

Ryker's attention was caught by his sister, and moisture blurred his vision. He audibly swallowed past the lump in his throat. He'd never thought he'd see her again in this lifetime.

"Hello, Ryker."

"Trina," he rasped out.

She knelt as he sat up, and they embraced. Her warmth and vitality allowed him to con himself into believing, if only for this one moment, she was well and truly alive. She wasn't, of course. This was just a trick of magic, but he could pretend.

"What is the meaning of this?" Councilman Smythe demanded.

Ryker slowly became aware of movement around him. The sound of muttering and speculation from those who had come to watch his trial matched that of the council members in their outrage.

With help from GiGi and Trina, he rose shakily to his feet. He nearly fell back down when Georgie Sipanil limped toward him in widow's weeds. She looked like a throwback to the eighteenth century in her long black dress and veil.

"Coming from a costume party, Ms. Georgie, or is that what they're wearing in the Otherworld these days?"

Amusement shone in the wide smile she graced him with. "It's about time you woke up and joined the party, dear boy."

He opened his arms and enfolded her into his tight embrace.

"I thought you were lost to us. You don't know how devastated I was." The gruffness in his voice was a clear indication of his emotion, and though he spoke low, for her ears only, Ryker had little doubt she recognized his feelings. A more perceptive woman he'd yet to find.

"I demand to know what is happening here," Smythe tried again.

Their group faced forward in time to see Harold rise up from the floor. His horror-filled eyes were focused on Trina. His head swung back and forth like a pendulum.

"It can't be."

Trina stepped forward with purpose. "Oh, but it is, Harold, you murderous bastard."

"I wouldn't... couldn't..." His eyes shot to Smythe and back to Trina. "I loved you... Alastair... he—"

"Enough of your lies, Beecham," Alastair barked. Menacing energy rippled across the room. "You murdered Trina. You tried to have Georgie Sipanil murdered. You kidnapped Leonie and forced Delphine Foucher to cover up your crimes, and in doing so, she murdered my brother, Preston." He stalked forward, a lethal beast after its prey. "You cheated my son of a mother, and Ryker of a sister. You almost cheated another little boy of his mother." He gestured over his shoulder to Leonie. "Now you stand there, trying to place the blame on *me?* I should strike you down where you stand."

The wooden council table cracked in four places, causing all the members to stagger back against the wall. Under the force of Alastair's anger, the air had become thick and the atmosphere crackled and sparked around them.

"Is this true?" Smythe demanded. Ryker half suspected Smythe wanted to subvert Alastair's rage. They all feared what he was capable of.

Trina joined Alastair. "Tell him, Harold. Tell him what you've done, all in your bid to rule the Council and cause a second Witches' War to cover your crimes. All because of your sick ambition and because one woman told you no."

When Beecham continued to shake his head in horror, she faced the rest of the council. "On the night I died, Harold came to my home. He told me of his intent to rule the witch community and said he wanted me to rule beside him. When I refused, he called me vile names and plunged a knife between my ribs. Not once, but seventeen times." She met Harold's fearful gaze. "*Seventeen.* Then he stood over me as I lay dying and told me he'd find a way to make Alastair pay for turning me against him."

"He did!" Harold shouted. "You loved me once. If it weren't for him... You loved me."

"No, Harold. I loved the man you pretended to be. You started to show your true colors long before Alastair stumbled into my life.

Your petty jealousy and meanness were already showing through by then. How twisted you've become!"

Some of this Ryker had known, but to hear his sister recount the grisly details, caused the herbal water to sour in his stomach. He hadn't realized just how tightly he was gripping GiGi's hand until she patted his arm and wiggled her fingers.

"Sorry, sweetheart," he murmured as he loosened his grip.

Georgie Sipanil limped forward to join Trina. "Obviously, it wasn't the first time you tried to frame another for your crimes, is it, Harold?" Without taking her penetrating gaze from Beecham, she addressed Smythe. "He commissioned council guards to kill me, Smythe. I've a list drawn up of who you can and can't trust. It's my understanding Mr. Beecham has quite a few on his payroll." She scanned the room with her eagle eye, then pointed to two men by the door closest to Harold. "Those two. They were in charge of the strike on my townhome."

Beecham surprised everyone when he withdrew a pistol from underneath his robes and leveled the barrel at Georgie. "I swear to the Goddess I'll kill her," he snarled.

Trina stepped in between the barrel and Georgie. "Put the gun down, Harold. You're finished here."

His dull gray eyes darted around the room and settled on Ryker and GiGi, who were closest to the doors. Ryker shoved GiGi behind him as Beecham pointed the gun at his chest.

"Come here, Gillespie."

"No!" GiGi shouted, trying to shove past him. He could feel her being ripped away from him by another.

"No!" She shouted again. "Let me go, Baz. Let me go!" Her cries mingled with those of the trial observers as they rushed toward the main set of doors to flee.

Ryker staggered forward, careful to keep GiGi out of harm's way. His eyes cut to Trina, and he registered her worry. He gave her a reassuring wink and turned his focus back to Beecham.

"Wilson, Miller, take him."

Too weak to fight, Ryker allowed the traitorous guards to apprehend him. They ushered him from the chamber through the rear council members' entrance while Beecham stayed behind to issue a warning that he'd kill the first person to follow him.

"Ryker Gillespie's life for your own, Thorne. That's the payment I require."

"Leave Ryker and take me now," Ryker heard Alastair respond. "Or are you too much of a coward to face me alone, Beecham?"

"Nice try, Thorne. But I'm not stupid enough to face you here with your family present. I know I'm no match against that type of power."

"You'll never be a match for me, you fool."

Upon his retreat, Harold shouted, "I'll tell you the when and where."

The second they were clear of the wards, Beecham gripped Ryker's arm and teleported. They arrived in a clearing very similar to the one between the Thorne and Carlyle estates.

"What do we do now, boss?" Wilson asked.

"Go get Perkins, Burnett, and Rivers. Once we secure the area, we wait. Alastair won't be able to help himself. He'll come for Gillespie, and when he does, we'll end him once and for all."

"You're a fool if you think so, Beecham," Ryker retorted. "Alastair will wipe the floor with you and not break a sweat doing it."

"Shut up, or I'll kill you right now and save myself the hassle afterward."

24

*G*iGi was enraged. One second, it seemed as if everything was going to plan, and the next, chaos. In one split second, Beecham had turned the tables. She struggled free of Sebastian's embrace and socked him in the gut. His grunt of pain did nothing to ease her fury.

"Don't you ever treat me like I'm helpless again. I will rip out your windpipe," she snarled.

"Got it," he croaked.

She stormed to where Councilman Smythe was running his hands through his thinning hair.

"I'm going to tear Harold Beecham apart limb by limb. If you have any objections, speak now."

Smythe paled. "Nope, no objections."

"Good." She didn't pause to consult with anyone else. Touching her bracelet, she connected with Quentin. Not caring who heard her or thought she was crazy for speaking aloud, she said, "I need a location. *Now.*"

"I'm on it."

"Get back to me, asap." She released the stone and shouted, "Knox!"

The double doors opened, and the man in question entered.

"I need you."

"I'm always of service to you, Ms. GiGi," he said with a half-smile. His eyes missed nothing as they scanned the room. His gaze settled on his fiancée in her old lady disguise. "You okay, love?"

"Harold Beecham abducted Ryker at gunpoint," Spring blurted.

"That was going to be my next guess," he muttered. "Go to Thorne Manor and stay there... please," he added with a soft smile. "I need to know you're out of danger."

"Of course."

Quentin teleported directly into the chamber, confounding everyone present.

"I have a longitude and latitude, Ms. GiGi," he told her.

"Where—?"

She was cut off by Smythe as he called for the wards to be checked.

"He's descended from Zeus, you bloody fool. It's only reasonable he can bypass the wards," Georgie snapped at him. "Go save your young man, GiGi."

Quentin gave Georgie a slow perusal and grinned. "Another prickly pear. Be still, my beating heart."

"I'm going to remove your heart from your chest if you pause to flirt, Quentin," GiGi warned.

He swept her into his embrace and kissed her temple. "Don't be jealous, Ms. GiGi. You're my main squeeze." With an inquiring look at Knox, he asked, "You coming?"

"Lead the way."

Alastair called her name. "We need a solid plan. Don't rush off. You could get yourself or Ryker killed."

"What about us? Are you not worried for me or Knox?" Quentin taunted good-naturedly.

"Pfft. You have the luck of the very devil, son. It's my sister I'm worried about."

"I *do* have a plan, Al. I've had it from the beginning. Don't get in my way," she told him. If she'd had a camera, she'd have snapped a shot of his startled countenance for posterity. Few questioned Alastair, and fewer still went against his mandate.

"Have a care, sister."

"I always do, brother."

Just as Quentin's magic fired up GiGi's cells for a teleport, Leonie rushed forward.

"Wait!" she called. "I'm going, too."

Quentin looked to GiGi for permission.

"I think it's better if you stay here," she told Leonie. "You have a son to think about."

"It's because of my son I want to do this. I don't want my mother's betrayal to be his legacy. I want to help, and if Harold is using black magic on Ryker, I believe I can."

GiGi met her brother's eyes across the distance. The silent question was answered with his nod. "Fine. Grab your bag."

The four of them arrived one hundred yards from the clearing and got their bearings. If GiGi squinted hard, she could make out figures in the glen.

"Where is this place?" she asked Quentin. "I can feel the vibration of the ground, and the air around us is practically crackling with the magic. It has to be a sacred spot."

"This land used to belong to the Beecham family about a hundred years ago. They went into debt from quite a few bad financial decisions. It seems not a one of them had a head for business."

"With Harold's ethics, I'd have thought he would've used magic for personal gain," GiGi murmured thoughtfully.

"Oh, he did. But he seems to be the exception to the rule. The Beecham clan was actually quite honorable throughout time." Knox inserted. When she sent him a questioning look, he shrugged and grinned. "Research is my passion."

"That and the lovely Spring," Quentin stated, grinning.

"Don't make me hurt you," Knox retorted.

"Are they always like this," Leonie asked, eyes wide.

"Pretty much." GiGi commanded everyone's attention and gestured to the men. "Both of you have the ability to stop or alter time. I think it would be a good idea to use this to take out the guards."

"Ah, the old one-two punch!" Quentin laughed.

Leonie opened her mouth, and GiGi forestalled her with a shake of her head. "No, he's never serious."

"I intend to confront Harold directly when all his backup is gone," she concluded. "Questions?"

"You should know black magic doesn't necessarily die with the practitioner wielding the power." Leonie's eyes darted from person to person as if trying to impart information of great importance.

It sunk in what she was saying, and GiGi wanted to lose the contents of her stomach. Instead, she crossed one arm under her breasts and rubbed the spot between her brows with her other hand. The struggle to stay focused and not panic was real. If Ryker died because of some black magic curse, GiGi's heart would break into a million pieces.

"What do you suggest?"

"A lightning strike."

All three stared at Leonie, mouths agape.

"Come again?" Knox demanded.

"Well, it d-doesn't have to be l-lightning, but it has to be strong enough to sever the c-connection," Leonie stammered.

"Explain," GiGi barked.

"It's like restarting the heart with paddles after a person has flat-lined. The current will reawaken a victim's magic to battle the invading magic." She threw back her shoulders and lifted her chin in the face of their disbelief. "There are other, better—or, er, safer—ways, but we don't have time for a ceremony."

"I can't believe I have to electrocute my husband," GiGi muttered with a shake of her head.

"I can do it," Knox offered softly.

She shook her head again, this time more firmly. "I need you to pause time for me to hand Ryker the knife. He should deliver the death blow to Beecham for what he's done."

They discussed various options and strategized as Leonie

squatted and dug into her bag. Once again, she removed the items she might need for a voodoo ceremony.

"I'll work from here and try to suppress Harold's magic." She held up a lock of hair and a stained scrap of paper. "Mother kept these in the event…" Her voice trailed off, and her large lioness eyes became misty. Clearing her throat, she continued, "…in the event she might need them against Harold."

"If they are what I think they are, why didn't she use them instead of attacking my family?"

"Lessening his magic wasn't going to bring me back from where I was being held," she said simply. "He might've killed me if he thought she was working against him."

Leonie was right. Harold Beecham was ruthless. Delphine had never held any true power in that whole mess. It still burned GiGi's ass that Delphine hadn't tried to obtain help from the Thornes before so meekly carrying out Beecham's directive. Preston's death was still an open wound.

"Let's go," GiGi ordered the men. She placed a gentle hand on Leonie's shoulder. "Thank you."

Calling up the power from deep within her cells, she quietly recited Granny Thorne's cloaking spell, adding a modification so the people with her now could see and hear her. Next, she called on her element and manipulated the wind underneath and around her to raise her up to the level of the treetops. When she glanced down, it was to see the stupefied expressions of her companions.

"Someone really needs to teach you young uns what you're capable of," she called down with a wink.

Arms straight down by her sides, she lightly circled her hands, one clockwise, the other rotating in the opposite direction, to generate the airflow she needed to move toward the clearing. She lingered ten feet above the spot where Harold held a gun on Ryker. From her vantage point, she could see and hear everything going on in the glen and surrounding area.

One by one, Quentin and Knox disabled the guards. Once Knox nodded in her direction, GiGi lowered herself to the ground. She withdrew a knife from her waistband and ran her hand along its length.

"Concelo!"

So as not to startle Ryker with her touch, she slowly walked in a half-circle around him, making sure the breeze was at her back to blow her light perfume in his direction. Recognition flashed in his eyes, but he was careful to keep his face blank.

Cautiously, she slipped the handle of the invisible knife within his grasp. It wouldn't do to cut him. There would be no way she could hide his spontaneous flow of blood. A flicker of a frown came and went on his face when she leaned in to press her mouth to his.

She backed roughly ten yards away and whispered the word to reveal herself.

"What... how..." Beecham recovered quickly. "Nicely done. I'm surprised you didn't attempt to disarm me. Where's your brother?"

GiGi detected the tell-tale sign of nerves in his voice and flashed him a smile full of wicked intent. "You aren't dealing with my brother today, Harold. You're dealing with me." Holding up her arms, she pulled ions from the surrounding air and supercharged her power. Blue light sparked between her fingertips.

"Oh, shit," muttered Ryker. "Give up now, Harold. It will go better for everyone."

Only her husband could joke with a gun pointed at his head.

GiGi wanted to laugh but curbed the impulse. "Put the gun down, Harold," she said softly. "Your reign of terror is finished. If you let Ryker go unharmed, I'll let you live," she lied.

"You're a liar. Your entire family is full of liars!" His eyes flared wide and spittle formed at the corner of his mouth.

The elements around them began to build; the wind picked up, and lightning flashed across the midnight sky. With only a single thought, GiGi sent a surge of power through the ground between them, creating a slight tremble in the earth's surface.

Tone hardened to show she meant business, GiGi snarled, "I won't tell you again, Harold."

His gun wavered between the two of them.

"If anything happens to me, my men will gun you down," he countered.

"That's a common mistake men make, believing loyalty lasts after they're dead. I mean, who is going to pay them? They have no reason to kill me after you're gone."

Blood drained from his face, but he tilted his chin up. "Even if you murder me, your husband's curse won't leave him."

GiGi had to give Beecham credit; he remained stubborn in the face of her impressive powers. "I'll take that chance."

"Guards!" Harold shouted. Silence was his only reply. He cast a nervous glance over his shoulder. "Guards!"

Sauntering in a half-circle around him, GiGi tutted. "Do you really believe I'm stupid enough not to remove your army first, Harold?" A small smile of satisfaction twisted her lips as she noted the bead of sweat on his forehead. She pulled more electricity into her fingertips, creating a glowing ball of energy.

"Sweetheart, while I am enjoying your game of cat and mouse, kneeling here has become uncomfortable for these old knees. Besides, your victim is positively green. Time for you to do what you came for." Ryker, although deathly pale, still retained a calm demeanor.

"You spoil all my fun, babe. But yes, I believe it's time to take out the trash."

Harold realized the exact second she intended to strike and turned his gun in her direction.

The report of the gun echoed off the trees lining the clearing, and the bullet stopped a mere foot from her heart. GiGi stepped to the side and shouted, "Now!"

Time corrected, and the bullet bypassed her. Without any flash or pomp, she hurled lightning at Harold and Ryker. Surprise stuck on her husband's face as the current coursed through his body. As his eyes closed, she shifted the arc to the earth and grounded the electricity.

"Restituere!" she shouted, running for him and placing her palm flat over his heart. She pushed revitalizing magic into him.

His lids lifted to reveal an amber glow in his mocha eyes. "Thanks."

"Time to end this."

RYKER FELT HIS WIFE'S ANCIENT FAMILY MAGIC FLOOD HIS CELLS AND restore his own power. Whatever dark magic Beecham had used on him was now fading, the connection having been severed by GiGi.

Harold had collapsed to his knees, the barrel of the gun pointing down. When he saw the knife in Ryker's hand, he struggled to raise his weapon.

Pure savagery filled Ryker's soul. With his right hand, he delivered a blow to Beecham's wrist. Using his newfound energy, Ryker plunged the blade under Harold's ribs and twisted up. As it pierced the lungs and sank into his enemy's heart, he said, "Die, fucker, and may you rot in hell."

Life left Harold's body in a whoosh, and his face became a frozen mask of horror.

Ryker drew the knife back a few inches and struck again, He repeated the action two more times.

"He's gone, Ryker," GiGi said softly. She laid a gentle hand on his lower back.

He swore and dropped the knife. The blood coating his hands caught his attention. Somehow, he thought it would be as black as Harold's soul. He also thought he'd feel more satisfaction when he brought that evil bastard down.

"It should have been Nash." His voice was raspy and raw. He feared he was on the verge of a breakdown and struggled to hold it together. "Trina… was his mom. He should have been the one to…" He gestured to the body in front of him. "I stole his revenge."

"No, babe. You did what was necessary. Gave Harold what he deserved."

A shout came from the tree line behind them.

They turned to see Knox carrying a limp Leonie toward them, Quentin beside him.

"No!" GiGi cried.

"She thought she could help you. She left her hiding spot." Quentin explained.

GiGi jumped up to check Leonie's pulse. When his wife placed her hands over her mouth, Ryker knew it was too late to help the poor girl.

"I can try to reverse time to save her. I was on the other side of the clearing, but it should count as being present."

A blinding white light filled the clearing, and they turned to shield their faces. When the light faded, Preston stood ten feet away.

"Pres? Why are you here?"

"I came to deliver a message from the Goddess." He walked to where they gathered. "If time is reversed, you take the chance of changing the outcome of this night's events." He gestured to Harold.

"She didn't deserve this. She's too young, and she has a son, brother."

"He'll need care," her brother said meaningfully. "Both the mother and father whom he should have belonged to."

Was Preston saying Armand was their reincarnated son? He hadn't realized he spoke aloud until Preston nodded.

"According to Isis."

"I don't want him back this way, Pres. Not at the expense of Leonie's life."

Preston gave them both a searching look. "Even if it means you'll not have children?"

GiGi covered her mouth, tears flooding her eyes. Ryker slipped an arm around her shoulders and hugged her close. They had a difficult decision to make. Either reclaim their son or give him over to Leonie's care. The choice was no real choice at all. They couldn't take a young woman's life for their own gains.

"Revive the girl," he croaked out.

GiGi's choked sob broke his heart in two.

"Place her here," Preston ordered Knox. A glow lit the fingers he used to probe Leonie's wound. Within seconds, the bullet was in his grasp. A red light arched between Preston's left palm and the hole in

Leonie's chest. When he was done, there wasn't a scratch on her chest.

Leonie's lids fluttered open. Her hands flew to where the entry wound should be. Confusion and a little fear lit her delicate features as she stared up at Preston.

"Welcome back, child," he said warmly. He gestured to their group with his thumb. "You have some people who are very happy to see you."

Her wide, golden eyes touched on each of them, pausing on the tearful GiGi before darting back to Preston. "Why did you save me?"

"Because my sister wouldn't be able to live with your death on her conscience. She tells me your son needs you."

GiGi pulled away from Ryker's arms and knelt by Leonie's side. "You're one of ours now, child. We take care of our own."

A thick ball of emotion settled in Ryker's throat as he watched the women embrace. His wife displayed such love and grace, he found it difficult to fathom.

Preston rose and moved to stand in front of him. "Your turn."

Placing the flat of one hand over Ryker's forehead and the other over the area of his heart, his brother-in-law blasted him with a celestial healing magic mere mortals weren't subject to. As his cells warmed to burning, Ryker couldn't prevent a cry of pain. It felt as if millions of tiny flames lit him from the inside and were forcing their way out through his skin. Sweat seeped from every pore, and for a brief moment, he feared he might faint.

Just when Ryker's knees were about to give out, Preston removed his hands.

The gentle morning breeze picked up, and Ryker could detect a distinct drop in temperature as it caressed his body. Opening his eyes, he met his wife's concerned gaze. "Thanks for that, sweetheart. Your brother lit a bonfire under my skin."

"I was removing the last of the darkness from your body, you pansy ass," Preston snorted with an elbow to the ribs.

"Don't make me look weak in front of my woman," Ryker returned. He grimaced as he rubbed the back of his neck. He lowered his voice and asked Preston, "Am I supposed to feel like I've been run over by a semi-truck?"

"You'll be fine in a day or two. I've literally burned all the blood magic out. It's going to take time for your cells to regenerate fully."

"Isn't that what GiGi did?"

"Her fix was only going to work in the short term, and since Leonie didn't have the original spell Harold used, she wouldn't have been able to remove it completely." Preston squeezed his shoulder. "Like a cancerous growth, it would have returned. Now it won't."

"Thank you, my friend."

"Don't mention it." Preston opened and closed his mouth as if he wished to say more.

"What is it?"

"I'm sorry about your son, and I'm sorry I led you to believe you'd have another child together."

Ryker cleared his throat. "He's alive and well. That's what matters most."

"I know, but GiGi…"

"She'll be fine. She's the strongest woman I know." Again, Ryker's gaze connected with that of his wife across the short distance. "Is it all truly over?"

"Yes. Trina has returned to the Otherworld, and the Council now knows Beecham was responsible for all the atrocities: Trina's murder, Georgie's attack, trying to stage a coup. I think you'll find that when you return, you'll be cleared."

"With the exception of this." He nudged Beecham's foot with his toe.

"Nah, you're good. You should've seen your wife, man," Quentin inserted, a wide grin playing on his face. "She was fierce. Told the Council she intended to rip Beecham apart limb by limb and asked if they had a problem with it. Fierce, I tell ya. I can see where my prickly pear gets her sass."

Ryker exchanged a wry glance with Preston. They both knew well that GiGi was a force to be reckoned with.

$\mathcal{G}$iGi woke slowly and rolled toward the warmth of her husband's body. Although he was asleep, he instinctively gathered her close. For a long while, she lay there with her ear resting on his chest, just over his heart, listening to the steady rhythm.

She'd come so close to losing him today. A small chill chased along her spine, and she shivered.

"You okay, sweetheart?" Ryker's voice was husky with sleep but still sexy as hell. It caused another involuntary shiver.

"Just thinking about the events of the last few days. It's been mentally exhausting, hasn't it?"

"Not to mention physically. I feel as if I could spend the next month asleep and still not catch up."

She lifted her head and grinned down at him. "The trials of getting old, babe."

He growled and rolled her over. Resting atop her, he buried his face in the hollow of her throat. "I'll show you old."

"Don't feel you have to wear yourself out proving you're a better man than Baz."

He lifted his head to glare down at her. "You didn't just go there."

Laughing, she pulled him down for a kiss. He didn't bother to resist, and GiGi knew he hadn't been offended by her teasing. When his lips claimed hers, she sighed her contentment. The feel of his tongue stroking hers, his minty-fresh breath, the way... She drew back with a frown.

"What?"

"How is it you have minty breath upon waking?" she demanded.

"Maybe because I was awake for a good ten minutes before you. I figured it would eventually lead to this, and I may have conjured some gum to battle my waking breath."

She grunted. "I thought you were sleeping." GiGi ignored his comment about anticipating their kiss; after all, that had been the standard morning routine when they were together, and she loved it.

"I know. I like how you rub up against me like an affectionate kitten when you think I'm out. It's pretty much the only time you're not argumentative."

"I'm not argumentative!" She would have continued to deny his claim, but his raised brow and smirk said she'd proved his point. "Fine. I may argue on occasion."

"And only when the rest of us are being obtuse," he declared loyally.

She pulled his head back down so he could explore her neck with his lips. "For that, you get to pick your favorite position."

"Hot damn!"

A knock sounded at the door, causing them both to groan their frustration.

"Let's teleport out of here and back to our place," Ryker whispered his suggestion.

"Don't even think about it," Aurora called through the door, apparently having anticipated Ryker's reaction to the interruption. "Georgie Sipanil has requested we all join her for dinner. You have fifteen minutes to get ready."

The click of her heels on the marble floor receded after a minute.

"How did we not hear Rorie approach?"

Ryker laughed and drew her into a sitting position. "Let's get a shower. You'd be surprised what I can do in fifteen minutes."

They raced for the en suite bathroom like a young couple in love —laughing and exploring every inch of exposed skin. Twelve minutes and two orgasms later, GiGi fell back upon the bed. "There's nothing as relaxing as a quickie. I'm too sated to go anywhere. Give Georgie my regrets."

"Oh, no. If I have to go, so do you. Conjure something black and slinky so I can dream about what I'm going to do to you when we get back here later tonight."

"Mmm, well, only if you promise I get more of the same." She gestured toward the shower.

He straddled her sprawled body and kissed her bared breast. "I think I can manage that."

"Ryker?"

The serious note in her voice caused him to lift his dark head and stare down at her.

"Do you think our baby was never truly meant to be ours?"

"What do you mean, sweetheart?" He climbed off her and sat on the edge of the bed.

"Isis had to have known I'd never let Leonie die, not just so I could have her son." She rubbed at the moisture building behind her lids. "And he was taken from us before he could draw his first breath. It's like he was never meant to be ours."

"I don't know." He heaved a sigh and stroked a gentle hand across her belly in comfort. "That's for us to discover when we cross over. Goddess willing, it will be a long time from now."

"Yes." She rose and pulled Ryker to his feet. "Goddess willing. Let's not keep Georgie waiting."

Within minutes, they were strolling down the corridor toward the main hall to join their family. The one constant thought in her brain was Leonie and Armand, and what they would do now that Delphine was gone. GiGi felt responsible, knowing their income would be drastically reduced since the voodoo priestess wasn't around to cater to the tourists of New Orleans.

She pulled Ryker to a stop and faced him. "What if we invite them to live with us?"

It spoke to how tuned into her needs Ryker truly was because he never asked who or why. Instead, he said, "I think that's an excellent idea." He lifted their joined hands to kiss her knuckles. "We can talk to her in the morning."

"Tonight. Let's talk to her tonight after dinner."

He studied her for a long moment, then nodded. "Tonight it is."

"Thank you, babe."

"No need. I understand what you feel you owe her because of Delphine, and I also think it would be great to get to know Armand. I just worry you'll feel the loss that much more keenly."

She mulled it over for a bit, weighing the pros and cons of having the boy who should have been her son so close, but also to hear him call another woman *mother*.

"I might. But the reality is, we never had him. Not really. Also, they deserve better than the hand they've been dealt lately."

"I agree. We'll find a way to persuade her to come stay with us."

DINNER WAS A CELEBRATION OF SORTS—IF THE DEATH OF A murdering scumbag could be deemed a celebration, considering the number of victims left in Beecham's wake. Ryker only wished he'd had more time with his sister. It was selfish because poor Leonie never had a second to say goodbye to her mother.

As he glanced around the table, he felt a rightness. Georgie was alive and, if not completely well, then on the mend. Trina's murder was solved and her attacker dispatched. There was only one true threat left on the horizon—Victor Salinger. Ryker had no doubt Alastair would handle that evil fucker soon enough.

"What has you thinking so hard, young Gillespie?"

The sound of Georgie's thready voice stirred him from his

musings. She was still recovering from her ordeal, and Ryker worried she'd pushed herself too far today.

"You. Beecham. Trina." He grimaced, unable to put into words the thoughts tumbling about in his mind. "I'm grateful you're still with us."

"Me, too." She cast a smiling glance down the table toward Knox and Spring. "If it weren't for those two, I wouldn't be."

"I still don't know why they didn't tell the rest of us you were okay." Ryker found it difficult to keep the hard edge of disappointment and anger from his tone. The belief that Georgie was dead had gutted him.

Georgie patted his hand. "Don't be upset with them, boy. It was my doing. The less people who knew, the better. It was the only way to draw out that sniveling coward, Howard."

The deep hurt was hard to disregard. She hadn't trusted him enough to give him a heads up. "I didn't think I was just anyone to you, Georgie."

"You are a consummate agent, Ryker. Gifted in all ways. But the fury you felt toward the injustice of the act and Beecham's part in my 'death' couldn't be feigned. You had to believe I'd died."

He had no real argument against Georgie's logic. GiGi's hand covered his knee in silent support. A single glance showed her sympathy in regard to his feelings. While he appreciated her support, he also hated to appear like a petulant child. He smiled to show he was fine when, in fact, he was stewing inside. Long ago, he'd learned to hide his gut reaction to situations and shelve his feelings until he was alone and could process his emotions. This would be one of those times.

"A toast," Georgie declared, rising unsteadily to her feet. Silence settled on the group so she didn't need to shout. "To Ryker Gillespie, the son of my heart. Thank you for caring as deeply as you do about this old woman." He gripped the trembling hand she held out to him and drew her gnarled knuckles to rest against his cheek.

"You're not old, Ms. Georgie. You're perfect," he declared loyally. And she was. For a woman who had to be pushing ninety-eight, she only looked to be fifty. The tell was her hands; they were far too misshapen to belong to a young woman. Even witches experienced arthritis and other maladies as they aged. No one lived forever.

She ran a loving hand over the top of his head as if he were truly her son. "Thank you, dear." Lifting her glass for the second time, she said, "To Knox Carlyle and Spring Thorne, you are a match made by the Goddess. Your brilliance saw us through this mess, and I'm deeply indebted to you."

Spring blushed as Knox whispered something close to her ear. She rolled her eyes, nudged him with her shoulder, and lifted her wine glass, ignoring his deep chuckle. "Thank you, Ms. Georgie. No debt is owed. You've been an advocate for our family for three generations. It's the very least we can do. I'm only sorry we didn't arrive in time to prevent it to begin with."

"Finally, to Sebastian Drake. Or should I say Councilman Drake?" Georgie countered his wide-eyed stare with a warm smile. "You'll take Beecham's seat. The intelligence and foresight you've shown through this mess have proven what an asset you can be."

"I believe that position should go to Ryker or Nash. They've been far more instrumental in keeping the witch community safe from our enemies," Sebastian demurred.

"I don't want it," Nash replied promptly. He met Ryker's gaze across the table. "Neither does my uncle." Facing Sebastian, he shrugged—the standard matter-of-fact Thorne response. "That leaves you. The only other person both the Council and the Thornes trust to have everyone's best interests at heart. And really, Drake, don't act like you don't want it. We all know you do."

GiGi leaned forward with a laugh. "Go ahead, Baz. Take the position. There's no one better suited for it."

Sebastian stared at GiGi's lovely face for a long moment before he nodded. Although he faced Georgie, his gaze lingered a little longer on GiGi before he finally dragged his attention away. "I'd be honored."

"Good," Georgie said. "The next order of business is to find you a suitable life partner. GiGi Thorne belongs to my boy here."

Everyone laughed with the exception of Sebastian, whose cheeks developed a distinctly pink hue. Ryker almost felt sorry for him. He might've expressed sympathy if the guy weren't half in love with his wife.

"I believe you've embarrassed our friend enough, Ms. Georgie," Alastair inserted from his end of the table. He rose and lifted his own crystal flute. "The next toast should be to you, dear lady. Thank you for always falling on the side of what's right and fair. Thank you for giving the Thornes the benefit of the doubt more often than we probably deserved. We adore you, Ms. Georgie, and we're happy you're still with us."

The elder witch blinked rapidly and cleared her throat. With a graceful nod, she sank into her seat and sipped of her wine. "Let's finish our wonderful meal, shall we?"

EPILOGUE

*R*yker popped into the kitchen where GiGi and Armand were busy mixing up the dough for chocolate chip cookies. After dropping a light hand on the little boy's shoulder, Ryker handed GiGi a folded piece of paper.

"Meet me here at seven tonight." When she would have questioned him, he held up a hand. "Nope. You'll have to wait and see." A devilish light flared in his eyes as a decidedly wicked smile curled his lips. He lowered his voice to add, "Wear something sexy and be sure to play along."

With all her heart, she wanted to forego the meeting and drag him to her bedroom for a lazy day in bed, such was the power of his sinful grin. But he walked away before she could form a coherent thought, much less voice it.

A glance at her watch showed she had a few hours to kill, so she stayed to supervise the dropping of dough on the baking sheets.

"Only twelve minutes and then you can ruin your dinner," she teased the boy.

He'd been exceptionally quiet in the week since he and his mother had moved into their place, and GiGi was left to assume the transition might be harder on him than anyone expected.

"Do you miss your old home?" she asked as she smoothed back his hair.

He nodded solemnly.

"And your gran?"

Tears flooded his golden eyes.

"Did she bake with you, too?"

Again, he nodded. "She wants me to tell you something."

GiGi froze in snitching a pinch of cookie dough. "What is that?"

"She says she's sorry." He curled his hand in his long-sleeved shirt and swiped it across his nose. "She says she understands why you did it."

Heart hammering, she lowered herself to the stool facing him. "She does?"

"She says to take care of me and her girl."

She cupped his small solemn face between her palms and kissed his forehead. "Tell her I always will."

"You believe me?"

"That you see your gran?" At his nod, she smiled and tapped his nose. "Yes, darling boy, I do."

As if a heavy brick was lifted from each shoulder, Armand's shoulders dropped and his tiny frame relaxed.

"Now, if Delphine doesn't have anything more to contribute, we'll finish our baking."

"She said you forgot the salt."

With narrowed eyes, GiGi pinched another bite of cookie dough. Damned if Delphine wasn't right. "Good call, cousin," she called out. Leaning toward Armand and flaring her eyes wide, she whispered, "Watch how we fix this." She pushed up her sleeves and waved her arms about in a dramatic display, causing her bangle bracelets to clank. Finally, she wiggled her fingers at the mixture and shouted, *"Abracadabra!"*

His giggle brought joy to her heart. She imagined, had life been a little kinder to her, she'd have had plenty of these moments with him. But love meant letting go. It meant allowing another to choose their path, and Armand had chosen Leonie as his mother when he was a lost soul in the Otherworld years ago.

"Miss GiGi?"

"Hmm?"

"I love you."

"I…" The words stuck in her throat, and all she could do was pull him in a tight embrace. Finally, when he wiggled in his impatience, she released him. "I love you, too," she managed. "But don't think it's going to get you cookies every time."

He grinned, and in that smile, she saw the deviltry of Ryker. "Yes, it will."

She narrowed her eyes. "Yes, it most likely will, and cake to boot."

They laughed together and gobbled more raw dough.

When the cookies were removed from the oven, she gave him a handful. "Go find your mother, you cheeky monkey. I have to clean up this mess and meet my husband."

He ran off after a hug and a wave.

After she'd dumped the dishes in the dishwasher and wiped down the counters, GiGi headed to the master bath for a long, luxurious soak in the garden tub. She sipped her wine and mulled over the events of the last few months since Ryker had stepped back into her life. A deep sense of contentment and peace flooded her. They would work this time around, she was sure of it. Both of them were committed to their marriage, and Ryker was now ready to put her first.

GiGi doubted there would ever be a lack of drama surrounding her family, and perhaps that type of disturbance would be enough for her husband's deep need for excitement. It was certainly more than enough for her.

She took great care with her appearance, creating a slinky, form-fitting dress that subtly caught the light with its iridescent material. The neckline plunged the right amount without showing off anything more than the cleavage between her pushed up breasts. A side slit ran from ankle to mid-thigh and gave a tantalizing peek of her smooth, shapely leg.

Leaving her hair loose and flowing down her back was perfect to offset her shoulders, bared by the halter dress. She applied a smoky eye in deep purple to highlight the brightness of her violet-blue gaze. A bubble-gum pink lipgloss finished the look as did the three-inch dangling earrings with their row of diamonds. GiGi Thorne-Gillespie was dressed to kill and not taking any prisoners tonight.

She blew a kiss to the fierce warrior woman in the mirror, then stepped into the closet for a purse and to slip on a pair of four-inch, fuck-me heels. Ryker would need an adult-sized bib to catch his drool tonight.

A call to her niece's husband, Keaton, confirmed he was in the driveway to deliver the present she'd ordered for her husband, and she stepped out the front door to admire the Corvette Keaton had found to replace Ryker's beloved car he'd been forced to destroy.

"Think he'll like it?"

Keaton snorted and handed her the keys with a light kiss to her cheek. "If Autumn ever wants to get me a gift of this nature, be sure to encourage it whole-heartedly, all right?"

She laughed and palmed the keys. "I'll keep that in mind. Any specific color?"

"Candy-apple red does it for me."

"And are you interested in finding one to restore with Chloe or one already finished?"

"You always ask the hard questions." He studied her for a moment and smiled appreciatively. "All I know is that if my wife showed up in a car like this, looking like you do now, I would be a happy man. Ryker won't know what hit him."

"That's what I'm hoping."

His handsome face dropped its teasing air. "We are all thrilled you've found each other again, GiGi. Be happy."

She cupped his cheek and smiled. "Thank you, dear. Now, I must be off before I'm late." With a twirl of the key ring, she opened the door and slid into the driver's seat. The motor growled as she started the engine, and GiGi laughed at the throaty sound. "Yes, this is perfect." With a wink and a wave, she drove away.

The place was busy, but she still managed to find a premium parking spot for Ryker's new toy. As she swung her legs around to stand, a wolf-whistle pierced the night air. Without acknowledging the sound in any way other than with an eye roll, GiGi headed for the entrance.

She'd only been perched on her stool for a few minutes when the men in the bar each thought to try their hand at wooing her. She never bothered to make eye contact with anyone but the twenty-something female bartender, who seemed harried and irritated by life in general.

A not-so-subtle surge of energy rippled the air surrounding her.

Ryker.

Her lips twitched in an effort to suppress her pleasure as she brought her martini to her lips. The aggressive guy next to her crowded closer, as if her half-smile was encouragement. She didn't bother to acknowledge him, instead shifting in the opposite direction to face her husband.

"Hi." His deep, warm tone curled her toes and woke the butter-flies low in her belly. Just as it always did.

"Hi."

Ryker held out a hand as if to introduce himself. "I'm Ryker."

She placed her palm in his. "GiGi."

"Hey, pal. I saw her first," the leech to her left protested angrily.

Ryker tilted his head, his eyes never leaving hers. "Should I be concerned?"

"Not in the least."

"Bitch," the guy muttered as he started to storm away.

Not bothering to verbally respond, GiGi flicked a finger his way. The man face-planted on the sticky barroom floor. He came up sput-tering and glaring at the crowded room before hastily making an exit.

"Nicely done," Ryker murmured. Leaning one elbow against the bar, he gave her the once-over. Inch by slow inch, his eyes traveled back up the length of her body. His half-smile turned into a wolfish grin. "You look lovely. May I buy you a drink?"

Unsure what his game was, she shrugged. "I'm waiting for someone."

"Really? Hmm. He's a fool to keep you waiting."

"Oh, I don't know. I think he's worth the wait," she replied meaningfully.

Their eyes locked.

"Really?"

"Absolutely." She stretched the short distance and settled a kiss on his mouth. "Want to tell me what this is about?"

"I thought we could start over. A clean slate, as if we were only meeting each other for the first time."

She settled a hand at the base of his throat and felt the hard hammering of his pulse. Looking at him in all his sexy self-assurance, no one would ever believe Ryker was nervous. But the pounding of his heart didn't lie.

"It's a lovely gesture, but…" She opened the small beaded purse in front of her, removed the keys to the Corvette, and dangled them in the air between them. "…then I couldn't give you this for an anniversary present."

His dumbfounded expression made her laugh aloud.

RYKER STARED AT HIS WIFE'S AMUSED COUNTENANCE IN A STATE OF utter shock. First, she'd remembered today was their anniversary. Second, if those keys belonged to the 'Vette he'd seen in the parking lot, he just won the damned lottery.

"Tell me it's that cobalt blue beauty in the front lot."

"Maybe," she teased, but he knew it was.

"I honestly wanted to wine and dine you to show you a good time after the nightmare we've been through." He could hear the indecision in his own voice. Damn, he wanted to drive that car. "I can wait."

"I can't. Let's go take it for a spin and come back."

"Goddess, I love you, sweetheart," he breathed as he snatched the dangling keys from her hand. "So much." He followed his words with a deep kiss, one that left her flushed and breathless.

"After a kiss like that, I believe you."

He grinned and reached for her hand. Although he wanted to run, he kept his pace slow, mindful of her sexy-ass shoes. Pausing halfway to the door, he leaned in to say, "Later, when we are in bed, I hope you consider leaving those heels on." He raked his gaze down her smoking hot body. "I..." Words failed him. "Yeah. Come on."

The throaty growl of the engine nearly made Ryker whimper. "GiGi, you are a goddess among women."

"Don't you ever forget it."

"Never," he promised as he lifted their joined hands to drop a kiss on her knuckles. "You shall be worshiped from here to the end of our lives, as is your due."

"You say the sweetest things."

They drove the backroads in silence, a mutual appreciation of the car's speed and handling. After twenty miles had passed, Ryker pulled off the road and let the engine idle. "Do we go back for drinks and dinner, or would you like to see my surprise for you?"

"You remembered?" Even in the darkness of the car's interior, he could see the sheen of tears in her brilliant eyes.

"Of course." He leaned forward to brush his nose with hers. "How can I forget the day you made me the happiest man alive?"

"Oh, Ryker," she breathed. GiGi rested a palm on each side of his face and pressed her forehead to his. "I love you so much more than I ever thought possible. Sometimes I'm terrified that I've lost my mind and this is all a dream."

"I feel the same."

She brought his head down for a kiss, and in that kiss, Ryker felt all their tomorrows. As he slowly pulled away, he pressed his lips lightly to the tip of her nose. "Back to the restaurant?"

"I could eat, *but* I'm also impatient to see this surprise of yours."

"Hmm. Well, I suppose we could always whip up some dinner when we get to where we are going."

"Is it the Grand Caymans? You know I love it there. Don't tease me."

He laughed at her eagerness. "No, but good to know a trip would go over well as a present."

He twisted slightly, looked both ways, then peeled out onto the highway. Utilizing Granny Thorne's cloaking spell, he broke the speed limit by a good fifty miles per hour. They arrived at their destination in record time.

"Where are we?" GiGi asked as she slipped out of her heels.

"The site of our new homestead—if you like it."

"Homestead?" She laughed and shook her head. "Ryker, it's dark, and I can't see a thing."

"Right. One sec."

He jumped out of the car and hustled to her side to open the door. With a nod to her now bare feet, he said, "You may want to conjure a pair of clogs or gardening shoes. The grass is likely to be damp."

"I don't care."

With a light laugh, he swept her into his embrace, secretly loving her little meep of surprise. "Come, my darling bride. There are things I wish to show you."

GiGi wrapped her arms around his neck and tucked her head under his chin. Her deep sigh spoke of contentment.

Ryker walked to the center of the area he'd mapped off then set his wife on her feet. With one arm raised horizontal to the ground and palm out, he slowly spun in a circle. One by one, the thousands of tea lights he and his nieces' husbands had painstakingly laid out came to life. The small clearing brightened enough to show the beauty of the setting around them.

"What is this? Ryker?"

"Since there are so many sad memories for us at the old place, I thought you might want to start fresh. Give our place to Leonie and Armand. If you don't want to build again, I understand, but I—"

She cut him off with her index finger to his lips. "It's a wonderful idea. Especially since things are heating up between her and Matt lately." She walked the tentative outline of the future structure. "This is east?" She pointed, and at his nod, she smiled. "A sunroom should go here, don't you think? It should be right off a massive kitchen with a window overlooking the garden that will grow just there."

"Whatever you want, sweetheart," he agreed.

"I want a large island to prep food, so when Armand visits, we can bake his favorite cookies."

"I predict he'll be over every day with as much as you spoil him. But don't forget my pies."

She laughed and practically skipped to where he remained at the center of their projected home. "I'll bake you at least one pie per month."

"It's going to have to be bi-monthly or no deal."

"You drive a hard bargain, babe." GiGi caressed his cheek with her fingertips. "But I get to keep my French sofa."

He groaned and acted put out. "Fine. But please promise no matter how angry you get, I'll never be forced to sleep on that POS again." He was unable to maintain his disgruntled look for long, and laughed at her saucy expression. "I don't care if we have boxes for furniture, sweetheart. Just as long as I am living with you, I'll be happy."

The love in her eyes glowed fiercely. "How is it you always know the right thing to say to melt my heart?"

For a long moment, he didn't answer. Instead, choosing to trace the beautiful bone structure of her face. Each curve complimented her loveliness, and the petal-soft skin begged to be caressed. Finally, he met her questioning gaze.

"From the moment I saw you, I was captivated." He eased forward and lightly brushed his mouth against hers, smiling slightly when her lips clung to his. "Nothing's changed from then to now. I'm still captivated. And I can't say what's right or wrong. I can only speak from my heart where you're concerned, GiGi."

"When do we conjure our new home?"

"Is tomorrow morning soon enough?"

"Perfect. I can't wait for our new beginning."

He grinned and tugged her within his embrace. "It's already begun."

TURN THE PAGE TO READ AN EXCERPT OF ESSENTIAL MAGIC. Nash's story is sure to delight.

ESSENTIAL MAGIC EXCERPT

*R*yanne Caldwell woke, heart pounding and mouth dry. What the hell had she just dreamed about? Two sisters—goddesses at that—and a cursed object? Snippets really. Someone declaring her "the Chosen," and then a vision of a necklace. The rest of the nightmare faded to obscurity.

A trip to the bathroom provided a much-needed drink of water for her sore, parched throat. She'd woken herself screaming, which was rare enough to make her question what she'd eaten the night before that might've triggered a nightmare of such magnitude. Nothing out of the ordinary jumped out at her. No caffeine after four p.m. No sugary goodness past noon. Yep, not food related.

Next, she ran through the list of shows she'd watched on TV. No murder mysteries, time travel, or unconventional movies to warp her thought process.

Dismissing the bizarre dream as simply that, she checked the clock.

Four-twenty a.m.

She swore under her breath, threw on her ratty old robe, and padded to the living room. No getting back to sleep after a dream of that nature.

"A full workload today on only three hours sleep is going to suck," Ryanne complained aloud to no one.

The sound of her own disgusted tone echoed off the barren walls of her tiny two-bedroom apartment. Plain white—ugh! She cast the room a distasteful look. Really, after three years in the same place, she could add some damned artwork or colored paint. Anything to make the space more habitable. More home-like.

Even after thirteen years, a home without her sister, Rylee, didn't bear thinking about. Maybe she should consider getting a cat?

With a dismissive shrug, Ryanne headed for the coffee maker.

Milk and sugar in the mug, she waited for the single brewer to work its magic and make her the drink of the gods. A shudder shook her. Yeah, better not to think about gods or goddesses. That dream had been wack. Who in their right mind would consider her a *Chosen*? What did that even mean?

She toyed with the idea of calling in sick to work. A mental health day. As a star employee of Thorne Industries for the last two years, she'd been the perfect little worker bee. She always showed up on time, stayed late, and hadn't used one single day of vacation.

"Maybe I'm due," she muttered.

Perhaps her brain was on overload and, as a result, was fried. It would explain the freaky visions her mind had conjured.

The more the idea of playing hooky bounced about, the more she warmed to it. She could lounge around, eating ice cream and catching up on rom coms. Let Nash pull a research assistant from the main floor. All his female workers were eager to be singled out. Her coworkers would backstab each other with letter openers in their desire to catch his eye.

And who could blame them? Nash was, well, *Nash.*

A sigh escaped, followed by a self-deprecating snort.

Working for the great Nash Thorne had made her immune to his charms. *Or nearly immune.* If, on occasion, she became short of breath in his vicinity, only she was the wiser. And if there were times when she would look up to find him standing over her, staring with those intense, all-knowing jade eyes, she was quick to suppress her lustful feelings.

Ryanne was certainly not as naive or as starry-eyed as she'd been when she first started working for him. A relationship was off limits. The arrogant little speech he'd honored her with on her first day made that quite clear.

"If you intend to be my top research aide, there will be no hanky-panky." He'd gone further to state that he didn't want her drooling over the ancient tomes in his possession.

Jerk.

Really, who used the term "hanky-panky" in today's day and age? He'd acted as if she'd be unable to control her baser urges in his presence. The conceit of the man had cured her of her brief fantasy almost immediately.

If she were forced to be brutally honest with herself—which she would go to the grave avoiding—she'd have to admit that on the days when he crowded in next to her to help translate a text, his unique scent turned her body into a live wire.

The musky, citrus smell of his skin had her wanting to bury her nose against his wide, muscular chest and inhale for all she was worth. And if, on her loneliest of nights, she fantasized about running her tongue along his corded neck or nuzzling his firm jaw with its perpetual two-day beard growth, who could fault her?

The blame could be firmly placed at the door of her dating dry spell. God, how long had it been since she got laid? She'd lost track around the two-and-a-half-year mark. Her vajayjay was ready to stage a strike.

Overly warm, Ryanne put the back of her hand to her sweaty brow. Maybe she really *was* coming down with something.

Screw it. She was calling off work today. Decision made. She grabbed her smartphone, whipped off a concise email to Nash, and copied Liz in Human Resources.

Both Nash and Liz tended to arrive early to work and would take the extra half-hour to check for new messages. They'd be shocked

Ryanne had asked for a day to herself, but her absence shouldn't cause a hardship.

She'd settled into her plush leather couch with her second cup of coffee and palmed the remote when a banging on her door caused her to jump. The splash of scalding liquid on her hand brought a curse to her lips and tears to her eyes.

Ryanne raced to the sink and ran her hand under cold water.

"Sonofabitch!" she muttered.

The banging sounded again. Who the hell was at her door before five a.m.? She ignored the intrusion.

The cold water took a small portion of the pain away.

"Ryanne?" Bang, bang, bang. "Ryanne! Open the door!"

Shock and Nash's frantic voice made her hustle to comply with his demand. Wrapping a dishtowel firmly around her right hand, she hurried to open the door.

Damned if she didn't have to catch her breath when she took in his tousled head of blond hair on top of those well-formed shoulders that made her mouth water. Clearing her throat was a necessity.

"Nash? What are you doing here?"

"Your email said you were sick."

"Oh-kaaay. And you're here *why?*"

His slashing dark blond brows dipped, and a deep frown line appeared in the center of his forehead. The scowl indicated he didn't appreciate the fine art of snark. If she hadn't been used to his thundercloud expression, she might've been a bit intimidated.

"You're never sick," he stated as if he was speaking to a dim child.

"Still not getting why you're here, Nash. It's not life or death if I was able to take the time to email you."

"You're ungrateful, you know that?"

She closed her eyes and counted to ten.

Really, she shouldn't be surprised. The man hardly slept and only lived twenty minutes away. She should've known he'd show up on her doorstep. Hell, if she'd taken the time to consider it, she would've been shocked if he hadn't.

That was the essence of Nash. He needed to control every aspect of his life. Nothing was allowed to derail the day. But the man seriously tried her patience. If he wasn't her boss... well, if he wasn't her boss, she'd probably be all over him like—*nope! Not going there!* That road was forbidden.

With a heavy sigh, she opened her eyes.

The intensity with which he was studying her caused her to swallow—*hard*.

When his frown deepened and he slowly raked her form with his gaze, her body went on high alert. Her breasts tightened with want, and her vagina became uncomfortably wet.

Crap!

She hated his ability to turn her on. No encouragement needed. For God's sake, he was only checking out her sleeping attire. Mr. Always-Impeccably-Dressed probably mentally faulted her mismatched tank, sleep shorts, and tattered robe.

Once again, she felt her brow to see if her forehead was overly warm.

"Do you feel faint?" Nash surged forward, scooped her into his arms, and kicked the door shut with his foot. "I've got you."

JesusMaryandJoseph! She was going to do it! She was going to lose control and lick him. As she leaned in, ready to take the plunge, he dumped her on the couch. Literally *dumped* her.

"Dude!" she yelped.

"Sorry. I lost my grip."

Nash nearly laughed at Ryanne's incredulous glare.

Whew, that was close! He'd nearly lost his ever-loving mind and succumbed to the overwhelming urge to kiss her.

He perused her scantily clad body at length for a second time.

While some people would consider her clothing cover enough, her ugly robe opened just enough to show off the outline of the pebbled tips of her breasts and created havoc in his mind—*as well as other parts of his anatomy.* She possessed the type of body to make a grown man weep. She had a petite, hourglass figure that short-circuited his brain.

Okay, focusing on her curves was not the smartest course of action.

In an effort to protect his sanity, he grabbed a quilt from the back of the sofa and tucked it around her. When she was wrapped from neck to ankles, he stood back and silently praised his quick thinking. A second glance showed that even her purple-painted toes were sexy as hell. He was in deep trouble.

Clearly irritated—her burning eyes said as much—Ryanne struggled to free herself from the heavy material.

He perched on the edge of the couch, hip to hip, hands on either side of her body, and held the quilt in place. "If you're sick, you should stay bundled up."

"I'm not that kind of sick, Nash."

Once again, he studied her—his favorite pastime when she wasn't looking.

Purple highlights blended perfectly with the nearly black hair. Her dark brows were shaped in a sharp arch, and her eyes were almost as dark as her hair and eyebrows. One had to look closely to make out her irises. They were a dark coffee-brown, practically black in appearance. Currently, they blazed with an unholy light.

Nash's lips twitched.

Ryanne's pique was a common enough occurrence—almost daily in fact.

Call him twisted, but he absolutely loved to see her fired up.

Those magnificent eyes would flash, and color would flood her cheeks. Her plump cherry lips would part in outrage and inspire fantasies no boss should entertain. Her passion brought to mind long, steamy nights spent in front of a fire, making love in every position known to man, then discovering a few extra for good measure.

His gaze fell to her mouth.

Whenever she smiled, her mouth split wide and showed a generous amount of white, lighting the room with its brilliance. But right now, when she was irritated and her lips were compressed as a result, he wanted to kiss the ever-loving hell out of her to bring back the joy to her face.

He recalled the first day he'd seen her in the conference room where she was being interviewed.

A goddess among mere mortals.

She'd looked up and beamed at him from her seat, clearly excited at the prospect of becoming his assistant.

Because he'd been in serious danger of falling at her feet and begging her for sexual favors right on the spot, he'd drummed up some stupid little speech about no romance and not drooling on his important papers or books. If he'd have dumped cold water over her head, he probably couldn't have shocked her more. His cousin Liz, who was conducting the interview, had shot him a horrified look as if he'd lost his damned mind.

Maybe he had. Maybe he hadn't been able to find it since meeting Ryanne two years previously. Really one year, eleven months, and twenty-two days if one wanted to be exact. When he wasn't thinking about business, his thoughts were consumed with her.

And wasn't that the crux of the matter? He'd been smitten the moment he saw her in all her technicolor glory, and nothing she'd said or done in the interim had changed his mind. No, time had only worked to reinforce his feelings. He was a Thorne, and family legend held that Thornes only loved once.

Oh, screw it! He was going in for the kiss. He'd waited long enough.

Angling his head, he shifted closer and released the blanket to allow her partial freedom. "I'm going to kiss you, Ryanne. If you object, speak now or forever hold your peace."

Her indrawn breath and wide eyes curled his lips. He couldn't help his self-satisfied smile. The sheer wonder on her face was a sight to behold.

"I'll take that as a yes."

He lowered his head to hers, and when her lips opened to accommodate him, he explored the depths of her mouth. The very earth seemed to shake when their bodies connected. Somewhere in the close distance, dishes rattled. Oxygen left his brain, and his lungs went into overdrive when she gently sucked on the tongue invading her mouth. Christ, he could lose himself forever in the incredible taste of her.

Lightning lit up the sky beyond the balcony door. Thunder boomed within a second of the flash, and a woman's laughter echoed about the room.

Icy fingers caressed his spine, and he nearly came out of his skin.

His head whipped up and about.

No one was there.

"Did you…hear that?"

Confusion apparent, she asked, "What?"

"I thought I heard…a woman…laughing," he panted out, short of breath from their kiss.

Ryanne jackknifed to a sitting position. Her forehead connected with his chin.

"For fu—" Nash bit off his curse and rubbed his throbbing chin. "Are you okay?"

"Yeah, sorry," she muttered. "This morning is getting weirder and weirder."

Her words caught his complete attention. Weird was never a coincidence in the Thorne world. "How so?"

"I had a strange dream. It's nothing."

"It's not *nothing* if you had to call in sick during the early morning hours." Unable to help himself, he traced her kiss-swollen lips with the pad of his thumb. "That's unlike you."

Her bewilderment was adorable. Did she not believe he was aware of his surroundings? Aware of her? Hell, most nights he couldn't get a full night's rest because he lay awake, replaying the day's events. He'd spend the entire time recalling every word they exchanged, every gesture she'd made. Of course, those thoughts brought to mind his ever-present desire for her. He nearly snorted in self-disgust.

All strangeness forgotten, he leaned forward. With his free hand, he cradled the back of her head in his palm. "Are you interested in picking up where we left off?"

Her soft whimper encouraged him to run the tips of his fingers down her long, graceful neck. He halted at the lacy edge of her top. "Say the word, Ryanne."

"No," she whispered seductively.

"Yes, I—wait, what? *No?*" Poleaxed, he pulled back. The husky quality to her tone had him wondering if he should go old-school alpha male and try to persuade her. He attempted to keep his petulant attitude in check when he asked, "Why not?"

"Because it could get messy at work. You know, I could drool all over your papers and books. We can't have that, Nash."

This time when he heard a woman's laughter, there was a wicked quality to the sound.

FROM THE AUTHOR...

Thank you for taking the time to read **FOREVER MAGIC!** If you love what you've read, please leave a review. To find out about what's happening next in the world of The Thorne Witches, be sure to subscribe my newsletter.

Books in The Thorne Witches Series:

SUMMER MAGIC
AUTUMN MAGIC
WINTER MAGIC
SPRING MAGIC
REKINDLED MAGIC
LONG LOST MAGIC
FOREVER MAGIC
ESSENTIAL MAGIC
MOONLIT MAGIC

You can find my online media sites here:

Website: tmcromer.com
Facebook: facebook.com/tmcromer
TM Cromer's Reader Group: bit.ly/tmc-readers
Twitter: @tmcromer
Instagram: @tmcromer

How to stay up-to-date on releases, news and other events…

√ *Join my mailing list. My newsletter is filled with news on current releases, potential sales, new-to-you author introductions, and contests each month. But if it gets to be too much, you can unsubscribe at any time. Your information will always be kept private. No spam here!*
Sign Up: www.tmcromer.com/newsletter

√ *Sign up for text alerts. This is a great way to get a quick, nononsense message for when my books are released or go on sale. These texts are no more frequently than every few months. Text TMCBOOKS to 24587.*

√ *Follow me on BookBub. If you are into the quick notification method, this one is perfect. They notify you when a new book is released. No long email to read, just a simple "Hey, T.M.'s book is out today!"*
Bookbub Link: bit.ly/tmc-bookbub

√ *Follow me on retailer sites. If you buy most of your books in digital format, this is a perfect way to stay current on my new releases. Again, like BookBub, it is a simple release-day notification.*

√ *Join my Facebook Fan Page. While the standard pages and profiles on Facebook are not always the most reliable, I have created a group for fans who like to interact. This group entitles readers to "fan page only" contests, as well as an exclusive first look at covers, excerpts and more. The Fan Page is the most fun way to follow yet! I hope to see you there! Facebook Group: bit.ly/tmc-readers*

ALSO BY T.M. CROMER

Books in The Thorne Witches Series:

SUMMER MAGIC

AUTUMN MAGIC

WINTER MAGIC

SPRING MAGIC

REKINDLED MAGIC

LONG LOST MAGIC

FOREVER MAGIC

ESSENTIAL MAGIC

MOONLIT MAGIC

Books in The Stonebrooke Series:

BURNING RESOLUTION

THE TROUBLE WITH LUST

THE BAKERY

EASTER DELIGHTS

HOLIDAY HEART

Books in The Fiore Vineyard Series:

PICTURE THIS

RETURN HOME

ONE WISH

Look for The Holt Family Series starting March 2020!

FINDING YOU

THIS TIME YOU

INCLUDING YOU

AFTER YOU

THE GHOST OF YOU

Lightning Source UK Ltd.
Milton Keynes UK
UKHW020801271220
375968UK00008B/210